Journey to Rhodes Castle

To Trevor and Elizabeth

Journey to Rhodes Castle

Best Wishes,

Patrick Wetenhall

PATRICK WETENHALL

authorHOUSE®

AuthorHouse™ UK Ltd.
1663 Liberty Drive
Bloomington, IN 47403 USA
www.authorhouse.co.uk
Phone: 0800.197.4150

Published by AuthorHouse   05/08/2014

ISBN: 978-1-4969-7907-0 (sc)
ISBN: 978-1-4969-7960-5 (hc)
ISBN: 978-1-4969-7961-2 (e)

"To the Reverend John Crawley, without whose encouragement this book would never have been written"

CHAPTER ONE

The little town of Cockermouth, on the north-western fringe of the Lake District, is normally a quiet town for most of the year until the summer tourists begin to arrive around about mid-July. In the late 'sixties the town was not frequented by so many tourists as it is nowadays in the height of summer, nor did many of the visitors come earlier, in May or June, as they now do. But at the end of June in the year after Jim Sandy joined the Police Force at Cockermouth the main influx of tourists had not yet begun. The town was not very busy; but the town's Police Station and its occupants certainly were exceptionally busy. There had been a murder committed at the railway station a few weeks earlier, and the police had a murder hunt on for a wanted man throughout the County of Cumberland; and the headquarters for this search was the Police Station at Cockermouth. Jim Sandy had decided that he wanted to leave the police as soon as possible, not because he disliked being involved in a murder hunt—that had nothing to do with it—but simply because he had soon found that the strict discipline for a Cadet in the Force did not at all appeal to him.

Police Cadet James Sandy left his house in Lorton Road, as usual, at half past eight that morning to set off walking down to the Police Station, where his day's work as a Cadet commenced at nine o'clock. The morning of June 30th was fine, but there were large, hard-edged clouds massing over the hills to the south and, although the sun was shining and it was already unusually warm for that time of day, there was in the air the ominous feeling of a storm to come presently. James Sandy, usually known as Jim by everyone who knew him, including his Sergeant at the Station, was a lad of only seventeen, one month off his eighteenth birthday. He had joined the Police at Cockermouth in December of the previous year. Physically he was well suited to be a policeman as he was a large youth, six feet tall, fairly heavy for his age, reasonably broad across the chest, and of a powerful, muscular build. His hair was very fair, not far off white in shade, and he had big blue eyes in a good-looking face. Jim came from a working-class background. His father was a Lakeland fell miner who worked at a mine near Keswick (some ten miles away) and was, at thirty-seven years of age, in charge of a small force of men at the mine. Jim had a brother and twin sisters, all younger than himself (and all still at school); his sisters lived at home with Jim and his father, but they had no mother at home. Just over a year previously Mrs. Sandy had separated from her husband after much bitter quarrelling and had moved down to London, taking Jim's brother with her. Now she lived there with another man.

Jim Sandy had one idea firmly fixed in his mind as he walked briskly along the pavement: if he found a reasonable opportunity to do so that day he would abandon home and job and take a train up to London. He would go and live at his mother's address while he looked for a new job in which he would be happier. He never doubted that in London he would find more than enough suitable new jobs to choose from. If he could somehow manage to catch the mid-morning train from Cockermouth, the 10.8 a.m., he reckoned that it should be possible to be in London before too late in the evening, although he had no idea of the times of the London trains from Carlisle; however, he reasoned that there must be at least <u>one</u> train which would be suitably timed for him. But was there really likely to be any chance to put such a wild plan into operation? Jim did not know, but he felt that he was already inevitably committed to trying it, because a week ago he had dispatched a trunk full of his belongings to his mother's address in Ealing, West London, as the first step towards his "escape" from the Cockermouth Police. If he did not manage to get away that day, he would try for the next day or a day soon after that; but the main thing was that Jim was now determined that he was shortly going up to London in the train by slipping away without informing the Cockermouth Police of what he was doing until he reached London. Jim almost always spent a good deal of his working time each day on the beat walking around the streets of Cockermouth, sometimes by himself, and sometimes in the company of a constable or of the station sergeant; so if he found himself on the beat alone in the neighbourhood of the railway station there would be the opportunity he wanted, if he could manage to be there at the right time.

He did not think that his plan to run away to London could in any way be called foolishness, although he did recognize that there was an element of irrationality in it, because his relationship with his father and his sisters was good, whereas he thought his mother had been very cool towards him before she had left the family home. So why did he want to go to his mother if he knew that he preferred living with his father? Jim had rationalised this question in his mind in a rough way like this: he hated doing police work, and he had come to hate the relative isolation and quietness of his home town (or so he thought), and therefore he would only use his mother's London home as a temporary residence for himself until he found, if possible, some good job in the Capital where he could "live in" at work. Jim had never visited London and consequently had a conception of the place which was typically romantic and naive for one of his age, but the important thing about <u>his</u> idea of London was that it would be a place where jobs would be easy to come by and plentiful and where it would be easy for him to make new friends. He might even find himself a steady girlfriend there, he thought, and perhaps marry her in time. Jim was a very shy person who, although he had been educated at a mixed school had never managed to make friends properly with any of the girls. He had, however, secretly admired one or two of them very much and had been very envious of certain boys at the school who, he felt, were the "steady" friends of the girls he would have liked to approach, but could not. Really, his principle emotional trouble at this time was that he was missing his mother more than he realised; also he lacked any close friends of his own sex and of around his own age. In short, he was lonely.

"Morning, Jim!" called a man's voice. It was his colleague, Constable Nickley who was keeping a watchful eye on people and traffic at a street corner near the Police Station.

"Hello," said Jim, and continued on his way. He usually had not much to say to his fellow officers.

Another minute, and he would have reached the Station. What'll it be this morning? he wondered. Square-bashing first and then out on the beat as usual, I suppose. Oh well, if I get a chance to slip away to the Railway Station . . . He had forgotten for the moment that his Police Station was the headquarters of a murder hunt, one of the rooms in it having been adapted for use as a murder Incident Room. However, the murder had taken place some three weeks earlier, and by now Jim was very little interested in the extra work of the murder hunt as it concerned him hardly at all. He knew the description of the Wanted Man well enough and was as familiar as any of his fellow officers with the "Photo-Fit" artist's impression of this Wanted Man; but because he was only a Cadet he was never involved in any of the detective work of the murder hunt. He knew that it was his duty, while at work, to be extra vigilant at this time in keeping a sharp look-out for that man, and to inform one of his superior officers immediately if he should even <u>think</u> that he might have spotted him. But since the time of the murder the Wanted Man, having been seen by several eye-witnesses running away along the railway track, had disappeared, seemingly without trace. The general public had been very co-operative in the task of watching out for the murderer, and the Cockermouth Police had been alerted two or three times to chase a suspect only to find that in each case it had turned out to be a false alarm. The Detective Inspector in charge of the murder hunt had noted down these incidents as "well-meant, genuinely mistaken sightings" rather than hoaxes meant only to waste police time and manpower on fruitless enquiries. Jim was becoming bored with the whole business. At first, for some days after the murder, he had consciously tried to look carefully at the faces of all the men he saw in the streets, but he had soon grown tired of such an intense level of vigilance, and then he firmly believed that their Wanted Man must certainly have escaped clean away from that whole area. That meant, he reasoned, that he need not trouble himself unduly to look out carefully for this man. Wherever he was, Jim knew that it was hardly likely that they would find him walking about the streets of Cockermouth.

Jim had to wait several seconds for a break in the traffic on the Main Street to cross over to the Police Station which was just opposite to where he was now standing. He saw a police car come out into the street through the archway from the yard of the Station. Two detectives were in the car; they recognized Jim Sandy and gave him a friendly wave before driving quickly off westwards down the street. Jim waved back, remembering as he did so that the murder hunt was still on; up to that point in his walk from home to the Police Station he had been thinking only of his private plan to escape to London. Now, if only there was a high speed chase in a car to catch that man, or something exciting like that, he thought, I shouldn't mind being in it. They don't think that this chap will be armed or dangerous if cornered. But I don't suppose there'll be anything like that. Just walking around these lousy streets is so awfully boring. But, of course, if I could get into the

10.8 train . . . I wonder when I could get a train from Carlisle to London?

He crossed the street and, seeing that the door marked "Enquiries" was standing partly open, entered the Police Station by that way. That morning a woman police constable was behind the Enquiry Counter. She was a powerful-looking woman of little less than Jim's height, about thirty years old, slim, with long golden-red hair which was, however, mostly hidden under her cap, where it was tied in a bun. Her name was Laura Apsley.

"Hello, Jim," she said. "You're just in time today by four minutes." She had a loud voice which might almost have been mistaken for a man's.

"Hello, Laura," said Jim, whose mind had been on other things, but he glanced at his watch as he said it. He was really supposed to be in the Station no later than five minutes before nine o'clock, and was then allowed five minutes to tidy up his appearance before reporting to the Sergeant for duty. The strict need for punctuality irked him considerably, but he usually managed to conform to the rules.

"How are you enjoying your work here, eh?" asked W.P.C. Apsley.

"Oh well, er, not all that much. I mean, it's quite all right, really," said Jim awkwardly.

"What! Do you mean you don't like it?"

"I suppose you could say that."

"Well, you do surprise me," said W.P.C. Apsley. "Do you know, Jim, I've heard Sergeant Koppel say that you're a very promising young recruit who should do well and get promotion in the Force?"

"Oh, has he really said that about me? But it's nice to know he thinks I'm doing all right."

"Right. You'd better hurry off and get ready to report for work at nine o'clock to keep doing right. But you ought to have more confidence in yourself, Jim, you know." She waved a ball-point pen at him by way of saying Good-bye, and immediately returned to some written work on the desk, while Jim hurried out through another door on his way to the Cloak Room. He did not exactly like Laura Apsley, but was rather in awe of her and almost a little afraid of her, for he thought she must be almost as strong as himself, and that perhaps, if he happened to annoy her, she might even knock him to the ground with a powerful rugby tackle. However, she had a pretty face, he thought, and although she could seem to be a little short-tempered at times she could also be gentle enough when in a good mood.

Jim was already wearing his full uniform, but now in the Cloak Room he carefully slipped a hand into the outer pocket of the tunic to check that those personal belongings which he could not do without, if he got a chance to get away on a train for London, had been transferred into it from his jacket. Yes, his wallet was there, and in it was thirteen pounds in notes, the result of having saved as much of his recent wages as possible for a train fare to London, and back, if necessary; he knew that thirteen pounds would be more than enough. That morning he had carefully stowed the wallet in the inner pocket of his police tunic and had put some small change into the trouser pockets. He realised that it would not be possible to bring his own jacket and trousers with him if he did set off for London, unless he were to run back home first to pick them up, so he decided that they would have to be left behind. No doubt they could be sent on to him later. Also Jim realised that he would find himself that night (if he got to London) missing one or two little items, such as his toothbrush, although he expected to find all those belongings which he had sent on in advance waiting for him at his mother's house in Ealing. As for the toothbrush and other over-night requirements which he could not bring with him: That's just too bad, he said to himself. I'll have to do without them, that's all.

A minute or two later, having rubbed a duster over his boots to improve the shine on them, Jim emerged from the Cloak Room to go to report for duty at the Station Sergeant's Office. There was a smile of anticipation on his face as he approached the Sergeant's door at the thought of his projected train trip to London. The smile, however, was soon to disappear.

"I have an indoor job for you to do this morning, Cadet Sandy," said Sergeant Koppel. "Some cards to file alphabetically for a card-index."

"Yes, sir." Jim's spirits had sunk immediately on hearing of an indoor job.

"Names of interviewees for our Murder Enquiry," continued the Sergeant. "There are hundreds of cards, I'm afraid, but you can take all morning up to lunch break on the filing, if you need to. I thought you'd like a change from going on the beat in the morning, so you can go out this afternoon instead."

"Yes sir, thank you."

"It's going to rain anyway, this morning, heavily too by the look of it, and probably quite soon. There would be no point in getting your uniform soaking wet out on the beat in heavy rain. It should be fine by this afternoon."

Jim looked out through the window, which was too narrow to see very much of the sky. Yes, there was no doubt that it <u>was</u> going to rain. He had seen for himself, just before he had come into the Station, that the clouds over the hills to the south were quickly moving up as if to cover the whole sky. Already the sun had disappeared and it was beginning to grow darker.

"It looks as if there might be a thunderstorm," said Jim.

"Yes, I think there might well be a thunderstorm," said the Sergeant. "Now then, run along to the Enquiry Office, my lad, and I'll get Constable Apsley to show you what to do with those cards."

Sergeant Koppel and Cadet Jim Sandy left the Sergeant's Office together, Jim in a much more sober frame of mind than he had been in only a minute earlier.

Five minutes later he was sitting at a desk and beginning the mammoth task of sorting through a great heap of what looked like hundreds of cards. The cards had names and addresses typed on them, and underneath each address a space in which various notes had been added; Jim's task was to put all the cards into strict alphabetical order under surnames. He knew that his projected escape to London was certainly off, for that day at least. The afternoon, he had decided, would be no use to him for catching a train at Cockermouth station because he wanted to arrive at Euston station no later than the early evening. That meant that it would have to be the 10.8 a.m. train or nothing. He felt thoroughly dejected as he began to go through all the cards to collect the "A's".

On a wall opposite to the desk where Jim was sitting was one of the posters with the artist's impression of the face of the man wanted in connection with the murder. There was a description in words underneath the picture, part of which read as follows:-

"Probably aged between 30 and 40, of slim build and medium height. Hair mid-brown, thick, slightly curly, showing no sign of baldness. Has a small fringe of beard and a moustache. Colour of eyes uncertain, thought to be blue . . ."

The circumstances in which this murder had been committed were not such as to lead the police to believe that it was likely that the murderer might strike again. On the contrary, it seemed to have been a one-off incident. Two young men, the younger probably in his twenties, had stepped off the last train of the day three weeks previously onto the down platform of Cockermouth station, apparently in the middle of a violent quarrel. After a brief struggle on the platform the older of the two men had brought out a knife and stabbed the other through the chest; then he had immediately fled eastwards along the railway line (the train was going on westwards). The younger man had been taken to hospital where he had died a few hours later from his chest wound. There had, of course, been many eye-witnesses of the attack; the police wanted to trace and interview every person, passengers, guard and driver, who had been aboard that last train of the day (the 9.18 p.m.) in their attempt to find further clues to the identity of the killer, who had totally disappeared.

Jim Sandy had been sorting his cards for the card-index for some ten minutes when Sergeant Koppel suddenly appeared in the room. Jim was finding the work monotonous and frustrating, but he looked up with a start when the Sergeant called his name sharply:

"Cadet Sandy!"

"Sir?"

"Come with me, lad, quickly. I've a job for you. Leave those cards at once."

Jim instantly jumped up and, wondering, hurried over to the door.

"We've a man to arrest," said the Sergeant. "You can come with us in the car. That's it, in the yard. Look sharp now."

Jim hardly had time to think as he was rushed out into the yard where a black police car was standing near the back door of the Station, its blue light already rotating and the engine already running. Two other policemen were standing out there beside the car. Who was the man they were going to arrest? Jim felt a somewhat confused sense of excitement arising in him. Anyway, a chase and possibly an arrest promised to be far more interesting than sitting at that dreary desk filing name cards.

"You drive, Sommers," ordered the Sergeant. "You get in the back with Nickley, Jim."

The four men got into the car and slammed the doors shut. A moment later the car roared out into the street, blue light flashing, and sounding the siren as the driver, Constable Sommers, took the Keswick main road out of the town.

"Constable Sommers thinks he may have seen our Wanted Man," explained Sergeant Koppel to Jim, turning his head round for a moment (he was sitting beside the driver); "so we've got to go and investigate."

All four men knew, of course, that it was highly unlikely that a man wanted for murder would be seen strolling about carelessly near the scene of his crime, but there was no question but that the Sergeant was right. The man would have to be detained and questioned, if only so that he could be eliminated from the police enquiries.

CHAPTER TWO

Earlier that morning Lord and Lady Dalmane, the Earl and Countess of Saint Helens, walked through the archway and onto the up platform of the railway station at Cockermouth. The taxi which had brought them there from Maryport, a small town on the Cumbrian coast, drove away from the station yard. Lord and Lady Dalmane were taking their summer holiday. The Earl was the owner of a small yacht which he kept in a boathouse belonging to a friend who lived locally and used to sail around the Cumbrian coast; but Lord and Lady Dalmane lived in the South: their seat was Rhodes Castle, a big old house and castle in the Dorset countryside. Lord Dalmane had for several years been coming up to the North every summer to go sailing with his friend in the Solway Firth and the Irish Sea, although sometimes they had gone cruising as far afield as Western Scotland, the Outer Hebrides, or even Saint Kilda. This year for the first time he had taken his wife with him instead of his friend, Dr. Martin Himmel. John Dalmane, the Earl of Saint Helens, had only been married a little over two months. His wife's name was Susan, a lovely young woman, only twenty-one years old, who had done some cruising before, and had been very eager to go with her husband on this occasion. They had been very fortunate with the weather, and the two of them had spent an extremely happy ten days sailing the boat, a smallish cutter with white sails, by themselves. Their voyaging had been on a somewhat more modest scale than John Dalmane's had been in previous years, but they had sailed along the Galloway coast almost as far as Stranraer, and crossed briefly to Northern Ireland from Portpatrick; then they had sailed into the Firth of Clyde, looked at Ailsa Craig in passing, and spent a whole day on the Isle of Arran, having landed at Brodick. On their return voyage they had put in to Kirkudbright, and early that morning they had sailed from there to re-cross the Solway Firth to Maryport, the port from which they had begun their cruising.

"It seems rather quiet here, a sleepy little place," said Susan Dalmane, the Countess.

"Yes, it does rather," said John Dalmane, "but mind you, my dear, you're forgetting how early in the morning it still is. It's only just gone ten to eight, but remember that we've been up and on the move since before five."

"Yes, I was rather forgetting that most people will hardly have finished their breakfasts yet, and the shops won't be open, I suppose, until about nine. What do we do now, John? Perhaps we'd better have a second breakfast here, a proper one, while we wait for the train. We didn't really get much to eat on board the <u>Osprey</u>, you know."

"Well, I think perhaps the <u>first</u> thing we ought to do, my dear, is to make sure about the time of our train," said Lord Dalmane. "Martin only told us he <u>thought</u> it went at 8.10, so we're in time enough if that's right: but he said he didn't really know. I'll just go and look for a Train Departure Times notice and then we'll know where we are."

Lord and Lady Dalmane had been standing on the platform near the entrance from the Booking Hall, and looking around them at the small railway station and what they could see of the town around it. Everything they could see was new to them. It had been a last minute change of plan to come to Cockermouth Station instead of travelling by the much more obvious and quicker rail route to Carlisle Station direct from Maryport. To do that had always been their plan: when they reached Carlisle Station later that morning they were meaning to travel on the "Royal Scot" express to Euston in London. Then they were going from London to Knebworth in Hertfordshire to stay for a few days with a great-aunt of Lady Dalmane's before finally returning home to Rhodes Castle at the end of their holiday. But, when they had brought their boat into the harbour at Maryport on the high tide at seven o'clock and had been met, as planned, by Lord Dalmane's boating friend, Dr. Himmel, while they were mooring their vessel at the quayside, Susan had said: "Oh, I do wish our holiday wasn't nearly over. John, couldn't we change the plan a little bit so that we could travel another way to Carlisle? It would be nice if we could see something of the Lake District when we're so near it, and we won't if we just go from here straight to Carlisle." It was then that Dr. Himmel had suggested that they could travel on the line from Workington through the Lakes to Penrith, starting by taking a train to Workington; or, better still, they could save time by taking a taxi direct to Cockermouth Station, as the train journey from Maryport to Cockermouth via Workington was not particularly interesting, and because in that way they could avoid a change at Workington. He told the Dalmanes that the line from Cockermouth to Penrith went through the northern part of the Lake District and was beautifully scenic, really something that they should not miss if they wanted to see lakes and mountains. The Dalmanes listened with interest. Dr. Himmel told them that they would be able to travel through to Carlisle that way without a change if they went by the morning train from Cockermouth which, as he thought he remembered, went at 8.10, although of this he was not sure. He was, however, certain that they would reach Carlisle Station by that way in ample time to catch the "Royal Scot." The Dalmanes had willingly agreed to this change of plan and Dr. Himmel had arranged the taxi for them.

So it was that Lord and Lady Dalmane had arrived at Cockermouth at ten minutes to eight in time for a possible train departure at ten minutes past eight. They had found that the Booking Office was open (they had seen the Booking Clerk sitting in there at a desk), but there was no one except themselves on either of the two platforms. Lord Dalmane turned from looking up and down the line to look at the wall behind him and, sure enough, there he saw what he wanted: various notices on wooden notice boards attached to the wall, among them the Train Departure Times. Lord Dalmane went up to it to read the details.

He was a reasonably good-looking man; at thirty-three, twelve years older than his wife. His appearance was, indeed, in no way extraordinary; yet it was to be the source of a good deal of trouble and embarrassment for him later that morning. John Dalmane had thick, slightly curly brown hair with a hint of red in it; hair which was not yet showing any signs of baldness. He had blue eyes, nestling under thick, ruddy-coloured eyebrows, a prominent nose, and fairly large ears. His height was medium for a man of his age, about five feet eight inches, and his general build slim. Altogether these features bore an uncanny resemblance to the police artist's drawing of the man wanted for the Cockermouth Station murder. There were, however, subtle differences between the face of the man in that drawing and that of the Earl of Saint Helens; for example, the description of the Wanted Man made no mention of any reddish tint of the hair, whereas such a tint was unmistakable in John Dalmane. Yet the two faces looked, on the whole, astonishingly similar; and it was nothing more than one of those strange chances of fate which had brought John Dalmane to Cockermouth on a day when the police were looking for a man whose description would very nearly have fitted his perfectly.

"There isn't an 8.10 train to Carlisle," said Lord Dalmane. "The next one is the 10.8. It seems that my friend at Maryport has remembered the figures the wrong way round." He turned to find that his wife, Susan, was at his side. "You see, Sue, there it is quite plainly: 10.8 a.m. through train to Carlisle."

"Oh, heavens!" said Susan. "That means that we've got ages to wait for it: over two hours in fact."

"Yes, I'm afraid so, my dear."

There was a short silence. Lord and Lady Dalmane held each other's hands, while for a few moments Lord Dalmane stared dreamily into his wife's eyes.

What he saw entranced him so much that it took only those few moments for him to forget all about the station and the next train to Carlisle. Susan was very beautiful, and Lord Dalmane found that the beauty of her face was something which never grew stale for him. There was some quality in that beauty which had often put him in mind of an exquisitely painted, fragile porcelain figure, so that it was almost instinctive for him to touch and kiss her very gently, as if he were afraid that she might break at a rough touch, like the most expensive bone china. In point of fact, Susan Dalmane was anything but fragile: rather she was strong and healthy. Her black hair was cut fairly short at the back of her head, where it just covered the nape of her neck, while in the front it was attractively parted in the middle. Her ears were partly hidden under her hair, and she always wore ear-rings in them, usually two gold heart-shapes, each with a diamond glittering in the centre. And her eyes, into which John, her husband, was looking with enraptured pleasure, were excitingly dark. He thought that her eyes were the loveliest of all her features. Susan herself described their colour as black, and in this John agreed with her. The very dark irises appeared almost to merge into the large black pupils. Her eyelashes were well made-up and there was eye-shadow (but not too much) around her eyes. Her eyebrows were very light and delicate, and she had the trick of being able to raise one of them slightly when she wanted to make her eyes look more exciting. As for the rest of her face, her nose was small and a little up-turned, her chin narrowed to a rounded point, and her lips were big, perfectly formed, and most inviting to kiss; indeed at this point, beginning to be lost in a reverie of the charms of his wife's face, John Dalmane without conscious thought suddenly lent forwards and kissed Susan on the lips.

But Susan was thinking of quite other things than kisses and hardly seemed to notice the contact of her husband's lips. "All that time to wait," she said, "unless we go for a walk, or something. Only I don't really want to, not just now anyway. I think I'm rather tired, actually, after that very early start this morning. And hungry too; and thirsty. What do you say, John? Shall we not sit down here and have a nice, leisurely picnic breakfast to kill most of the time while we wait for this train? Look, there's a bench over there." She pointed up the platform to where a bench stood just beyond the station buildings on that side of the station.

"Okay, good idea, Sue," said John Dalmane. "I could do with some breakfast too. Tea and biscuits on board ship at five-thirty a.m. don't count for very much by eight o'clock, do they? Although they were very nice at the time, taken in the cockpit, while we were slowly leaving the Galloway coast behind on a nice, smooth sea. Mind you, now that I think about it, I'm glad the wind came when it did. If it hadn't we'd still be drifting about somewhere on a flat calm out there in the Solway Firth."

"I wish we were," said Susan. "At least, I wish the sailing didn't have to be over. It's been really gorgeous. We must go again next year, John, and we could go further."

"I don't see why not. You've been pretty good as a crew, Sue, so we could take Osprey almost anywhere around these coasts. But, you know, I was really a bit bothered by that calm this morning. And the weather doesn't look to me all that kind now, either."

"But why were you bothered?" asked Susan. "We could have run on with the engine, couldn't we, all the way across if we'd had to, if the wind hadn't come when it did?"

"We couldn't," said John. "We hadn't nearly enough petrol left to do that. If that light air from the south hadn't strengthened when it did we could never have managed to beat our way across close-hauled on the starboard tack against the incoming tide. We'd have drifted up the Solway north-eastwards. And there are shoals and shallow water further up that estuary, so we could have been in trouble if we couldn't steer properly so as to avoid going aground on a mudbank. No, we've been a bit lucky this morning. But maybe it's a good thing that we're back on solid, dry land now. Look at those clouds over there, Sue." He pointed towards the hills to the east of the town. Most of the sky was clear and blazingly blue, but in that quarter only was a bank of clouds: white cumulus clouds, darker towards their base line over the hills, but John Dalmane judged by their shape and hard-looking outlines that they were quickly rising and moving out over the rest of the sky. The morning sun was now not very far clear of the bank of clouds.

"Well? They're just clouds, aren't they?" said Susan.

"It looks to me as if it might turn thundery presently," said Lord Dalmane. "There's not much wind now, but it could get up a great deal if there's a thunderstorm in the offing. I may be wrong, of course, but I think those clouds have a distinct look of thunder about them, and that might mean fierce squalls of wind, not exactly what anyone wants when sailing. We've been jolly lucky with our weather . . . oh look, there are a few other people here now."

A small group of people were standing near the middle of the other platform. Lord and Lady Dalmane had by this time strolled up their platform to the seat and had sat down on it. They had taken the knapsacks, which they had been carrying, off their backs; among other things these knapsacks contained plenty of picnic food (mostly sandwiches) which Susan had prepared the evening before while their boat, the Osprey, had been at anchor at Kirkudbright.

"How did they come there?" said Susan, looking at the people on the other platform. "I never saw, or heard, anyone crossing from this platform. Perhaps you can get onto the other one direct from that road bridge."

"I don't think you can," said Lord Dalmane. "I think I saw the entrance to a subway just in there, by the Booking Office. They must have walked underneath the tracks and come up on that side."

"What train do you think they're waiting for, John?"

"I suppose, for the 8.19 to Workington. I think that's what I read on that notice. But it doesn't concern us, of course. We're going to Carlisle, not Workington."

"I suppose we <u>are</u> waiting on the right platform for the 10.8 to Carlisle?" said Susan.

"Oh yes, definitely so," said Lord Dalmane. "It said Platform One for the 10.8, and that sign up there says this <u>is</u> Platform One. By the way, Sue, we mustn't forget that we haven't bought our tickets yet. We came straight onto this platform when we arrived here to have a look at the place. Shall we get the tickets now, so we don't forget them?"

"There's no need," said Susan. "We shan't forget them. Let's have some breakfast." She was already unfastening the straps of her knapsack. "I'm fairly dying of thirst, and pretty hungry too, so we'll have that flask of coffee out for a start. Hello! There's this too." She brought out of the knapsack a little flat-shaped bottle with a small amount of a golden liquid in the bottom of it.

"The rum? Shall we finish it now?" said Lord Dalmane.

"Yes, we'd better have it now. It won't do much to quench thirst, but it would be rather comforting to drink it. There's only a drop left anyway, and there'd be no point in carrying it all the way down to Knebworth."

Susan had brought the small bottle of rum with her from home to have as a medicinal stand-by, if necessary, on board the yacht. As it had not all been consumed while afloat, John and Susan drank the last drops of it directly from the bottle in turns. Then Susan brought out a flask of coffee and poured out two drinks of that into plastic mugs; then she took a packet of sandwiches out of her knapsack.

While the Dalmanes were enjoying their breakfast picnic a few more people gathered on the opposite platform until presently they saw the 8.19 train to Workington come into sight, rumbling across the ugly concrete bridge, which stood just outside the station to the east, spanning the River Cocker. The train made a brief stop at the other platform while people got in and out, and within a minute was going on its way again. For a little while the station seemed to be quite a noisy, busy place, as it appeared that a small crowd of passengers had disembarked from that train. John and Susan Dalmane went quietly on with their picnic, taking little notice of anyone else. They knew perfectly well that they would look to all these other people just like two ordinary, common tourists; in fact, that was what they wanted to look like. Not one of those people could have guessed that the solitary pair sitting on Platform One of that station and eating sandwiches out of a knapsack were the Earl and Countess of Saint Helens, a peer of high rank and his consort. It was more likely, because of the knapsacks and because they were both wearing sturdy outdoor boots, that they were being mistaken for hikers or fell-walkers. Susan's five feet eight inches figure (she was about the same height as her husband) was clad in a pair of old jeans and a thin blouse, which fitted her top parts well enough to do justice to her ample and shapely bust. Lord Dalmane wore an old tweed jacket over his shirt and a pair of grey trousers which did not match it at all; and he had left the shirt open at the neck. He never liked to wear a tie when he considered that one was not really necessary, and for many informal occasions preferred a cravat to a tie.

Within about two minutes from the departure of the Workington train the small crowd of people had completely vanished. A porter who had been over there amongst those passengers had disappeared into the station buildings. The quietness which the Dalmanes somehow thought natural to that small branch line station was restored. The wind too had dropped to nothing, adding to the effect of sudden silence after the brief period of bustle. The noise of motor traffic in the streets of the town seemed peculiarly muffled and remote in the slack, sticky air. They were startled by a clang of the signal on the opposite platform changing to the danger position behind the departed train, a loud noise in the windless air. Then there was silence for a minute or two, a silence which seemed to hum in their ears until it was disturbed by the sudden loud roar of a lorry passing over the road bridge which spanned the single track just beyond the western end of the platforms.

Meanwhile John and Susan Dalmane continued to eat their breakfast picnic, being careful not to hurry over it, while they talked over their sailing holiday and discussed some tentative plans for a rather more ambitious cruising holiday for next year, or the year after. After about twenty minutes they felt they had eaten a good, solid meal, and had drunk the last of their coffee; this still left them with more than enough food and drink for another picnic meal at lunch time. Then they went along to the Booking Office and bought themselves through single tickets to London Euston. The clerk at the ticket counter confirmed their opinion that the 10.8 train was the correct connection for the "Royal Scot". "That's right, sir," he said to Lord Dalmane, who bought the tickets. "Your train to London is the 11.57 a.m. from Carlisle. The 10.8 from here gets in at 11.34 to connect with it."

"Here you are, Sue," said Lord Dalmane, handing her a ticket. "You'd better have yours just in case we get separated in the train when a ticket inspector comes along."

The Dalmanes wandered back onto the up platform of the still deserted station and returned to sit again on their bench. They again discussed the possibility of taking an after-breakfast stroll around the streets to see what the town was like and to fill up some more time out of their long wait, but neither John nor Susan really wanted to walk at that time so they agreed to rest their legs on the platform seat instead.

"And perhaps I might even drop off for a short nap," said Lord Dalmane, "if you could be sure to wake me in good time for our train, Sue. You're sure you're not sleepy now, my dear?"

"No," said Susan, "I don't feel at all sleepy now. But I'd rather stay here for a while, sitting down all the same."

After that neither of them spoke again for quite some time.

CHAPTER THREE

Lord Dalmane felt himself being gently prodded in the side.

"John, dear, do wake up."

He heard Susan's voice, opened his eyes, and sat up with a jerk.

"Hello. Have I been asleep?"

"Yes, I think so."

"What's up, Sue? Time for our train?"

"No, it isn't that," said Susan. "It's only just after nine. But there are two people up there who have been looking at us—or rather, staring at us."

"Where?"

"Up there on that road bridge."

Lord Dalmane looked up at the bridge and saw a man and a woman standing there, looking over the parapet, apparently watching them.

"Why shouldn't they look at us?" he asked.

"Oh, I just thought that it was rather odd because they must have been standing up there looking down at us for about four or five minutes," said Susan.

"Well, they're moving on now." They saw the man on the bridge pick up what looked as if it might be a heavy suitcase as the couple walked on down the road, disappearing from the Dalmanes's view. "Maybe they're coming here," added Lord Dalmane. "They looked to me like travellers if that was a suitcase they're carrying."

About a minute later the Dalmanes looked round towards the entrance from the Booking Hall on hearing a sudden sound of footsteps and people talking. The porter came out onto the platform carrying a large suitcase which he set down not far from the platform edge; with him came the man and the woman who had been staring down at the station from the road bridge.

"That's quite a fair weight," said the porter.

"Well, we needed to take a lot of stuff with us," said the man.

"Are you going far?"

"We're going down to the South to live with my parents, until I can get a house of our own down there."

"What! You don't mean to say you're <u>leaving</u> us, Nigel?" said the porter.

"Yes, we are," said the man. "We're leaving this area altogether, and probably we'll never return."

"Well, I'm right sorry to hear that you're going, Nigel. It's the first I've heard about it. What about your job?"

"Oh, I'm not giving that up. They haven't actually given me a transfer <u>yet</u>, but I'll be getting a driving job somewhere down there presently."

"I see. Well, you'll have to excuse me, Nigel, but I'm busy just now on a job in the Office. I'll see you later. You're in very good time anyway for the 10.8. So long!"

"They're the couple who were looking at us from the bridge," whispered Susan to her husband when the porter had gone back to the Office. John nodded thoughtfully. The Dalmanes had overheard all the other people's conversation in the windless air and realised that the porter seemed to be a close friend of theirs. The woman, who had said nothing, and was carrying nothing except a shoulder-bag, seemed to be looking for something. They noticed a worried expression on her face as she kept restlessly turning round, looking now up or down the platform, now at the buildings behind her. Susan saw that the strange woman had obviously been pretty when she had been a few years younger, but she thought that her face looked old and careworn prematurely. Probably over thirty, Susan said to herself, but I doubt if she's passed forty. In fact, Susan's guess was accurate, for they learned later that the woman was only thirty-seven. She was tall and very thin. Her cheeks were very pale and looked rather hollow; her lips lacked colour. Susan could not be sure about the colour of the woman's eyes, but her hair was dark, yet not as dark as her own, and although not long, the hair was certainly very untidy. Altogether she was still, in a way, attractive, but she appeared to Susan to be seriously ill—as, in truth, she was.

"I <u>must</u> sit down," they heard the woman say to the man whom they had heard addressed as "Nigel"; clearly she was his wife.

"Well, my dear, there's the Waiting Room," said the man. "We could sit in there."

"<u>Not</u> the smelly Waiting Room, Nigel," said the woman. "I want to sit out of doors."

The husband looked rather helplessly around. But Susan, followed immediately by John Dalmane, quickly stood up.

"Come and sit here," said Susan. "There's plenty of room for three on this bench."

"Yes, do," said Lord Dalmane. "We don't mind."

"Thank you," said the pale woman.

"That's very kind of you," said her husband.

The woman, unsmiling, sat down on one end of the bench.

"But what about you?" asked Lord Dalmane, addressing her husband. "I think we could fit four in, with a bit of a squeeze. Or I could stand up or walk about for a bit."

"No, please don't do that for me," said the man politely. "I'm quite all right standing up for a while. I'll sit on my suitcase when I want to sit down. I'm going to walk about for a while, though."

Rather uncomfortably the Dalmanes sat down again on the bench, Susan in the middle beside the thin, pale woman, and Lord Dalmane at the other end. The other man was walking away towards the eastern end of that platform. He stopped close beside the signal post and they noticed that he looked up at the semaphore arm of the starting signal in a familiar sort of way, as if he knew all about railway signals. He was a fairly lightly-built man who, Susan thought, might have been around fifty or in his early fifties, although in fact he was only forty-four. His hair had been black but was now turning grey and considerably receding, and he was rather short for a man of his age: he was noticeably several inches shorter than his wife. They had seen something of a worried look in his pale, hazel-coloured eyes which was emphasised, perhaps, by the furrows on his forehead which appeared to be a permanent feature.

But, having sat down beside that man's wife, Susan felt much more concerned about her than about him. The woman sat there, rather slumped forwards, looking down at the paving stones around her feet. Susan had little doubt that she was shy with strangers and feeling awkward at having to sit so close to her, but also she felt again that her new companion looked ill. But a little conversation would no doubt help to ease the tension.

"It looks rather like rain, I think," said Susan by way of opening the conversation, glancing up briefly at the sky.

"Yes," mumbled the woman dully without looking up from her feet.

It was not an encouraging start for breaking down the barrier of shyness with a stranger. Susan looked up again at the sky as if for inspiration. The sun had disappeared some time ago, and now more or less the whole sky was cloudy, but it was not yet becoming significantly darker. There had been little or no wind for a while, but just then there came a light breeze out of the south, stirring the close air; it rustled the leaves of a line of little willow trees between the station and the park which lay immediately to the south on a steeply rising bank of neatly mown grass, in which were set well-kept flower beds; the little willow trees grew in a row along the station perimeter fence at the foot of this incline.

There was also a group of larger trees around the station-master's house at the western end of the main platform. Here too a sound of leaves rustling in the wind was heard: a pleasant sound to listen to, but it only lasted about a minute before dying away into a silence which was almost tangibly a threat: as it were, a quietness before an inevitable storm. Both Susan and John noticed a sudden flickering brightness in the south-eastern sky, the reflection of distant lightning amidst the dark clouds which were still swelling over the range of mountains which lay hidden from sight below the horizon to the south-east. There was a hot, sticky feeling about the motionless air, an unpleasant stuffiness, strongly suggestive of approaching thunder; but they never heard the thunder which must have followed that far-away lightning flash.

Susan looked round for a few seconds following the lightning, and then tried again to make polite conversation.

"It's rather oppressive, isn't it? I believe it's going to thunder."

But this time the woman merely shrugged her shoulders as if in complete indifference to the possibility of thunder.

"It begins to look very much as if there's a thunderstorm brewing up here," said Lord Dalmane. "At least it looks very like rain—really heavy rain, probably, though perhaps it won't come for another half-hour or so—but I expect we'll get wet if we just stay here."

"So do I," said the man's voice. He had come back from the end of the platform and was standing beside Lord Dalmane. "But I think the rain's not going to come for quite a while yet. The train should get here first."

"Are you waiting for the 10.8 train too?" asked Lord Dalmane.

"Yes," said the man.

"Going far, are you?" Lord Dalmane glanced towards the large suitcase as he pretended not to have overheard that earlier conversation with the porter.

"Indeed we are. We're going down to a little place called Knebworth in Hertfordshire to see an aunt of mine who lives there, and then we're going on tomorrow to live for a while with my parents who also live in that part of the country." The man was puzzled to see the expressions of considerable surprise on the faces of both of the Dalmanes as he said this.

"Well, that is a really amazing co-incidence," said Lord Dalmane, "because Knebworth is where <u>we</u> are going today."

"There could hardly be two places called Knebworth in the South of England," said Susan, "so we must, all of us, be travelling to the same destination. How extraordinary!"

"Indeed, yes," said the man. "But as we shall be travelling, I suppose, in the same trains all day—you're going up to London on the 'Royal Scot'?"

"We are."

"Then we ought to get to know each other a little, I suppose. Our name is Beck; I'm Nigel, and this is my wife, Norma." Mrs. Beck looked round and nodded vaguely as if to acknowledge that her name was indeed Norma Beck, but still she did not say anything. She had looked up on hearing that, by a strange chance, all four of them were travelling to Knebworth that day, but hardly any sign of surprise or other emotion had appeared on her sullen face.

The Dalmanes stood up.

"No, please don't get up," said Susan quickly, seeing that Mrs. Beck was also thinking of standing up. "You look awfully tired."

"Pleased to meet you," said Lord Dalmane. "Our name is Dalmane. I'm Lord Dalmane, John, and this is my wife, Susan, who is Lady Dalmane, but please don't be put off by our titles. We're the Earl and Countess of Saint Helens, but really we're very ordinary people, you know."

It was now Mr. Beck's turn to look surprised. "How do you do, my Lord?" he said politely and a little awkwardly. "Pleased to meet you, my Lady." He made a little bow with his head.

Susan smiled and took his hand, and shook it. Then she smiled a little more broadly at seeing Mrs. Beck stand up for a moment and curtsey to her and her husband. A shy little smile appeared on Mrs. Beck's face for the first time as she said, rather nervously: "How do you do, my Lady?"

"Lovely to meet you," said Susan, taking her hand and shaking it warmly. "Well, now we know each other," she added, "by name, at least. Look here, do sit down with us, Mr. Beck. We can make room for you here."

"Thank you," said Mr. Beck. A moment later he found himself sitting down between Lord Dalmane on his left and Lady Dalmane on his right. It certainly was rather a tight fit for four of them on the platform bench, but Mr. Beck felt less awkward sitting there than standing and trying to converse with three seated people.

"Will you have some tea, Mrs. Beck?" asked Susan kindly. "And you, Mr. Beck? And would you like anything to eat? We've got plenty of food."

The Becks accepted mugs of tea but took nothing to eat. Mr. Beck, as he took his plastic mug of tea and thanked Susan for it, said that as there was still a lot of time to wait for the train he would shortly take a walk, and he invited either or both the Dalmanes to join him. "You don't want to walk anywhere, Norma, I take it?" he added.

"No, I don't," said Norma.

"Thank you for asking us," said Susan, "but I don't know whether I'll go for a walk just now: I rather think not. I think I'd prefer to stay here and talk with your wife if you two men are going walking. Only don't go too far! Remember to watch the time, John."

"Yes, of course, my dear."

"By the way," said Susan, "if you don't mind me asking, Mr. Beck, why did you two stand up there on the bridge looking down on us for so long? I noticed that, and thought it a little odd that you didn't move on for maybe five minutes."

"Well," said Mr. Beck, "for one thing we'd left our house really quite ridiculously early to catch the 10.8 so we had masses of time to spare. But stopping to look down on the station from up there was just pure nostalgia on my part."

"Nostalgia? You mean, you know the place very well?"

"Indeed I do," said Mr. Beck. "We're going away, you see, possibly never to return to Cockermouth. We're going to live down in the South, as I explained before. But the thing is, I used to work here, so I know this old station very well indeed."

"Oh, really? What was your job, Mr. Beck?" asked Susan.

"I used to be a porter here to begin with. I first came to Cockermouth from the South twelve years ago, back in 1947, when the old L.M.S. was still running the railways in these parts. The railways were nationalised the year after that, and for a year or two British Railways kept me on as a porter at Cockermouth. But I'd always wanted to be a driver and so I started my training on the footplate—I can't quite remember when, though it might have been in '50 or '51—and then I began travelling all over the place on the railways, sometimes handling the controls under supervision, and sometimes stoking—the fireman's job, you know. And so, at last, I became a fully qualified engine-driver. This last year I've been driving the little diesel-hauled trains which are used now for all the passenger services on this line. I reluctantly gave it up only about a month ago when my health wasn't too good—it's better now—and when Norma's condition was becoming a really serious worry. My poor wife suffers from dreadful depression which she says is made much worse by living here in such an isolated part of the country— that's right, dear, isn't it?"

Mrs. Beck nodded her head slightly but said nothing.

"So I gave up my job driving on this line," continued Mr. Beck, "and we agreed that we'd leave the area altogether and move down to Hertfordshire, which is where I originally came from. I got British Railways to agree to keep me on as an employee on sick pay temporarily until I can resume work."

"You mean, you hope to be given a job driving trains down in Hertfordshire?" asked Lord Dalmane.

"That's right: in Hertfordshire, London, or somewhere in the Home Counties," said Mr. Beck. "Somewhere more on my native ground, as you might say, or nearer to it."

"How very interesting to hear that you're an engine-driver, Mr. Beck," said Susan with genuine interest. "I do hope they'll give you another driving job without too much difficulty. Now, my husband, John, loves railways, and I think that if he had not had to be an Earl he would have been an engine-driver. Isn't that so, John?"

"Yes, indeed, Sue," said Lord Dalmane, "if I hadn't happened to be born into an aristocratic family, the heir to an hereditary earldom, I might well have decided to work on the railways. I love trains, and particularly steam engines. Mind you, I'm usually a very busy man, with little time for any train watching or anything like that. My work in the House of Lords often takes up most of each day; I'm on various committees of the Lords. But my wife and I are on holiday now."

"Yes, I thought that you two must be strangers holidaying here," said Mr. Beck. "Have you been here before?"

"No, it's our first visit to Cockermouth."

"Have you been here long?"

"No, we only came here today."

"What? By the 7.22 train?" (the first train of the day from Workington).

"No, not by train," said Lord Dalmane. "We arrived here by taxi at about ten to eight from Maryport. When I said 'our first visit to Cockermouth' I only meant that we're passing through. We haven't stayed here at all, although I'd certainly like to some time as it looks quite a pretty little town, what you can see of it from here—and the glimpses we had from the taxi."

"You say you only arrived here this morning—from Maryport?" queried Mr. Beck, apparently surprised to hear this.

"Yes," said Lord Dalmane. "We've just come to the end of a very enjoyable ten days of sailing. I own a small yacht which we keep up here, although we live down at my seat in Dorset—Rhodes Castle, near Sherborne."

"Sailing," said Mr. Beck thoughtfully. "How very pleasant it must be to go on a sailing holiday at sea." Mr. Beck knew nothing whatever about yachts or sailing, but it occurred to him that there would indeed be something very enjoyable in experiencing being cut off from all one's familiar surroundings on land while sailing on the sea in a small boat. For a few seconds he was silent, turning over in his mind with relish his idea of what sea sailing in a yacht would be like. One would escape from all the familiar, dreary things—and people too—which normally made up an inevitable part of daily life: that must be the great virtue in a sailing trip, he thought. He glanced at his wrist-watch, and saw that it was between a quarter and twenty minutes past nine.

"I say," he added, "time's getting on. Did you say that you'd like to come for a short walk with me, Lord Dalmane? We'd better go straight away, if we're going."

"Yes, I should love to come with you," said Lord Dalmane. "You know somewhere nice to walk, I expect?"

"Yes, we'll walk along the line. We can get right out into the country in ten to fifteen minutes, and beyond the Cemetry you get a magnificent view towards Skiddaw. It's a pity that the weather looks so glum, of course, but it _is_ a little brighter now over to the east. The rain will hold off for a while, perhaps even miss us altogether." Mr. Beck tossed down the last mouthful of his tea and handed the mug back to Susan. "Thank you," he said. "That was very refreshing. Are you staying here, Lady Dalmane?"

"Yes," said Susan. "Your wife and I can have a little chat while you go for your walk." Susan had already started a second conversation with Mrs. Beck, while her husband and Mr. Beck had been talking. She had felt very sorry for Mrs. Beck on learning that she suffered from depression, and imagined that Mrs. Beck would feel better for having the opportunity to talk about herself to a stranger.

Mr. Beck stood up.

"Shall we go, my Lord?" he said.

"But we can't walk along the railway line, can we?" said Lord Dalmane.

"Yes, we can. I can walk on the railway line any time I like, because of being employed on the railways. But it'll be all right for you, Lord Dalmane, accompanied by me. You needn't worry about trespassing: nobody will mind, I assure you."

"Very well, then, let's go. Good-bye, Sue."

"Don't be late back," Susan called after him as they set off. "Don't go too far."

"All right," called Lord Dalmane over his shoulder.

The two men stepped down onto the gravel of the trackbed at the eastern end of the platform.

"Hello, there, Nigel!" called a voice. The signalman was leaning out of a window of his box. "Going for a walk along the line?"

"Hello, Bill," said Mr. Beck. We're only going as far as Bridge Number Eleven, or maybe a little further. There'll be no traffic on the line to run us over, likely?"

"Nay, you're all right, Nigel," said the signalman. "There'll be nowt until the 10.8."

"So that's all right," said Mr. Beck as they walked on. "I thought it was."

"How far is Bridge Number Eleven?" asked Lord Dalmane.

"About half a mile. We've got plenty of time," said Mr. Beck.

They walked on past the place where the two sidings on the left were connected by points to the main line and so came to the high concrete bridge over the river. As they reached the bridge the sun appeared through a rift in the storm clouds. For some time little seemed to have changed in the sky above them although, in fact, slow and imperceptible changes were all the time altering the outlines of the clouds, revealing the presence of powerful thermals in the upper air. Down at ground level they felt an occasional light southerly air stirring the closeness. Mr. Beck and Lord Dalmane paused on the bridge to look down over the high parapet to the north, over the town. The sudden shaft of light was like the narrow beam of some gigantic searchlight; it glinted off the deep pools of the river far below the two watchers with unexpected brilliance. As the bright rays pierced down into the close air Mr. Beck and Lord Dalmane felt their spirits noticeably lightened, although neither had really been aware that the thundery feeling in the air was having a depressing effect on them; yet undoubtedly it was.

"It's nice to see a glint of sun," said Lord Dalmane. "Perhaps the storm will pass over without breaking, do you think?"

"I doubt it," said Mr. Beck, glancing up for a moment. The sun's disc was still just hidden by cloud but that brilliant beam, pouring through a widening chink between the turbulent cumular masses, looked almost like a tangible thing. "But the storm will hold off, I think, for perhaps another half hour or longer. Well, there's the little market town of Cockermouth, Lord Dalmane. You can see it quite well from up here. That spire is on the parish church of All Saints."

"Oh, yes," said Lord Dalmane. "What's that smaller stream called?" He pointed to a tributary of the river on the east (right-hand) bank, a stream which came down a little waterfall to empty itself into the River Cocker (the river banks thereabouts were rocky and precipitous).

"That's the Rudd Beck," said Mr. Beck. "The railway follows its valley eastwards from here. I expect you know that 'Beck', apart from being my surname, is the usual word for a small stream in these northern parts: what one would call a 'brook' in the South."

"Yes, I've gathered that," said Lord Dalmane.

"There's not much water coming down those waterfalls, as you can see," continued Mr. Beck, "or in the river either, come to that. It's been very dry around here for several weeks now. But, of course, all that could change dramatically this morning, I suppose, if we catch this impending storm. That beck might be a muddy brown torrent in an hour's time or so. But we'd better press on. You want to go on don't you, Lord Dalmane?"

"Oh yes, I'd like to go as far as this Bridge Number Eleven that you mentioned. Which bridge is this?"

"Number Nine. Numbers Ten and Eleven cross the Rudd Beck."

"Oh, I see."

They walked on, scrunching along the gravel of the trackbed beside the single pair of rails which carried the line eastwards to Keswick. It was curving round to the left. Lord Dalmane glanced behind him two or three times and soon noticed that the station platforms were now hidden from his sight round the gentle curve of the railway line. Mr. Beck and he were now walking along the bottom of a cutting; ahead of him Lord Dalmane saw a road bridge spanning the line, and noticed that beyond that the track curved round to the right and was lost to view. They were not talking now, but trudging steadily along the easy, level, but narrow path beside the rails. Both men had seen the figure of a man standing on the bridge but had not really noticed him. Mr. Beck and Lord Dalmane neither knew nor cared that this figure leaning on the bridge parapet was watching them intently as they approached, nor did they notice that he wore blue police uniform and had a police motor cyclist's crash helmet on his head. As the two walkers approached the bridge they were mostly looking ahead of them; they did not look up. But the watcher on the bridge had caught a glimpse of both of their faces.

Police Constable John Sommers had stopped on the railway bridge in Lorton Road to have a chat with a friend who happened to be passing that way on foot. His police motor cycle was propped up beside him at the edge of the kerb. Presently the friend went on his way. P.C. Sommers was on the beat in that part of the town and so, although he had his motor cycle with him, he was in no hurry to go anywhere in particular. He looked down at the railway line in its cutting and saw two men down there coming round the curve from the river bridge. They were trespassing on the railway, of course, so he would have to shout out a warning to them to get off the line. Then he recognized the figure in front. Oh, its Mr. Beck, he said to himself. It's all right for him to be down there, of course—but who's that chap following him? Got no business to be walking on the railway, likely, even at Mr. Beck's invitation. But—. Suddenly the policeman caught his breath and stiffened. He had just caught a glimpse of that man's face. No! he gasped to himself, It's HIM! On the instant he recalled the face of the Wanted Man on the posters at the Police Station. If that was not that same man down there then it was certainly someone who looked remarkably similar to him. But it can't possibly be our Wanted Man, he thought. A chap wanted for murder would hardly be walking about quite openly—in the company of someone else—hardly a quarter of a mile away from the scene of his crime. As the two walkers on the railway line came right up to the bridge P.C.Sommers tried and failed to get another chance of a good look at that man's face. Yet from what he could see of him, the policeman could not help feeling convinced that this man was the one they had been looking for during the past three weeks.

The policeman saw Mr. Beck and the other man disappear underneath the arch. What should he do about it? P.C. Sommers thought quickly through various possibilities. Do nothing, assuming that the man was merely an innocent, co-incidental look-alike? No, that would be unwise although this was probably the truth. Dash down there and arrest him? No, he couldn't do that when he was so unsure whether this was the right man. Right, he thought, That's it. I must have another proper look at that man's face first. He knew now just what he had to do. There was a place just around the bend of the line where a road in a new council estate ran close beside the railway for a short distance, separated from it only by an area of short grass like a lawn and the railway fence. He could dash round there on his bike in less than a minute and be there before those two could get there, walking along the railway.

Three minutes later he started up the engine of his motor cycle again with a loud roar. A second look at the face of Mr. Beck's strange companion, seen at fairly close range from the patch of grass at the side of the road through the new houses, had convinced him that immediate action had to be taken to apprehend that man. A moment later he was riding his motor cycle as fast as he could back to the Police Station, the headlight of the machine switched on to warn everyone to keep out of his way.

CHAPTER FOUR

The police car with Cadet Jim Sandy, the Sergeant, and two constables in it, accelerated rapidly along a straight stretch of main road leading eastwards out of the town. Jim was still feeling a little bewildered by the great speed at which he had been bundled into this new adventure. Had Constable Sommers really seen their Wanted Man somewhere around or near the town? It seemed to Jim a most unlikely possibility. Still, it meant a high-speed chase in an attempt to catch and question <u>someone</u>, and that was clearly going to be interesting while it lasted. Possibly too this outing might give him the chance he wanted to slip away to the railway station. There was still plenty of time left before that morning train was due to leave Cockermouth.

"So where, exactly, did you see this fellow?" asked the Sergeant, who was sitting in the front passenger seat beside the driver, Constable Sommers.

"I saw him from the railway bridge in Lorton Road," said P.C. Sommers. "That was where I first spotted him, walking eastwards along the railway line."

"First?" queried the Sergeant.

"I hurried round to Bellbrigg Lonning immediately afterwards to get a second look at the man's face," continued P.C. Sommers. "You know, that place where there's a patch of grass with a children's slide on it, just opposite the new houses. You can see a bit of the railway line there from the road—only about twenty or thirty yards away—a good viewing point."

"Yes, I know the place. But where are you taking us now?" P.C. Sommers had put on the right-turn indicator, slowed down, and was turning off the main road onto a small, rough road.

"I thought we'd best go down here, past Anfield, and then follow the track across that field to Bridge Number Eleven on the railway," said Constable Sommers. He looked at his watch. "We've been pretty quick: only just over seven minutes since I left Bellbrigg Lonning, so we'll maybe get just ahead of them, assuming that they're still not hurrying."

"Them? I thought we were only chasing after <u>one</u> man."

"No, Searj, I saw two men walking on the line: the other one was Mr. Beck."

"Which Mr. Beck was that?"

"Nigel Beck, the engine-driver and railwayman."

"Oh, him! Good heavens, but what would <u>he</u> be walking with our Wanted Man for? This is going to turn out to be just a wild goose chase, Sommers, it seems to me."

"I expect so, Searj, but we've got to make sure."

A few seconds later, slowing down considerably, the car came into a very muddy farmyard which seemed to have buildings all the way round it. Jim Sandy had just been thinking that twenty-five miles per hour, as shown on the car's speedometer, was a reckless speed over such a rough surface: the farm lane was full of pot-holes. He was, however, increasingly interested in the outing, and was looking keenly around. Jim had lived all his life in Cockermouth, yet he had never been down this particular farm lane before, and was wondering exactly where they were going to strike the railway line. They would probably have to walk or run along it when they got there.

The driver had to pull the car up in the farmyard because he was suddenly uncertain of which way to go next. There seemed to be no way out other than the lane down which they had just driven.

"Which way now?" asked P.C. Sommers desperately, looking round at his passengers. But Constable Nickley in the back seat was pointing to a gap between two farm out-buildings where there was a gate, luckily open.

"There," he said. "There's a track through a field if you go through that gate. I've been here before."

"And turn that blue light off, man!" said the Sergeant sharply. "We'll be in sight of the railway in a few seconds, and we don't want them to spot us approaching if we can help it."

P.C. Sommers flicked a switch upwards to stop the rotating light on the roof. As they drove through the gateway carefully (it was a narrow exit between the gateposts) Jim Sandy glanced back and saw a man in wellington boots and dirty overalls standing gawping at the sight of a police car with four officers in it crossing the farmyard and entering a field. He's wondering what the devil we're up to, Jim chuckled to himself.

The field in which they found themselves sloped gently downwards to a level bottom where a broad stream flowed; Jim guessed rightly that it must be the Rudd Beck. Down there also at the bottom of that field they could see a stretch of railway line on either side of a bridge over the beck. The car, now being driven cautiously in first gear, was following a rough muddy track which slanted down the field and lead to that same bridge. There was no sign of anyone walking on the railway.

"They'll be here in a minute, I expect," said Constable Sommers. "My word, it's lucky that the ground is so dry. If it was wet we could easily get stuck in the mud here." He looked anxiously at the sky ahead to the south.

"It's all right," said the Sergeant. "It won't rain yet. Look, it's a bit brighter in the east, and there's even a shaft of sunlight breaking through the clouds. We should be back at headquarters before this storm breaks. Look, you'd better stop here, Sommers. We'll have a good look before going any nearer to the railway."

P.C. Sommers pulled the car up and put the hand-brake on. Three pairs of unaided eyes were turned to the right, focused intently on the point where the line of the railway disappeared into the evergreen trees around the Cemetry, the place where the railway walkers might at any moment appear; but Sergeant Koppel opened a glove compartment and took out of a case a powerful pair of binoculars, which he applied to his eyes, and presently focused onto the railway line near the bridge. There followed several tense seconds of silence. Jim noticed in the silence that his heart seemed to be beating very loudly and quickly in his chest, ample evidence that the mounting excitement of this adventure was bringing more adrenalin into his bloodstream.

"There they are!" exclaimed Constable Nickley, just as Jim and Constable Sommers almost at the same moment saw the small figures of two pedestrians on the railway line, two figures who had just emerged from the Cemetry trees.

"By the level crossing, sir," said Constable Sommers to the Sergeant, who had not yet got the binoculars trained onto the right spot. "They must be the men I saw before."

A moment later Sergeant Koppel had the notice board by the Cemetry Level Crossing (which was an ungated pedestrian crossing) clearly in his binocular focus.

"By Jove!" he said, "he is our Wanted Man. Must be him. He's the splitting image of our artist's drawing if he's not the same man. And the other one's Nigel Beck all right."

"What do we do now, Searj? Drive on?" asked Constable Sommers.

"Yes, drive on, man, drive on! Get down to that bridge and we'll park it under the arch. With luck they may not see us coming."

The car was already on the move again.

"I'll just let them know at headquarters that we've sighted him," said the Sergeant. He put down the binoculars and picked up the microphone of the car's two-way radio link with the Police Station.

Lord Dalmane and Mr. Beck, having passed under the Lorton Road Bridge, saw a fence to their right on top of the cutting and a hedge of laurels and rhododendrons.

"What's up there?" asked Lord Dalmane. "A park?"

"No, that's the Cemetry," said Mr. Beck. "The other end of it is only a short step away from Bridge Number Eleven over the Rudd Beck, and out in the country."

They walked on, rounding the next curve of the railway line, and a minute or two later saw a bridge carrying the line over a lesser stream.

"Is this the Rudd Beck too?" asked Lord Dalmane, pausing for a moment to lean on the iron railings of the bridge while he looked down at the stream which at that point was far below them in an ugly concrete culvert.

"Yes," said Mr. Beck, "but it looks much prettier a little higher up at the next bridge where it's in its natural channel instead of this nasty culvert."

"H'm, yes. And the next bridge is Number Eleven?"

He had seen a number "10" on an oval metal plate attached to the iron railings on the cemetry side of the bridge. But for a moment Mr. Beck did not answer as at that moment they were startled by the sudden roar of a motor cycle engine, which abruptly stopped.

"Only a police motor cyclist over there, on that housing estate road," said Mr. Beck. "Sorry, what did you say? Yes, the next bridge is the eleventh one. We'd better press on."

About a hundred yards further on they came to the place where the railway lay closest to the road on the edge of the new housing estate, separated from it only by the narrow strip of grass. Just before they reached this point, Mr. Beck and Lord Dalmane saw a man, who was clearly dressed in police uniform, jump onto his motor cycle and roar away from them as if in a race. They had noticed, but with little interest, that he had seemed to be looking straight at them for several seconds.

"It sounds as if that chap were in a frightful hurry about something or other," said Lord Dalmane.

"Maybe," said Mr. Beck, not bothering to look round. They had not stopped walking but were still trudging steadily along the gravel which made the ballast for the rails. "If you look along to the end of this straight bit, Lord Dalmane," added Mr. Beck, "you'll see a notice board where a footpath crosses the line between the end of the Cemetry and the end of the housing estate."

"Yes," said Lord Dalmane. "What about it?"

"It marks the place where we come out into the fields," said Mr. Beck. "The end of the town as a train heads eastwards along the line."

Lord Dalmane glanced at his wrist watch. It had been about twenty minutes past nine when they had started their walk, and it was now only 9.32. That was all right. "Of course you must know this line incredibly well," he said. "I think you said you'd been driving on it for about a year. I suppose this walk is something of a fond and rather sad farewell for you to very familiar territory."

"It is: it is indeed that," said Mr. Beck. "Really I wish we weren't leaving, but for Norma's sake . . ." He broke off his sentence, sighed, and trudged on silently for a while. Lord Dalmane looked for a moment to his right and saw rows of hundreds of tombstones, very neatly kept graves, and well-mown lawns amidst many gloomy-looking trees. It was, he thought, a trick of the curious light at that time which gave him the impression of the trees being gloomy, because many of them were fine, tall, deciduous trees: lime, birch, sycamore, and beech were among those he recognized, but there were many others there in the cemetry as well as the sombre-looking evergreens: yew, cypress, laurels and others. Perhaps, he thought, those dark-leaved evergreens always have a rather depressing effect when one sees them in a graveyard, but this is certainly very funny weather, not at all pleasant. He looked ahead, past the footpath-crossing at the end of the Cemetry, at the sky in the east and south-east. Up there that rift which had appeared in the clouds, letting through a narrow searchlight-beam of the sun, had widened considerably. There was now a fair sized area completely clear of cloud which looked to Lord Dalmane not only odd but somehow quite wrong before a storm. The sun had come out again and was lighting up some hills somewhere beyond the level crossing with a light so vivid that it did not look like daylight at all but like some exceptionally brilliant artificial lighting; and the green of the grass where it was irradiated by this peculiar illumination seemed to glow with a shade reminiscent of luminous green paint.

Soon the two men came to the ungated level crossing at the end of the Cemetry but Lord Dalmane, staring mostly at the sky and somewhat lost in his thoughts, hardly noticed the crossing; but suddenly he saw that there were now fields level with the line on either side of it.

"There's Bridge Number Eleven," said Mr. Beck, and Lord Dalmane started at hearing him speak: neither had said a word for several minutes.

"Where? Oh yes, I see, just a little way ahead."

"We could perhaps walk a little further than the bridge, if you like," said Mr. Beck. "It's only nine thirty-six so there's time enough, but I think that we ought to turn back at least by ten to ten. But, you see, it's really very pleasant out here. That's Skiddaw, the mountain that you see over there."

"Yes, it's a fine sight," said Lord Dalmane. "But for heaven's sake don't let's run it too fine for catching our train. I certainly can't think of missing it having left my wife, Susan, on the platform."

"And I certainly wouldn't think of letting myself get left behind leaving poor Norma to go on her own," said Mr. Beck. "Don't worry, Lord Dalmane, we'll be back there in time. The trains never leave early on this line, but we can still easily be back there by ten."

They walked on. Lord Dalmane saw that on this stretch of the line between the Cemetry and the next bridge over the little river new sapling trees had been planted, a regular row of them along the railway fence on the right-hand side, presumably so that they would grow up to form a wind-break from the prevailing south-westerly winds. The little trees were only about three to five feet high, obviously very newly planted, and quite close together so that presently they would make a hedge: most of them were cypress trees but the row was interspersed with some deciduous varieties, mostly beech and hawthorn. Neither Lord Dalmane nor Mr. Beck noticed a police car which was standing on a rough track in a field to the left of the line: not the field now immediately adjacent on their left, but the one beyond it, a field which had a gentle slope down towards the railway line. Lord Dalmane did not look much to his left; he kept looking up anxiously at the sky, and when he was not looking up he was mostly looking to his right, at the line of new saplings, at the course of the Rudd Beck (a little way off to the right), and at the hills. The police car started to move forwards, coming along the rough track towards the place where it passed under the railway at Bridge Number Eleven, but they neither saw it nor heard the low hum of its engine as it approached cautiously in first gear.

In the car Sergeant Koppel hung up the radio microphone and spoke to his men.

"Right, lads, we'll take them by surprise," he said. "We'll spring an ambush on them. They haven't seen us, or they wouldn't be walking along the line to meet us. That's it, Sommers, park it under the arch." Bridge Number Eleven had been built with an arch wide enough for both the stream and the rough track to pass under the railway. The rough track crossed the stream first on a bridge a few yards upstream from Bridge Number Eleven: this other bridge was nothing more than a low brick arch without any parapets.

"All right," said P.C. Sommers, the driver. "But why bother about an ambush, Searj? It'd be a lot quicker, wouldn't it, for one of us simply to go straight up to our man and arrest him? One to arrest him, and the other three could be ready to dash in to help in case he tries to make a bolt for freedom." He switched off the engine, having parked the car as carefully as he could in the narrow space available for it under the arch. The stonework of the bridge was hard against the doors on the near-side of the car, but on the off-side there was a narrow strip of dry mud between the track and the beck.

"No, no, no! That wouldn't do at all," said Sergeant Koppel. "Listen, Constable Sommers, and you other two: I'm in charge of this operation and I'll give the orders. That man is to be taken back to the Police Station to be questioned by the Chief Inspector himself. That's <u>his</u> orders and we've got to do it. You heard what I was saying to him just now, didn't you?"

"Of course, Searj," said P.C. Sommers.

"Well then, let's have no more argument about it. Cadet Sandy, could you do some scout work for us?"

"I'll try to, sir," said Sandy eagerly.

"Right, out you get then, lad, quickly, and shin up that embankment on the other side of the stream, and get into hiding behind the stonework of the parapet so that you can get a look at those two on the line without being seen yourself. I'll be right behind you in case of trouble. Understand? You've just got to let us know when they've got onto the bridge, and we'll take the operation on from there when we know what their next move is. Can you manage to do that?"

"Yes, sir."

"Off you go, then."

Jim stepped quickly out of the car through the off-side rear door (he had already seen that there was a sufficient gap between the car and the beck to do this without having to stand in the water). He ran back the few yards to the other bridge, the low brick arch over the stream, to gain the other bank (it was much too wide to jump across, and although clearly shallow along the muddy edges, looked quite deep in the middle, too deep for comfortable wading). He ran bent well forwards, and kept glancing at the two men walking along the railway line on the top of the embankment, knowing that they had only to turn their heads that way to spot him; but they did not turn their heads. They were both looking the other way; one of them, the man they were about to arrest, was pointing to the low clouds over the Embleton Fells and obviously saying something to Mr. Beck about the threatening look in the weather, although Jim did not catch the words. A few seconds later Jim was again safely hidden from those two as he climbed nimbly up the steep side of the railway embankment by the stone pier of the bridge on the opposite side to where their police car stood parked under the arch.

"Look!" Lord Dalmane was pointing to a peculiar cloud-formation above Sale Fell and the hills behind Embleton and Wythop. He and Mr. Beck had almost reached the little bridge over the Rudd Beck.

"Well?" said Mr. Beck, his gaze following Lord Dalmane's pointing finger into the sky.

"Why, that towering white cloud seems to have such an extraordinary outline," said Lord Dalmane. "It must mean something pretty sinister from the weather point of view, I should think. It reminds me of . . . I don't quite know what that shape reminds me of."

"It looks a bit like a spiral candlestick, I suppose," said Mr. Beck, "with that broad base, down on the hills, and that bit that goes up and up—I should think it must look something like a waterspout or a whirlwind, or something like that."

"What! You don't really think we're going to be struck by a sort of whirlwind, do you?" said Lord Dalmane anxiously. He was thinking that never in all his experience of sailing had he seen any cloud of quite so sinister a shape.

"No, I'm sure we're not," said Mr. Beck. "There'll just be a strong wind coming with that thing, and probably that's all."

"And rain too," added Lord Dalmane. "Look, lightning over there." He pointed more to the south, to the fells over Buttermere way. What they had seen was not so much a stroke of lightning itself as a momentary flickering brightness against the dark background of clouds, a reflection of distant lightning. Over that way, from Grassmoor well around towards the south-west, the low cloud base, obscuring the upper parts of the higher mountains, had a distinct hint of purple in its darkness. Mr. Beck and Lord Dalmane were now standing by the southern parapet of the bridge, observing the stormy portents in the sky. If either of them at that moment had turned round suddenly, he would have seen a face under a police cadet's cap peering at them from behind one of the stone pillars on the other side of the bridge; but neither man turned quickly from looking at the view to the south. Lord Dalmane turned slowly round to the east to look again at that odd patch of clear sky in which the sun was still shining; and as he turned young Sandy lowered his head a little more, ready at any moment to duck his head completely below the level of the top of the embankment on which his body was lying at an awkward angle. Lord Dalmane looked along the next stretch of the line, a long, straight stretch across the fields with a flat-topped mountain, Skiddaw, filling in the horizon behind a clump of trees where the line lost itself to view. The broad base of the candlestick-shaped cloud began just to the right of Skiddaw, as Lord Dalmane looked at it, but it was odd that Skiddaw itself had no more than a detached cap of white cloud, shot through with a dull red, hanging around the high summit. The broad base of the "candlestick" of thunder cloud was also inflamed by a sullen red light, a light which could mean nothing but a threat of violence shortly to come when the storm should break; but above this flattened base it was as if some gigantic invisible arm had pulled the hard-looking material of the cloud upwards and upwards in a strange, spiral motion, making a helix pointing towards the icy regions near the bottom of the stratosphere. Lord Dalmane gazed at this strange piece of nature's handiwork with some fascination and a certain awe. "It's all incredibly beautiful, in a way, as well as threatening," he murmured, not really meaning to speak his thought aloud.

"What?" said Mr. Beck. "Oh, that peculiar, spiral-shaped cloud. Yes, it's a thunder cloud, if ever I saw one, and there'll be wind with it very likely." He had hardly finished speaking when they felt a fresh breeze, stronger than any they had yet felt that morning, come out of the south-east; it ruffled their hair and set swaying the smaller branches of a hazel tree which grew hard beside the bridge. "Anyway," added Mr. Beck a moment later, looking at his watch again, "it's nine forty-three now, so I suppose we'd better go on . . . or back?"

Jim Sandy made hand signals to his companions below the bridge; the two constables were standing by the car, watching out for his signals but the Sergeant had come round to his side of the stream and was waiting just below him on the embankment. Jim whispered a few hurried words to him.

"Let's go back," said Lord Dalmane. "At any rate, I'm going back to the station now. I'd rather not get soaked in the downpour that looks like happening soon, and I'm getting a bit bothered too about being back in time for that train."

"Right, I'll come back with you," said Mr. Beck, but for a few moments more he remained where he was, looking eastwards along the line towards Skiddaw, unable to tear himself away from that well-known view. When he had been sitting in the driver's cab of the local diesel multiple-unit passenger trains, until his recent cessation of work, he had always thought of this particular stretch of the line from Bridge Number Eleven to Strawberry Howe Farm as his favourite view between Cockermouth and Keswick. It was, he thought, a view particularly pleasing because of its relative simplicity. Further on there was Bassenthwaite Lake to be seen, and more fells and mountains than could be seen from here; but looking along this straight stretch of railway line there was Skiddaw sitting very handsomely on the eastern skyline, with just the low fells above Embleton and Wythop to the right of the valley (if one did not look round as far as the Buttermere Fells) and Slate Fell to the left of the valley. Mr. Beck had a good eye for natural beauty and the low green eminence of Slate Fell, seen from this angle, with its tall deciduous trees growing near its rocky summit, had always given him particular pleasure when he had driven a train, steam or diesel hauled, eastwards out of Cockermouth. He was looking at this scene with almost unbearable nostalgia now that strange clouds were in the sky and a sudden wind was blowing and forewarning a storm. the idea of saying Good-bye to it all seemed positively tragic to him. He forgot for a moment Lord Dalmane standing beside him, impatient to be returning to the station, as his eye followed the course of the Rudd Beck across the meadow to the left. That was very pleasant almost park-like country where a few large, old ash trees grew in that gently sloping field and by the banks of the meandering stream. In the field beyond that one he saw the slope of the ground downwards from left to right gradually increase until it passed by degrees into that small outlier of the Lakeland Fells, the little Slate Fell, only some two hundred feet above the nearby railway line through the valley. Altogether it was a pleasing prospect which Mr. Beck was loth to turn his back on; but just as he was about to make the effort to do this, he spotted two figures in blue police uniform. There was a small cutting about a hundred yards east of the bridge, and he saw the two policemen jump down onto the line from the sides of this cutting and begin to run towards them.

"What on earth . . . ?" he gasped.

"What?" said Lord Dalmane, turning sharply on his heel. He had been about to start walking back on his own.

"Stay just where you are! You're under arrest!" shouted a stern man's voice from behind them.

They both wheeled round in time to see that two other police officers had appeared on the line: one, a cadet, and the other, the one who had just spoken, Mr. Beck recognized as the Cockermouth Sergeant. It seemed that these two policemen must have climbed onto the line up the embankment at the Cockermouth end of the bridge where, presumably, they had been hiding.

"What the devil's this?" said Lord Dalmane.

"This is a Murder Enquiry," said the Sergeant. "You, sir," (he indicated Lord Dalmane) "are required for questioning at Cockermouth Police Station."

"What, me?" Lord Dalmane's tone was more surprised than indignant.

"Yes, you. Your name, sir, if you please." The Sergeant had pulled out his notebook and opened it.

"Look here, what the hell do you want to know my name for? I know nothing about your Murder Enquiry—absolutely nothing."

"There must be some mistake, Sergeant," said Mr. Beck. "This is my friend, Lord Dalmane, who is a visitor here and a stranger; and he's got absolutely nothing to do with the recent murder here."

"Is your name Dalmane?" asked the Sergeant, ignoring Mr. Beck's last point.

"Yes it is. My name is John Dalmane, if you must know, and I'm the Earl of Saint Helens. Now look here, Sergeant, I'm in a hurry if you don't mind. I've a train to catch. I'm sorry, but I've no time for questioning at your Police Station, and anyway, I've told you I know nothing that would help you. I'm not a local."

"H'm, I see." The Sergeant wrote busily in his notebook. He looked up.

"Constable Sommers!"

"Yes, sir?"

"This is the man you saw on the railway line from the Lorton Road bridge and again from Bellbrigg Lonning? You confirm that?"

"Yes, sir. Very definitely so, sir."

"Look here," said Mr. Beck. "I must go; I want to catch that 10.8 train too. I take it I'm not being arrested."

"No, but I'd just like to ask—"

"Then for heaven's sake let us both go, Sergeant," interrupted Mr. Beck. "I'm sure it must be all a dreadful mistake to arrest my friend here for murder."

"It most certainly is," said Lord Dalmane.

"I'm not charging anyone with murder," said Sergeant Koppel. "Definitely not. Lord Dalmane is to be detained and taken back to the Police Station to be interviewed by the Detective Chief Inspector; that's all."

"But why—?" began Lord Dalmane, but the Sergeant waved a hand at him to silence him. "Just a minute. Now then: Mr. Beck, how long have you known this man?"

"Oh, hardly for an hour! I only happened to meet Lord Dalmane this morning at the railway station, and we were taking a little walk together to fill in the time . . . Look here, it's nearly ten to ten. I must go."

"'Hardly for an hour,'" repeated the Sergeant, again making a note in his book. "Very well, you may go, Mr. Beck. We may need to question you again later, but you can go for your train now."

"But what about me?" said Lord Dalmane angrily. "I told you that I've got to catch that train too. Why should I answer your Chief Inspector's damned questions? Why should I? How could I know <u>anything</u> about a murder here when I've never been here before today?"

"I'm sorry, Lord Dalmane," said the Sergeant, speaking now more quietly and more politely. "You must forgive me, my Lord, for any inconvenience caused, but in this matter I must tell you that I'm under orders myself. You <u>must</u> come with us immediately, Lord Dalmane, to the Police Station. I'm sorry about your train but it can't be helped. When once you've satisfied the Inspector as to your innocence you will be set free straight away; so the sooner you come along, the sooner you can go again. We have a car here waiting to take you to the Police Station."

Lord Dalmane sighed and looked wearily around him. To the south the sky over Grassmoor and the Loweswater and Buttermere fells looked darker than it had appeared before. He saw a thread of bright fire stab its way downwards towards the earth, a momentary white brilliance against the dark purple curtain of cloud. The Sergeant, he knew, was waiting for him to answer, to say Yes, he would go to the Police Station; and Mr. Beck had not gone, but was still looking at him anxiously, not wanting to have to walk back to the railway station without him. And then there was Susan: what would she think if he failed to turn up for that train and she had to learn that the police had arrested him in connection with a murder enquiry? A few tense seconds passed and there came a louder clap of thunder, obviously a nearer one than the many indistinct distant rumblings they had already heard, but still Lord Dalmane had not given his answer.

"Oh, very well," he said at last. "I'll come along to the Police Station and answer your questions; I see I've got no choice about it really. Look here, Mr. Beck, can I leave it to you to explain to my wife what's happened? Tell her I'll be following on the first train I can get as I'm bound to miss this 10.8 one. I suppose I'd better write her a quick note which you could hand over."

He looked hopefully at the Sergeant.

"Here you are, Lord Dalmane," said Sergeant Koppel immediately, tearing a page out of his notebook as he spoke. "Have you a pen?"

"Yes."

The policeman handed him the piece of paper and his notebook on which to press it. Lord Dalmane scrawled a message to Susan on the sheet of paper as quickly as he could. Then he handed it to Mr. Beck who took it without attempting to read what Lord Dalmane had written. Mr. Beck had been anxiously glancing at his watch.

"Right, you hand that to my wife, and explain that I'll be following as soon as ever I can," said Lord Dalmane.

"All right, I'll explain to her," said Mr. Beck. "I'll say that you'll catch her up at Knebworth anyway, if not before. Well, I'm really sorry that our little walk should end like this with an unintended parting, but I really must hurry away now. Good-bye, Lord Dalmane." He waved a hand and immediately set off walking quickly back towards the railway station.

"Come along, Lord Dalmane," said the Sergeant. "You can step across the fence here and climb down this embankment. The car's parked under the arch of the bridge." He swung a leg over the fence, which luckily was rather delapidated at that point, as he lead the way down. The two constables, Sommers and Nickley, had already climbed down that way and returned to the car. Lord Dalmane obediently followed the Sergeant over the fence and began to scramble down the steep grassy slope, but Cadet Jim Sandy remained standing on the bridge, looking along the line after the already receding Mr. Beck. He was on the very brink of taking a momentous decision, one which he knew might well alter the whole course of his life for better of worse, but it was going to be a great struggle for him to bring himself to say what he meant to say.

"Come on, young Sandy!" called the Sergeant from below the embankment. "What are you waiting up there for?"

"Sorry, sir," Sandy shouted back, "but may I go with Mr. Beck to the railway station?"

"What for?"

"Well, sir, we still want to interview Mr. Ruddock, don't we? I could go and see if it's him driving the 10.8 and, if it is, perhaps I could give him a message from you?"

"Why, that's an ingenious idea, young Sandy! Yes you can do that if you find him on the 10.8: tell him from me to report to any police station within twenty-four hours, and that we can send some of our chaps out to interview him unless he cares to call at Cockermouth Police Station." Mr. Ruddock was a train driver on the Cockermouth line; he had been the driver of the train at the time of the railway station murder but the police had not yet interviewed him as a potential eye-witness of the incident.

Jim Sandy was grinning broadly as he set off running along the line to catch up with Mr. Beck, who was by now at least a hundred yards ahead on the way back to Cockermouth Station; but although Jim was grinning he was not really very happy about what he was doing.

CHAPTER FIVE

Susan Dalmane and Mrs. Beck watched their two husbands as they walked away from them through the sidings.

"Oh look, the sun has almost come out again," said Susan. "Look how that narrow beam of light is coming through the clouds." She was looking at the two men who had stopped while they leaned over the parapet of the river bridge; they were lit up in the sudden shaft of light as if by a searchlight. "It's rather cheering, don't you think, to see a glint of the sun?"

"That's as may be, Lady Dalmane," said Mrs. Beck, "but we're still going to get a storm presently, I expect."

"Do you dislike thunderstorms?"

"Doesn't everyone dislike thunderstorms? Yes, of course I do. Well—really, they upset me."

"You mean you feel frightened in a thunderstorm?" said Susan. "Well, Mrs. Beck, I must admit that I often feel frightened in a thunderstorm, especially when the thunder comes very near. There's really nothing to be ashamed of in feeling like that, you know: it's a very normal sort of human fear."

"Oh, don't talk to me about fear," said Mrs. Beck. "I'm afraid of almost everything in spite of the pills I have to take. You see, Lady Dalmane, it's the way my illness affects me . . ." She rambled on for a while, talking about her illness, and telling Susan that her doctor was not optimistic about her chances of a full recovery from depression and her various phobias, but that he had encouraged her to consider the idea of leaving that part of the country for the South, as she and her husband were now doing. She told Susan that she herself, as well as her husband, Nigel, originally come from the South: she had been born in Bournemouth. She said that of late she had found that her restricted environment living in the small town of Cockermouth had been making her more and more depressed, because of seeing what she called "the same dreary old surroundings" day after day. In spite of a fear of travelling, so that she had seldom left the town recently, she felt that she therefore desperately needed a change of surroundings.

Susan found it boring enough to listen to this discourse, and quickly realised that Mrs. Beck was only interested in talking about herself; nevertheless she tried very hard to attend to what Mrs. Beck was saying, and to make it sound as if she took an interest in Mrs. Beck's condition. To this end she frequently interrupted to ask questions, hoping always to divert the trend of the conversation away from the topic of illness and depression but, it seemed, with little success. In point of fact, although she sometimes found it hard to listen attentively to Mrs. Beck's words because she spoke always in a dreary monotone, not raising either her head or her voice, Susan was, on the whole, thoroughly sympathetic in her response to Mrs. Beck. She suggested that since they were going to be travelling together in the same trains all that day, they could continue their discussion on how it might be possible to help Mrs. Beck overcome her depression. Susan even suggested that if Mr. and Mrs. Beck were to return to Bournemouth some day to live there, after a temporary stay with Mr. Beck's parents in Hertfordshire, they might like to come to stay occasionally in Rhodes Castle. "You'll find that we're not very far from Bournemouth," she told Mrs. Beck. "It's only about an hour's run in the train to Stalbridge, the station for Rhodes Castle. We could meet you there and I'm sure you'd enjoy a visit to our place."

Then Susan attempted to change the subject by again drawing Mrs. Beck's attention to the weather.

"It looks rather better now," she said. "Look at all that clear sky over there." She pointed to the east. The two men on their railway walk had long since disappeared that way.

"Oh, but I don't like it," said Mrs. Beck. "Look at those awful stormy colours, that dull red and that sort of purple over there. And look at the strange twisted shape of that tall cloud. I wish Nigel would hurry up and come back. It'll be awful if this beastly storm breaks and he's not here to comfort me."

Susan tried to comfort her by pointing out that as it was now a quarter to ten, Mr. Beck and her own husband would soon be back, and that perhaps they would all get away in the train before the storm broke.

Suddenly both the ladies looked round towards the river bridge. A man had come into sight running with an easy stride around the corner of the line leading onto the bridge.

"Hello! Who's that?" said Susan.

"It isn't Nigel," said Mrs. Beck. "Oh, there he is, I think," she added a moment later as a second man appeared, running along behind the first one who, they thought, might possibly be a policeman; but at first both the figures were too far away to be distinguished with any certainty. The women saw them cross the bridge. It looked as if the leading figure was running easily at a steady jog-trot, as though he were well accustomed to exercise; but the other one looked as if he were exhausted, out of breath, and having difficulty in keeping up with the first runner.

"It is Nigel," said Mrs. Beck a few seconds later, standing up the better to see him.

"But where's John?" said Susan, also standing up. They had been sitting on the bench while they had been talking.

A few seconds later the first runner slowed down to a walk as he approached the ends of the platforms by the signal-box; as they could now see, he was a young Police Cadet with a broad smile on his handsome face. He was scarcely out of breath at all, being in an excellent state of physical fitness. Some fifty yards behind him Nigel Beck had also slowed to a walk. He waved a weary hand to them and came plodding slowly on.

The sun went in again, disappearing behind the storm clouds which were rapidly advancing across the clear space of sky in the east, and it grew darker; but Mr. Beck, walking away from Bridge Number Eleven, head down and thinking, hardly noticed that it was getting darker. He heard steps behind him and looked round for a moment.

"Hello! Aren't you going back to the Police Station?" he asked as Jim Sandy, the Police Cadet, came up to him, not at all out of breath as he slowed down to a walk.

"I'm coming with you to the railway station," said Cadet Sandy.

"Oh." Mr. Beck did not bother to ask the youth why he was also coming to the railway station; that, no doubt, was his affair, and Mr. Beck was content to walk on in silence. But about a couple of minutes later, when they had passed the Cemetry level crossing, Jim decided that he ought to confide his intentions in Mr. Beck.

"Mr. Beck," he began.

"Eh, what's that?"

"Are you travelling far by train, Mr. Beck?"

"I'm going down to a small place in Hertfordshire, near London, so I'm taking the 10.8 first. Why?"

"May I come with you?"

"What?"

"May I come with you to London in the train?"

Mr. Beck stopped walking and looked at the youth; a look of amazement was in his face. Jim Sandy stopped too and looked hopefully at Mr. Beck; his mind was made up on the matter of going to London, but it would be much more pleasant to travel there with people he knew.

"What's all this, young Sandy?" said Mr. Beck. "May you come with me to London? But you're meant to be doing a day's work here, aren't you?"

"No, I'm not. I hate being· in the Police here so I've decided to run away to London; my mother lives there."

"What! You must be quite out of your mind, Jim! That's a crazy idea, if you mean you're thinking of dashing off to London without telling anyone. I should certainly advise you most strongly to think again about it."

"But I have told my mum I'm coming," said Jim. "I sent some of my things down to her address a week ago, and I sent a letter with it explaining and saying that I'd be coming. I'm going to look for a better job, you see. Father knows too that I'm meaning to go there, and I'll let them know at the Police Station, of course."

Mr. Beck was fairly dumbfounded to hear all this, and for a few seconds he answered nothing. He knew Jim Sandy and his father well and liked them, but he was not sure for the moment whether he ought to take any active steps to discourage the boy in his sudden wild idea to run away from home and job. He looked away from him for a moment to his left at a thick screen of evergreens with a few taller deciduous trees which partially concealed the rows of tombstones. The sound of the police car taking Lord Dalmane away—easily audible in the quiet air—was gone; the gust of stronger wind had stopped as suddenly as it had begun, and both Mr. Beck and Jim Sandy had heard the car being driven away up the rough field track. But it was too late now to send Jim back to the Police Station that way. Mr. Beck for a second or so turned over in his mind the words he had just heard. He shook his head and turned again to Jim.

"No. That's no way to go looking for a new job," he said. "How old are you, Jim?"

"I'm eighteen."

"And whereabouts in London does your mother live?"

"In Ealing."

"H'm, Ealing. So that would be a three hundred mile rail journey from here to Euston and then you'd have to find your own way to that part of West London . . . you know you really are mad to think of running off all that way on a sudden impulse."

"It's not a sudden impulse," said Jim. "I've thought it all out carefully."

"Have you? So you're only eighteen: a bit young, perhaps, for the Police. All the same, surely it's not such a bad job? What about the promotion prospects? I should think twice before I ran away from a good steady job like that if I were in your place, my lad."

"It's no good, Mr. Beck, I'm not changing my mind. I'm quite absolutely determined to go by the very next train to London, if I can, and by the 10.8 from here. Mum's expecting me now, so I've got to go."

"Oh very well, then; have it your own way!" said Mr. Beck. "At least you seem to know your own mind, although the scheme sounds crazy to me, but that's your affair." He sighed, and a moment later added: "But let's be practical. I suppose I'd better help you, if I can, as I can't stop your wild scheme. Now, what about money?"

"On, that's all right, Mr. Beck, thank you very much. I've got quite enough money for the fare to London and plenty to spare. And I'll be able to find some sort of work down there. What I don't know is the time of the next train there, I mean from Carlisle. But you know all about trains, Mr. Beck. Is the 10.8 from here the right train to connect with the 'Royal Scot'?"

"Yes, it is. The 'Royal Scot' is the 11.57 a.m. from Carlisle to Euston, and this local train, the 10.8, is timed to connect with it, getting into Carlisle at 11.34. Then it's a really grand run up to London non-stop on the 'Royal Scot'. I know that West Coast

Main Line almost as well as I do our local line here. I've driven on it once or twice, over short sections, as an apprentice driver, still under instruction, you know; but many a time I've stoked those big engines they use on the 'Royal Scot' and the other Glasgow to Euston passenger expresses. My word, it's quite some job being the fireman on that run on board a 'Duchess'—damned hard work, but great fun, of course! Heavens, I'm getting quite carried away by my memories! Let's be practical. What about clothes—and baggage? Haven't you any clothes, barring the police things you're wearing—or other possessions?"

"It's all right about clothes," said Jim. "I packed plenty of them and other personal possessions in the box I sent off to my mother's address. It should be there by now."

"Well, I suppose you know best what you're doing, young Sandy," said Mr. Beck. "You're old enough to look after yourself. And if you're quite determined that you're going up to London in the 'Royal Scot' you'd better come with me and Mrs. Beck. Eh, what's that?"

"It's just gone five to ten, Mr. Beck. We'll miss the train if we don't look out." Jim had just looked at his watch.

"Come on, then, we'd better run!" They set off immediately jogging steadily along the gravel of the trackbed on that stretch of line between the Cemetry and the road beside the grassy space. "Heavens!" muttered Mr. Beck as he did his best to keep up with the athletic youth who seemed to run as easily as he could walk. "I was forgetting the time—talking—with you." After that Mr. Beck did not attempt to say anything more; he was very soon out of breath and feeling the whole of his body protesting at the sudden physical effort to which it was not accustomed. He soon felt as if he would collapse if he did not allow himself to slow down to a walk, but knew that with the time fast approaching ten o'clock he could not afford to do that. By grim determination he managed to keep running. The short distance to the station—about a quarter of a mile—seemed to him to be impossibly far to run, and the various landmarks by which progress could be measured were left behind with sickening slowness: the bridge (Number Ten) over the beck in its culvert, the bridge under Lorton Road, the post of the down home signal . . . there was the concrete bridge over the river just yards ahead and there beyond it the station platforms. Yes, he was going to be able to make it, and he reduced his speed a little. He felt his legs aching, his chest aching, and he had an irrational fear that he might be on the point of collapsing with heart failure unless he slackened his pace. He knew that this fear must be irrational as his heart was sound and had not been in the least affected by his recent illness, but altogether his general physical state was more out of condition than he had reckoned it to be. He crossed the river bridge well behind Jim Sandy at a speed little more than walking, saw the two women on the platform get up off their bench, and decided thankfully that he could walk the last few yards back to the platform.

"Where's John?" called Susan as soon as she thought that Mr. Beck was near enough to hear her. But Mr. Beck had as yet no breath to answer her; he waved a hand vaguely behind him. Jim Sandy had waited a few moments by the signal-box for Mr. Beck to catch up with him; then they walked slowly together up onto the platform end by the starting signal.

"Oh, Nigel," said Mrs. Beck, seeing how her husband was still gasping for breath. "You look awful. Are you all right? You really shouldn't have gone off like that."

"I'm—all—right," panted Mr. Beck in answer.

"Come and sit down," said Mrs. Beck.

Jim Sandy looked from one to the other of the two women. He knew which one was Mrs. Beck: she was the one who had spoken in agitated tones to her husband, calling him "Nigel." So the other one could only be Lady Dalmane, the wife of the man they had arrested who had said he was the Earl of Saint Helens. So this was the Countess of Saint Helens: but what a beauty she was! Indeed the impact of her beauty on his feelings was immediate. Phew, he gasped to himself, What a gorgeous girl! She must be Lady Dalmane, but I somehow didn't think she'd look so young and so beautiful! His heart was beating faster now, more because of the sudden surge of excitement he felt as he looked for the first time at Susan Dalmane than because of the run from the Cemetry just completed. Heavens, what a sweet face she has! he said to himself, And what a magnificent figure! Gosh, I hope she'll talk to me in the train! But his thoughts were most unexpectedly interrupted at that moment as she turned to him and addressed him.

"Who are you?" Her voice was quite sharp, noticeably upset.

"My name is Jim Sandy, my Lady," he said politely and rather nervously.

"Have you seen my husband, John, the Earl of Saint Helens— Lord Dalmane to you?"

"Yes, my Lady, the Police have arrested him."

"What?" said Susan.

"Oh, you needn't worry about it," said Jim quickly. "I'm sure he's innocent; they'll very soon let him go free again."

But Susan was no longer listening to him. Stunned by what she had just heard about an arrest, she had turned to Mr. Beck, hardly knowing what she was doing.

"What's happened?" she asked.

Mr. Beck was sitting on the bench beside his wife, head down, and breathing very heavily after his exhausting run, but in fact he was recovering very quickly. He raised his head as he replied in a weak, breathless voice: "They've arrested him. I'll explain everything . . . in just a minute." He put a hand into a pocket and seemed to be searching for something. Susan, understanding that he was still too breathless to speak properly, turned again to the young policeman. Spots of red were on both her cheeks, indicating her mood of surprise and indignation as she again spoke to Jim.

"So your colleagues have arrested my husband? You're part of the police force here, I take it?"

"No, my Lady, not any more," said Jim. "I <u>was</u> a cadet based here but I'm leaving the Police and going up to London."

"Yes, but where is my husband?" asked Susan impatiently.

"They've taken him to Cockermouth Police Station."

"Right. I'm going there at once. They've no right to arrest John like this; he's a senior Peer of the Realm <u>and</u> a perfectly innocent man too!"

"Just a minute!" said Mr. Beck, who seemed to have recovered his usual voice, more or less. He stood up, a little laboriously, and flourished a piece of paper. Susan stopped abruptly. She had already started to walk off along the platform.

"What is it?"

"A message from your husband," said Mr. Beck. "He wants you to go on by this train, not to go to the Police Station. Here, you'd better read it." He handed a rather crumpled sheet of paper to Susan. She unfolded it and found a message in John's handwriting hurriedly scrawled in ballpoint pen:-

> Sue, darling, do please go on by the 10.8 train. Mr. Beck will explain everything properly, I'm sure, but I'm bound to miss this train by the time the Police let me go. It's all absolute nonsense, of course, arresting me, but it <u>can't</u> take long to convince them that I'm <u>not</u> the person they're looking for in this Enquiry. Then I'll follow you on the very next train if I can and we'll meet at Knebworth or perhaps I might even catch you up somewhere on the way, with luck. So, <u>do go on ahead</u>, darling, and I'll see you very soon.
>
> All Love, John.

Susan read the letter through twice and then looked at Mr. Beck, frowning slightly, evidently considering what such a disgracefully unexpected arrest by the local Police could possibly mean when she knew that her husband could not have done anything to justify it.

"I suppose I'd better take this train, as my husband tells me that he wants me to do that," she said rather glumly, "although I do hate the idea of leaving poor John behind at the Police Station. But what on earth is it all about, Mr. Beck?" While she was saying this a few large drops of rain began to fall, heavy drops of water well spread out so that they hardly had any wetting effect at all on the warm ground. Susan, very worried about her husband, did not even notice them, nor did she seem to realise how very dark the sky had become in the last few minutes.

"There's a murder hunt going on here," explained Mr. Beck, "so, you see, over the last three weeks the police have been extremely busy interviewing hundreds of people, trying to collect the evidence they want to convict whoever it was who did it."

"Yes, but why did they want John? He's nothing to do with it, is he? Unless—I say, you don't think that perhaps they may have mistaken him for someone who's a suspect—the one who they think may have committed this murder?"

"Oh, good heavens, no! I'm sure it isn't like that at all," said Mr. Beck. "No, I think that what's happened is this: the police may have mistaken him for some key witness they were trying to get hold of. I suppose your husband's face must very closely resemble the face of this witness they were trying to trace."

Mr. Beck had never seen the police artist's photo-fit picture of their Wanted Man so it had never occurred to him that Lord Dalmane in fact <u>did</u> resemble him very remarkably in his facial features and general appearance. But from what he had heard the Sergeant say when arresting Lord Dalmane it was clear that a mistake of this sort must have been made. However, as soon as Lady

Dalmane put the idea to him that the police might have mistaken her husband for their suspect, he decided to alter the facts of his account slightly in order to allay Lady Dalmane's worst fears and soothe her a little, for her agitation was very evident to him. His conscience and his mind were at ease about this; he had looked at his watch just before he had told Susan about the murder hunt and had seen the hands of his watch pointing to three minutes past ten so he knew that, after all, he had made it back to the station in fair time for the train. The few heavy drops of rain which were falling from the thunderous looking sky were as yet hardly wetting either them or the platform, so he was not too worried by the weather either: with just four or five minutes until the train was due there was, he thought, a fair chance that they would be able to get into it before the inevitable downpour of rain began in earnest.

"Well," said Susan, "I suppose it must be something like that: the police mistaking John for someone else they wanted to interview. But surely it won't take them more than a minute to find out that John's the wrong man. Will he be at the Police Station now, Mr. Beck?"

Mr. Beck looked quickly at his watch again before answering her. It was five past ten.

"Yes," he said, "they probably got him back there several minutes ago."

"Then maybe they've already found out their mistake. Perhaps they might bring him here in a car and, just possibly, he might still be in time for the train. Or shall I dash round to the Police Station on foot to make sure that they're setting him free? My instincts tell me I should in spite of John saying 'Don't' in his letter. I'd miss the train of course, that way, but—gosh, look at that!" At that moment there came a blinding brilliance of forked lightning, stabbing its way downwards towards the ground, a flash in the purplish sky to the south-east which looked so alarmingly near and bright that they all blinked their eyes for a moment. "I'd miss the train but it wouldn't matter," said Susan a second later, picking up her broken-off sentence. She was just going to continue speaking, to ask Mr. Beck for his advice, when she was again cut short by the peal of thunder which followed that flash. It was a crash so ear-splitting that the little group in the gloom looked at each other in considerable alarm. It was such a shattering, cataclysmic peal that it seemed as if something must fall down under its shock waves, a tree, perhaps, or part of the old station buildings, but nothing did fall down. However, the rainfall was still minimal; the imminent downpour was still holding off, and only a light scattering of big, warm drops had splashed down onto the platform driven by a strong southerly wind which had sprung up with the rain.

The little group around the bench on the platform looked at each other with startled eyes as the reverberations of the great thunder clap sounded in their ears; all except for Mrs. Beck who had shut her eyes, put her head down, and placed her hands over her ears. They could hear her wailing on when the sound of the thunder had passed. "Oh help, it's horrible! I can't stand it, Nigel, I can't stand it . . ."

But Mr. Beck was taking no notice of his wife for the moment. "I should certainly advise you not to rush round to the Police Station, Lady Dalmane," he said. "For one thing you'll get absolutely soaked through to the skin, probably, in the rain that looks like coming on; but in any case, if I were in your position, and it was my wife who had been arrested and she'd written a note saying 'Go on ahead', I think I'd do just that." He looked again at the threatening sky and noted that the cloud with the strange outline like a tall spiral candlestick had been absorbed without trace into the lowering mass which covered the whole sky. Susan also glanced up at the clouds. The rain was already beginning to fall a little more heavily.

"Yes, I think you're right, Mr. Beck," she said. "I must do what my husband says." But she still had some doubts in the back of her mind about it until, a few seconds later, the rain came on really heavily, and with the downpour her mind was finally made up that she would go on in the train without John if he did not turn up in time for it. She remembered that he would at least be able to keep perfectly dry inside the Police Station where he would no doubt remain to take shelter from the rain until it eased off.

"It's coming on really heavily," said Jim Sandy. "We'd better all take shelter."

They were just in time. Mr. and Mrs. Beck, Susan Dalmane, and Jim Sandy rushed together for the small covered part of the platform and were underneath the roof just before a torrent of warm rain lashed down onto the old platform like the turning on of a huge tap in the sky; puddles formed in seconds and large bubbles showed in them. Another brilliant flash illuminated the semi-darkness as they ran for the wooden annexe to the booking hall, a structure like a sort of porch over a little bit of platform. They saw that the few other passengers who had turned up to wait for the 10.8 were also waiting under shelter further in, by the booking office counter; the porter was standing there too with a set of wooden steps. He would take these out onto the platform when the train arrived in order to make it easier for passengers to board the train as the platforms at Cockermouth were too low for boarding a train comfortably without the assistance of steps.

Jim Sandy had since his arrival at the station been content for the most part of the time to listen rather than to speak, and to look at Susan Dalmane, although he tried to do this without obviously staring at her. He had seen the marks of indignation printed on her face when she had spoken to him outside by the bench, the spots of red gathered around each cheekbone, the slight frown above her eyes, and he had thought that these signs made her look perhaps more beautiful than the smile he had not yet seen. It did not worry him in the least that she had offered him no vestige of a smile; he knew how upset and worried she was feeling at the moment, but he knew too that this mood would pass. She would surely give him a little smile before too long. He wondered how far she was intending to travel by train. What luck if she's going as far as Carlisle, he thought. That would give me—let me see—about an hour and a half I should think with her. Was it inconceivable that there might be a further opportunity to talk with her in the train, later on, when she would have forgotten about being so worried by the arrest of her husband? To talk with her when her mood was more relaxed and cheerful? No, it was by no means inconceivable that this might happen. All eyes in the little group of people around Jim Sandy (except for Mr. Beck who was again chatting with the porter) were turned towards the platform and the rain, Jim's eyes among them; but really he was at least as much concerned with watching Susan as he was with looking at the station and the weather. She was standing just in front of him, while he was looking at the back of her head, at the luscious sweep of her dark hair down onto her neck, and having occasional glimpses of her face. He was wondering whether he was going to continue to enjoy the company of this lovely woman in the train as far as Carlisle; or would she get out before that at Keswick or Penrith or one of the smaller stations at which they would stop? At any rate it was clear that she was about to be a passenger in the 10.8 train, just as he was, and he was preparing himself on that account for a very enjoyable journey.

They had been sheltering from the heavy rain under the wooden annexe on the platform for not quite two minutes when Mr. Beck put his head round the opening onto the platform. He thought he had heard the familiar sound of a two-car diesel-unit train approaching during an interval of relative silence after one of the loud rolls of thunder, and he had not been mistaken. At that moment he saw the train come into sight around the curve to the west of the station, its single headlight flaring through the gloom.

"Here it is," he called to the others.

Mr. Beck hastily said Good-bye to his friend, the porter, and shook his hand. Then the porter carried the wooden steps outside to the platform edge, apparently heedless of the rain which, mercifully, seemed to be not quite so heavy after the first minute or so of the deluge, although it was still splashing down noisily into the pools of water which now seemed to be everywhere. The train rumbled under the road bridge and slowly pulled in to their platform; Mr. Beck and the others were watching it from the open doorway of the booking hall annexe, and did not hurry out onto the platform until they saw the train stop. Jim had been watching it carefully through the windows of the annexe. He saw an oldish-looking man sitting at the controls in the driver's seat and recognized him as Mr. Ruddock. It had certainly been a brilliant idea of his to give Mr. Ruddock a message from his Sergeant, but because of the heavy rain, and through a certain feeling of shyness, he did not at all fancy the idea of hailing the driver from the platform to pass on the message. No, he would do all that later; what mattered now was to get in quickly. He deliberately let Susan go out onto the platform in front of him, thinking of seeing whereabouts in the train she would choose to find herself a seat, so that he could sit somewhere near her. Susan, however, instead of getting straight into the train via the wooden steps positioned beside an open door, stopped at the platform edge to look desperately around to see whether, at the very last moment, her husband would come running onto the platform in time for the train. But there was no sign of Lord Dalmane and Susan beckoned impatiently to Jim to board the train ahead of her.

"Hurry up, Lady Dalmane, if you're coming!" called Mr. Beck from inside the leading carriage of the two-car train. Susan abandoned her last hope that John would be able to come with her and, thankful to step inside out of the rain, entered the train and slammed the door shut behind her. A moment later Jim heard a buzzer sound twice in the driver's cab as the guard gave the driver the signal to re-start the train. The front carriage was still almost empty, the other new passengers having just entered the rear carriage. Mrs. Beck had plumped herself down straight away into a window-seat facing forwards on the right-hand side of the train, but Mr. Beck was standing there, politely waiting for Susan to choose a seat before he sat down himself; he gave a last wave to the porter through the windows. Jim Sandy had to think very quickly about where he should choose to sit down, having entered the train ahead of Susan. He immediately saw that she would sit down in the middle of the carriage, where Mr. Beck was offering her a seat, either beside Mrs. Beck or opposite her in a backward-facing seat; however, obeying some obscure sub-conscious motivation, Jim went forwards to take a seat right at the front, just behind the driver's cab on the right-hand side: the seat with the best view forwards through the glass partition in the whole train. As he came there the driver gave a short blast on his horn, and Jim saw him move his gear lever into first gear upon which, with a roar of diesel engines, the train began to move forwards. Turning round for a moment before he sat down, he saw Susan standing and staring through the windows to the left. Jim was not too sure what thought had prompted him to go right to the front; true, it was usually a favourite position for him because of the view forwards, but this time, with the windscreen wipers pushing away sheets of water from the front windows of the train, there really was not much view to be seen. Another thing was that the thought had come to him that he did not yet know the beautiful Lady Dalmane and that therefore it would not be proper for him to sit too near her. But, as soon as he sat down, he regretted his choice of a front seat because he could no longer see her—at least not without turning round. Drat it! he said to himself as the platforms slipped away behind them, I should have chosen a seat at the <u>back</u> of this carriage, but it's too late now!

CHAPTER SIX

As soon as Mrs. Beck took her seat in the train, and while her husband was still standing, she quickly but furtively took a pill bottle out of a pocket, extracted a tablet from it, and hurriedly swallowed it. She thought that her husband had not noticed her swallowing this pill, but in fact he had noticed; however, Susan, who sat down beside Mrs. Beck a moment after the pill bottle had been hidden away again, had noticed nothing of this. Susan was still thinking about her husband being left behind. She looked hard through the windows on the left-hand side of the train, hoping even now after the train had started that she might get a sight of her husband rushing up to the train, soaking wet and exhausted; then she would bang on the door of the driver's compartment, if necessary, to make him stop to pick up John. Susan saw sidings with cattle and sheep pens follow the platforms, and the concrete parapets of the river bridge follow the sidings, but there was no sign of anyone on foot in the downpour near the railway lines. After the river bridge she saw, for a moment, what looked like a small oil storage depot on the left immediately at the foot of an embankment, but a moment later the embankment had given place to the side of a cutting. She finally gave up looking for her husband. This is just silliness, hoping to see John here, she told herself. He'll be in the Police Station, keeping dry until the rain's over. He <u>should</u> get a really handsome apology for mistaken arrest, and then he'll come back to the railway station by road, not walking along beside the line again. Susan looked round and saw that Mr. Beck was politely waiting for her to sit down before he sat down himself.

"May I sit beside you?" Susan asked Mrs. Beck.

"Yes, do, if you like," said Mrs. Beck in a dull voice. The pill bottle had just been thrust away into a pocket.

Mr. Beck knew that Norma had just taken an extra tranquillizer, one which, strictly speaking, she should not have taken. But he was not concerned about it. Probably Norma would soon fall asleep under the effect of a double dose of sedative, and that, after all, would be no bad thing, he decided (he knew that she had taken her after-breakfast pill as usual before they had left their house for the station). Mr. Beck knew that it was mainly Norma's fear of the thunder which had induced her to take an extra tablet; that and, perhaps, the excitement of getting away in the train from the town from which she had so much wanted to make her escape.

Mr. Beck sat down in the seat opposite his wife's seat. It was at this moment, just as the train passed under the Lorton Road Bridge, that Jim from his front seat turned his head round for a moment to glance at the group in the middle of the carriage, the first of many such glances. As he had expected, there was that delightful Lady Dalmane sitting beside Mrs. Beck. He thought that, if anything, she looked even more striking than he had thought at first. Should he get up and move to another seat somewhere behind Lady Dalmane? He half got up, and then reluctantly changed his mind, sneaking another quick sideways glimpse of that enchanting face. Just then he noticed that the train was passing the place beside the Cemetery where Mr. Beck and he had stopped to talk before running back to the station. It was certainly interesting to compare the time the train had taken to cover that stretch—probably between a half and one minute—with the time he had taken to cover it himself on foot, about two minutes. So they were still travelling quite slowly as they approached the Cemetery Level Crossing, probably at not more than twenty miles per hour, Jim thought. His lively mind (he had a good aptitude for mental arithmetic) was usually fascinated by considering little problems such as this, but this time he was too pre-occupied with other matters for the estimation of the speed of the train to be more than a quick passing thought. It would not do for him to change his seat now. If he did, the Lady would know that he had changed his place simply in order that he could stare at her from behind—or so Jim argued to himself. Oh blast it, I'll have to stay where I am, he thought. I'd look silly if I walked back to another seat now having chosen this front seat.

"Well," said Susan as Mr. Beck sat down in the seat just in front of her's and Mrs. Beck's, "that's it. John's left behind. It really is a most extraordinary way to end a holiday to have one's husband suddenly snatched away by the police when he's done nothing wrong. The sort of mistake you'd think couldn't happen to you, but it has to me. Anyway, <u>surely</u> he'll be able to get the next train from here, don't you think, Mr. Beck?"

Mr. Beck had been only half attending to what Susan was saying as he looked out of the window and, like Jim Sandy, noted how the train was rapidly passing one after another the main landmarks of his recent railway walk, although the speed was not great; but he pulled himself together, and turned his head round to answer Lady Dalmane's point.

"Of course he will, Lady Dalmane," he said soothingly. "Now, don't you worry about it any more. It's all a mistake, and your husband's sure to convince them very quickly that he's not the witness they were looking for. Look, Lady Dalmane, we're just coming to the place where the police stopped us: that bridge."

"Oh. You and John had walked quite a long way then?"

"Yes, about half a mile from the station."

The little train rattled over the bridge and Susan, looking down, had a glimpse of quite a wide-looking stream, almost a small river.

The water looked deep and already somewhat muddy after less than five minutes of really heavy rain.

"I expect you'll know, as you're a driver, when John can get the next train from Cockermouth," said Susan a moment later. "Will it be long for him to wait if he gets to the station about now?"

"Yes, I'm afraid it would be a long wait," said Mr. Beck. "The next train to Penrith is the 11.48, and he'll have to change there to go on to Carlisle."

"We don't have to change at Penrith on this one?"

"No, this one goes right through to Carlisle in time for the 'Royal Scot'."

"But John'll miss the 'Royal Scot' too, I suppose?"

"I'm afraid so, and by a long way too. He'll get to Carlisle, after changing at Penrith, at around half past one; but, you see, the 'Royal Scot' goes out for London just before midday, at 11.57 to be precise. However, never worry, Lady Dalmane, your husband will certainly be in time to follow us on the 'Mid-Day Scot'. It leaves Carlisle for London just before five o'clock—4.56, I think it is."

"Good heavens! But that's hours later! Isn't there another train to London before that?"

"I don't <u>think</u> so," said Mr. Beck slowly as he tried to remember how the Timetable went. "Well, possibly there might be a slow train with one or more changes to make <u>en route</u> to London; I can't really remember that without a Timetable. But the 'Mid-Day Scot' gets into Euston at 10.30 p.m."

"Oh dear, how awfully late. So at that rate it's going to be about midnight before poor John gets to Knebworth . . . But perhaps I'd better not come with you in the 'Royal Scot', Mr. Beck. Perhaps I'd better hang about in Carlisle Station while I wait for the 'Mid-Day Scot' if you think I'd meet John on it."

"Oh, I wouldn't do that if I were you, Lady Dalmane," said Mr. Beck. "I think that would be most unwise when your husband's message told you to go on. 'Meet you at Knebworth' was what he said, wasn't it? And then, you see, if you <u>did</u> wait for him for the 'Mid-Day Scot' you might wait in vain, because he <u>might</u> find some other way to go up to London."

"Yes, you're quite right, Mr. Beck," said Susan. "I'd better not do that. His message <u>did</u> say that I was to get along ahead of him in the 'Royal Scot' as we originally planned . . . Do you like travelling by train, Mrs. Beck?" Susan felt that they were rather leaving Mrs. Beck out of things unless an attempt was made to draw her into their conversation; after all, Mrs. Beck was sitting right beside her, but she sat there so quietly that Susan, talking to Mr. Beck about train times, had all but forgotten her.

"Sometimes." Her answer sounded oddly vague and dream-like.

A flash of lightning came just then over the fells to their right, followed some four or five seconds later by a rumble of thunder. It may have been partly due to the fact that they were now hearing the thunder from inside the moving train, or else it may have been further away but, for whatever reason, it was nothing like so loud as those first resounding crashes they had heard from the station.

"I think the worst of the thunderstorm is over now," said Susan. "At any rate, it isn't deafening now, like it was, and the thunder and lightning are coming much less often."

"But the rain certainly isn't over," said Mr. Beck.

"No, but it's hardly frightening any more, is it, Mrs. Beck?" said Susan.

"H'm."

Susan looked at Mrs. Beck. It seemed that she was scarcely attending to what was being said, or hardly cared any longer what the weather might be doing. Her head was turned towards the window but her body was rather slumped in her seat; she had not turned round to answer Susan. Susan thought that she must be feeling tired.

"Are you feeling rather tired, my dear?" asked Mr. Beck, who was evidently thinking along the same lines as Susan.

"Yes, very tired," murmured Mrs. Beck, only her lips moving as she answered.

Mr. Beck nodded to Susan, as much as to say: "We'll let her drop off to sleep, shall we?" Then he turned round to look behind him for a moment, and saw that the Guard was coming forwards into their carriage from the rear one where his compartment was. Mr. Beck recognized the Guard as an acquaintance, though not a very old one; his name was Tim Blencow, and he must be coming forward to have a word with the Driver. And the Driver? Mr. Beck was sure that he must know him too, probably very well; but he could only see the back of the man's head from where he was, and he had not yet managed to catch a glimpse of his face. I think he must be old Tom Ruddock, he said to himself, and then: Hello! There's the Embleton Distant Signal. So we're just coming to the first stop. We seem to have got here quite quickly.

★

It did not take the Detective Chief Inspector much longer than ten minutes of questioning to satisfy himself absolutely that a serious mistake had been made: they had arrested the wrong man; the interviewee, who had given his name as John Dalmane, the Earl of Saint Helens, <u>was</u>, without doubt, the Earl of Saint Helens, and nothing whatever to do with their Murder Enquiry. What made the mistake on the part of the police worse was that, as the time now stood at seventeen minutes past ten, Lord Dalmane had missed the train he had been wanting to catch because of the arrest and interrogation. Not that the Chief Inspector had a mind on that account to caution or discipline the constable whose mistake had been responsible for the whole unfortunate episode: really his sharpness in that he had spotted a man who, from his appearance, <u>might</u> have been their Wanted Man, made him worthy of commendation. But what mattered immediately was to apologise profusely to Lord Dalmane and to find out without another moment's delay whether the Earl had indeed missed his train. The Chief Inspector rang the railway station and the porter, who answered the telephone, confirmed that the 10.8 train had left the station punctually, and reminded the Inspector that the next up train left at 11.48.

"So that's that," said the Chief Inspector. "I'm <u>very</u> sorry, my Lord, but we <u>have</u> made you miss your train, and we were wrong in bringing you here for questioning. I would like to offer you our most sincere apologies, Lord Dalmane, for this mix-up; and if there's anything we can do now to help your travel plans, I hope you'll mention it, and I hope you'll forgive us for the inconvenience we've caused you."

"Thank you for your apologies, Chief Inspector," said Lord Dalmane. "Yes, I'm prepared to forgive your men for bringing me here. But I'm not quite sure what I should do next, seeing that I've missed my train. Take the next one, I suppose." Now that his adventure with the police was more or less over, Lord Dalmane felt no bitterness towards the men at Cockermouth Police Station in spite of the fact that they had made a mess of his travelling plans for that day by making him miss his train. A little earlier the idea had occurred to him that perhaps he should take some retaliatory action against the police for his wrongful arrest when he got home, perhaps even sue them in court for damages or at least threaten them with "legal action" by his solicitor. When they had brought him into the Police Station he had really been somewhat annoyed when he found that he had to sit and wait for some six or seven minutes, apparently because the Detective Chief Inspector had not been in his room at that time; but even then he had not really wanted to take any vindictive action. Now that his innocence and ignorance of everything that pertained to this Murder Enquiry were definitely established, Lord Dalmane had no desire to do anything other than to accept the Chief Inspector's apologies and to continue his journey as soon as he could.

The Chief Inspector did not seem to have heard Lord Dalmane saying that he proposed to take the next train.

"By the way," he said, "I'd like you to see a copy of our artist's impression of the man we really are looking for in connection with this Enquiry. I've no doubt you'll understand better how this mistake arose when you see the picture."

"Yes, do show it to me," said Lord Dalmane. "I'd like to see what this chap looks like who's supposed to resemble me so closely."

"Bring us a copy of the poster, Sergeant," said the Inspector. "You'll find some spare ones in the top long drawer of the desk where Constable Apsley usually works by the Enquiries Counter."

"Yes, sir," said the Sergeant, and went out. He had been standing quietly to attention by the door of his superior officer's little room, in case the Inspector needed him for anything. Normally that small room on the first floor was only used to store things in, but when the Police Station had received an influx of extra officers at the beginning of the Murder Enquiry, an office had been hastily set up there for the man from the Police Headquarters who was to be in charge of the whole operation at Cockermouth. Consequent upon the temporary nature of this office was the surprisingly sparse appearance of the furniture in it. There were curtains for the window, but the desk in the middle of the room (a spare desk which by luck had been kept in that room) stood on carpetless floorboards, although a small mat had been found for the Chief Inspector's chair, and for his feet to rest upon. A picture of a typical Lakeland scene, reproduced from a colour photograph, had been found to liven up the otherwise bare walls; and on the wall to the right, as seen from the door, a large noticeboard had been put up, with a calendar and various sheets of paper memoranda attached to it by drawing pins.

During the few minutes while Sergeant Koppel was out of the room, Lord Dalmane's eyes roamed around the nearly bare walls, noting as he did so a certain lack of symmetry in the positioning on the wall opposite him of that one picture. He sat in the only other chair in the room, drawn up to the desk on the opposite side to the Chief Inspector's larger wooden chair (which was a revolving chair).

"Well," said the Chief Inspector as the door closed behind the Sergeant, "it's a lucky thing I haven't told the Chief Constable anything about this morning's misadventure. I had been thinking of ringing him to say that we'd found our man. But it would be as well for him not to know how we've bungled things by arresting an innocent stranger." He smiled for a moment, thinking of the amusing side of the mistake, but then he added in a more serious tone: "You weren't thinking of taking any legal action against the police, were you, Lord Dalmane? You might have a case, you know. We were undoubtedly in the wrong to arrest you."

"No," said Lord Dalmane. "I'm bringing no action against the police over this. We'll call the matter closed."

"That's very good of you, my Lord."

Meanwhile Sergeant Koppel had picked up one of the spare copies of the poster of the Wanted Man. But he did not go straight back to the Chief Inspector's Office. Where's that boy, Sandy, got to? he wondered. Should be back here by now. Gone for a further walk around the town, I suppose—doing some shopping maybe. Or perhaps he's stayed at the station to shelter until the rain stops, though it's beginning to ease off now. But I never gave him leave to hang about. It would only have taken him a minute or so to run back here, and he wouldn't have got really wet in that time. I'll have to give him a good ticking off . . . He had a quick look round the one or two rooms where Jim Sandy might possibly be waiting and then, not finding him, put him out of his mind again as he took the poster back to the Chief Inspector's Office.

"Good heavens!" said Lord Dalmane a moment later when the poster had been handed to him. "The resemblance is, I must say, quite astonishing. Yes, I can only suppose, having seen your artist's drawing of this chap, that this morning's mistake was almost bound to happen with your sharp-eyed constables keeping a good look-out for their 'Wanted Man'." He looked closely at the face in the drawing and chuckled at the thought of all the trouble his appearance in Cockermouth had caused.

"I'm glad you say that you think there was something inevitable about our mistake, Lord Dalmane," said the Chief Inspector. "Not that I think that altogether absolves the police in a case of this sort. Now that I look at you again, more carefully perhaps, I can see that there certainly <u>are</u> some subtle differences between the appearance of your face and this one in the poster."

"H'm, yes," said Lord Dalmane thoughtfully. "My hair is, perhaps, a little redder than this fellow's . . . and maybe his beard is slightly narrower than mine . . . but we seem to be very alike, worse luck. However, I'll be well out of the way of your murder hunt in a few hours' time unless, of course, you have to extend it as far as the South of England."

"Were you intending to travel beyond Carlisle, Lord Dalmane?"

"I was going up to London. I'd meant to travel in the 'Royal Scot' with my wife, but I gave her a note by Mr. Beck to say 'Go on without me'. I'll have to catch her up by taking the next London train and by taking the next train from here—the 11.48 I believe it was."

The Inspector suddenly looked up, smiling.

"No need for you to do that, my Lord," he said. "One of us will run you to Carlisle Station in a car, if you like. You're going through to Carlisle this afternoon, Sergeant Koppel, aren't you?"

"Yes, sir," said the Sergeant, "I was going to go after lunch in any case to Carlisle Police Station to pick up those papers we want.

I can easily take you with me in the car to the railway station, Lord Dalmane."

"Well, that's very kind of you to offer me a lift," said Lord Dalmane.

"Right, so we only need to know the time of the next London train from Carlisle, the one after the 'Royal Scot'," said the Chief Inspector. "It can't be helped now that you're bound to be too late for the 'Royal Scot', and we're very sorry about that; but I'll give Carlisle Station a ring right away and see what they can do for you." He picked up the telephone receiver on his desk and started dialling a number.

Lord Dalmane could not help feeling a little disappointed that he was being offered a lift in a police car to Carlisle Station. The walk with Mr. Beck along the railway line eastwards out of Cockermouth had made him even keener than he had felt before to travel that way by train through part of the Lake District. And now, at that very moment, Susan was somewhere along that line, travelling comfortably in the 10.8 train from Cockermouth. He had been thinking that he would at least be able to travel in the next local train; but now, by accepting the offer of the lift, he was going to miss his chance altogether of seeing what the branch line through Keswick and Penrith was really like. Of course, the Cockermouth Police were seizing an opportunity to make amends, in a way, for their dreadful mistake, but Lord Dalmane knew that the offer of a lift was nevertheless a generous gesture, and he decided at once to accept it with good grace.

A few minutes later his revised travelling plans had all been worked out for him to go as far as London; he would have to find out when he got to King's Cross whether it would still be possible to get to Knebworth by train that day, or whether he would have to take a taxi there. The Chief Inspector told him that the next departure for Euston after the 'Royal Scot' was the 4.56 train from Carlisle, a train called the 'Mid-Day Scot'. Oh heavens, thought

Lord Dalmane, I've got hours to wait here in Cockermouth! There's nothing very mid-day-ish about four fifty-six in the afternoon!

"—and it gets into Euston at 10.30 p.m." said the Inspector, concluding what he was saying. "I hope that will be all right, Lord Dalmane?"

"It'll do fine," said Lord Dalmane shortly. He realised that it would <u>have</u> to be all right because there was now no way (other than by plane, perhaps) in which he could reach Central London before half past ten that evening. Even if he had been offered a lift all the way to London in a police car, starting straight away, he thought that he still could not have arrived there any sooner. There was no point in saying anything more about it.

It was just after half past two when Sergeant Koppel drove away from the Police Station at Cockermouth with Lord Dalmane sitting beside him in the front passenger seat of the police car. The Earl had found the four hours of waiting in the small town which he did not know very boring, and had managed to pass the time by walking aimlessly around the few streets, alternating his walks with two visits to a hotel for morning coffee and for lunch. He had on both occasions sat for a very long time at the hotel table so that there would be less time for wandering about. Lord Dalmane thought, in fact, that the four hours around the middle of the day, between ten-thirty and two-thirty, were one of the longest four-hour stretches of time that he ever remembered. At last he looked at his watch and saw that it had reached twenty minutes past two. He had paid the bill for his lunch more than half an hour before, so now he left the hotel without pausing again to go back to the Police Station for his promised lift to Carlisle. He thought that there was something rather odd in that he felt decidedly cheerful when W.P.C. Laura Apsley, who was behind the Enquiries Counter, said as he came into the Station: "Hello, Lord Dalmane. Just take a seat, please, while I go and tell Sergeant

Koppel that you're here." It was somewhat inappropriate, he thought, to feel his spirits rising on coming into that police station when he remembered how he had been feeling when he had been brought in that morning from the railway line; but there could be no denying that he was beginning to feel cheerful again at the thought that he was about to resume his journey up to London, and thence to Knebworth to meet Susan again.

CHAPTER SEVEN

As the train left Cockermouth behind Mr. Blencow, the Guard, was standing in the gangway coupling the rear carriage to the front one while he was watching the small group of passengers in the middle of the front carriage. He recognized Mr. Beck as someone he knew, although he had not seen him at work for a while; but he had seldom worked as guard on a train driven by Mr. Beck: the shifts had not worked out like that. Most usually he worked with old Tom Ruddock, as he was doing this morning, as a regular train crew. Although he had seldom seen her, he knew Mrs. Beck by sight too. She was the thin woman with untidy dark hair sitting in a window seat and looking out of the window. But who was that younger-looking woman sitting beside her? Mr. Blencow certainly did not recognize this other woman although he saw that she was remarkably pretty. But at only thirty-six years old, and single, Mr. Blencow fancied that he always had an eye for a pretty woman; and now here before him was a really beautiful young woman. He assumed that, as she was sitting beside Mrs. Beck, she must be a friend of the Becks.

Tim Blencow glanced at his watch and then for a few moments looked out of a window. A farmyard right beside the track on the south side had just been left behind and then, seconds later, they passed under a little wooden bridge carrying a footpath from the wood to the south side over to the sloping field to the north. The steep little mass of Slate Fell rose up on the left through the slanting lines of rain into a cloudy top; it was a small, grassy knoll about two hundred feet high, the first outlier of the hilly country into which the railway wound its easterly way. Mr. Blencow knew almost every yard of the route. Just passed Strawberry How Bridge, he said to himself; Tom's not making very good speed on these wet, slippery rails, so we'll make Embleton in about another two minutes. He looked again at that pretty young woman who was sitting next to Mrs. Beck. Don't ever remember seeing such an eye-opener in one of my trains before! he thought happily. This might well have been true as he had only quite recently been promoted to the position of Guard; previously he had been a porter at Workington at the western end of the line. He had nothing particular to do at the moment, however, so he thought that he might as well take his chance, and for a minute or so longer continue to stare at that good-looking young woman from his unobtrusive vantage point in the doorway leading through from the rear carriage.

When the train had nearly reached Embleton Station, the first stop after Cockermouth, Mr. Blencow came forwards into the leading carriage, knowing that he would be needed to give the "all-clear" to the driver after the stop. It was just then that Mr. Beck turned round and saw him.

"Hello there, Tim Blencow!"

"Well, bless my soul, if it isn't Mr. Nigel Beck!" said the Guard, pretending that he had only just recognized him. "Haven't seen you for many a month, Mr. Beck." Susan looked round for a moment to see who it was that Mr. Beck was talking to. Mrs. Beck did not look round. Her hands were resting on her lap, and her chin had fallen forwards onto her chest although her head was still turned slightly towards the window; she was almost asleep.

"Going through to the Driver, are you?" said Mr. Beck. "That is old Tom Ruddock driving us, isn't it?"

"Yes, Tom's our Driver. I'm just going through to have a word with him after the Embleton stop." The Driver had applied the brakes and the train was coasting towards a single short platform as Mr. Blencow said this. The only person standing on the platform in the rain (which was now definitely not so heavy as it had been at the onset of the storm) was a railway official holding out a single-line token, which was a thing with a large loop for easy catching from a moving train. "Why not come forward for a word with Tom yourself?" added Mr. Blencow, and then: "Just a minute!" The train stopped and the Guard walked quickly forwards and opened a window and leaned from it to see whether any passengers were getting either into or out of the train, but there were none; while Mr. Ruddock, the Driver, stood up and leaned from his window to change tokens with the man on the platform. Before he resumed his seat at the controls, Mr. Ruddock looked round briefly through the glass partition at his passengers in the front carriage and at once saw Mr. Beck, who at that moment had left his seat to come up to the cab; and he also noticed, just for a second, a strikingly beautiful young lady among the passengers. He signed to Mr. Beck to come into the cab, saw Mr. Blencow wave his green flag vaguely in his direction, and sat down again to re-start the train.

Mr. Blencow stuffed the green flag, still rolled round its little stick, into one of the ample pockets of his railwayman's jacket and turned again to Mr. Beck as the train passed over the level crossing which followed the Embleton stop. "Look here," he said, "aren't you going through to have a word with Tom? He signed for you to come through to the driver's cab."

"Yes," said Mr. Beck, "but not right away. If you're just going in there I'd better wait; there aren't meant to be more than two people at once in the cab."

"All right," said Mr. Blencow. "Oh, by the way," (here he lowered his voice and came a little closer to Mr. Beck) "who is that delightful young woman who's sitting next to your wife? A friend of yours, I suppose? But, I say, Nigel, she looks absolutely superb! What a lovely face! And what magnificent breasts! My word, she's a piece of crumpet and make no mistake—"

"'Sh! Be quiet, she'll hear you," hissed Mr. Beck with a certain degree of irritation detectible in his voice. They were standing well up to the front of the carriage, near Jim Sandy's seat, but Mr. Beck looked round anxiously to the place where Susan was sitting, and saw that she did not seem to have noticed that her appearance was being discussed. He had only known her himself for a little over an hour, but had carefully refrained from expressing aloud to anyone his own feelings about the lady's undoubtable attractions, so that he found it offensive to hear such coarse remarks concerning Lady Dalmane coming from the mouth of a complete stranger.

"But who _is_ she?" whispered the Guard.

"You'd better be careful, Tim," said Mr. Beck. "She's her Ladyship, the Countess of Saint Helens."

"A countess? You mean she really is a titled lady? Or are you just pulling my leg?"

"No, no, she really _is_ a countess. Susan Dalmane is her name, so she's Lady Dalmane to you. So you jolly well mind your words, Tim, you dirty old man!"

"All right! Here, steady on, Nigel! I was only curious to know who she is . . . as anyone might be."

"Well, you know now that she's Lady Dalmane," said Mr. Beck. "Look, I'll sit here while you're in the cab. Tell Tom I'll come in for a word after you." He sat down on the left-hand front seat, immediately behind the driver.

Mr. Blencow, rather taken aback by what Mr. Beck had told him, put his hand to the handle of the door leading into the driver's cab and paused a moment, glancing at the other front seat where young Sandy was sitting and indulging himself in amorous fantasies about the beautiful Lady Dalmane. He likes her too, he thought, seeing the youth half turn his head round to catch a squint backwards towards Lady Dalmane's seat. Mr. Blencow opened the door of the cab and went in.

Jim Sandy had had time enough, now that the first few seemingly fast-moving minutes of the journey were over, to begin to think about what he was doing. However, he still had no regrets, other than a vaguely felt unease, at having run off from his job with the Cockermouth Police, not intending to return to it, and without a word to anybody. He felt less worried about leaving home because he had hinted to his father that he intended to go up to London in the train "soon" to see his mother and to look for a new job; and his father, although he had not exactly approved of the idea, had made it clear that he would not try to stop his eldest son going up to London. Mr. Sandy had told Jim that as far as his proposed job hunt in the capital was concerned he had grave doubts, but he had thought that it would not be a bad thing for Jim to visit his mother, if he wanted to. Jim had left home that morning not knowing whether he would be off to London that day or not, so he had not said a special Good-bye to his father. Mr. Sandy was, of course, under the impression that Jim had given his notice to the police in order to look for a new job. As he also knew that Jim had sent off a trunk full of his personal belongings by Passenger's Luggage in Advance to his mother's address, it was clear to Jim that his father was not going to be surprised when he told him that he had reached London. His plan was to ring up his father as soon as he reached his mother's house in Ealing to inform him where he was. There should be no difficulty about that, he thought. The Police Station at Cockermouth would also have to be rung up, but that was a rather different matter which Jim did not at all want to think about at that time.

One might have thought it a curious thing that Jim Sandy's action in being, to all practical purposes, a deserter from the police force, was bothering his conscience remarkably little. In fact, the reason why his conscience was so little pricked over this matter was simply that his mind was too full of other thoughts to allow the thought· "I am behaving disgracefully in what I'm doing" to trouble him seriously. It was there vaguely, in the back of his mind, and Jim was quite happy to let it remain there, quietly dormant. His active thoughts were mainly pursuing a quite different subject. He had been slyly turning his head round to catch glimpses of Susan whenever he could. She had become quite naturally a totally absorbing fascination for him. When the Guard suddenly looked at him before going through to the cab, Jim hurriedly turned his head and pretended to be looking with interest at the rain-soaked valley and at the looming mass of Skiddaw right ahead, completely hidden in the clouds. But there really was not much to look at through the windscreen, across which the windscreen wipers slapped to and fro, pushing aside the streams of water; and, of course, the youth was not really interested in the scenery, fine though it would have been but for the clouds and the rain. The lightning flashes were by now hardly noticeable and the thunder no more than an occasional distant-sounding rumbling, but still the rain came down steadily and fairly heavily in lines which would have looked nearly vertical but for the motion of the train; the wind had dropped to nothing. They were passing now down the flat-bottomed valley between the village of Embleton and the lower end of Bassenthwaite Lake. There were low hills to the north and the south, hills which rose up steeply from the floor of the valley into the low-lying blanket of cloud which covered everything above about two to three hundred feet up the hillsides: Sale Fell and Ling Fell to the right, and the Embleton Quarry ridge to the left. Altogether the view just then was something of a dismal prospect, but that meant nothing to Jim. He was regretting more than ever that he had taken a seat right up at the front, and longing to move to a seat a little behind Lady Dalmane, to be as near to her as he dared; and yet he could not quite bring himself to move. He thought that he had never before seen such a beautiful woman, and probably he had not. All his other thoughts and feelings, such as prickings of conscience and the enjoyment proper to a pleasant train journey, were being swallowed up in a burning infatuation for that woman.

Mr. Ruddock, the Driver, was sixty-five years old, but hardly looked as old as that. He was a very fit man and hoped to continue driving trains for another three years before retiring, by which time he would have achieved fifty years of service on the railways. Not that he had been working on the footplate and in the cab for anything like all of the time since he joined the London and North Western Railway in 1912 at the age of eighteen as an odd-job boy at the Company's Carlisle Depot; he had progressed through several other jobs with the Company before he had first become an apprentice engine driver in 1919. He had been, in turn, apprentice signalman, signalman in charge of a country box, and fireman; and then he had started his training as a driver. Since his early years with the London and North Western Railway he had worked for the London, Midland and Scottish Railway and, latterly, for British Railways for many years, driving many different kinds of trains. He was a conscienscious man, and his forty-seven years on the railways were so far unblemished either by accident or by reprimandible incident. Tom Ruddock was a fairly small, squat man with nondescript greyish hair which in spite of his years showed little sign of baldness. He had blue eyes and a kindly-looking face.

"Well," he said, "isn't Mr. Beck coming in?" Mr. Blencow had just entered the cab and shut the door marked "Private" behind him.

"Not just yet," said Mr. Blencow. "He's coming in after me, as there shouldn't really be three of us in here together."

"Ah, yes, he's quite right really." Mr. Ruddock for a moment took his eyes off the line ahead to look backwards into the carriage. "By the way, Tim," he added, "have you gathered who that gorgeous piece is? The big girl with dark hair and dark eyes and big breasts?"

"That's Lady Dalmane," said Mr. Blencow. "Mr. Beck says she's the Countess of somewhere—I forget where."

"She's <u>very</u> pretty! But surely she isn't a real Countess? Doesn't look the right sort to me. I mean, you wouldn't expect a Countess to look like a buxom wench like that, would you?"

"Really, Tom! You shouldn't say things like that about Lady Dalmane!" Mr. Blencow was grinning broadly as he said this but he managed all the same to make his mock indignation sound fairly genuine.

"Oh well," said Mr. Ruddock, "if she really is a Countess, far be it from me to say anything rude about her. The aristocracy deserve our respect, Tim. But is there an Earl of wherever it is? Because if so, he doesn't seem to be travelling with us. Or is this all a joke?"

"Oh no, I don't think it's a joke. Mr. Beck sounded perfectly serious."

There was a short silence in the cab while Mr. Ruddock sounded the horn as the train approached the level crossing of a minor country road. Then the two railwaymen began to discuss railway matters, but Mr. Ruddock soon broke off the conversation as he again turned round to admire Lady Dalmane's beauty for a few more seconds.

"D'you know what I'm going to do?" he asked. A mischievous glint had come into his eyes.

"Well, what are you going to do?" asked the Guard.

"I'm going to invite that young lady to sit beside me here in the cab!" said Mr. Ruddock, smiling broadly.

"Tom, you can't do that! It's against regulations, you know, to allow passengers to ride in the driver's cab."

"Damn the regulations! I'm going to ask her."

"But what about Mr. Beck? He's coming in here just now."

"Yes, I know," said Mr. Ruddock, "but I had in mind to ask Lady Dalmane to come in later on—maybe when we've got to Keswick. I think the finest scenery on the whole line comes just after Keswick in the Greta Gorge, don't you? I expect she'd be very glad to have a grandstand view of that from the front, as you might say. So why not?"

"Why not? Because you're meant to be driving this train, Tom Ruddock, not seducing young women. So, if you insist on having her in here, you'd better be careful to see that your hands keep to the controls so that they don't stray towards her private parts!"

"Oh shut up, Tim Blencow, you old woman! You know damn well that I wouldn't allow my hands to 'stray,' as you put it, off the controls, or behave indecently in any way at all. As a married man I know how to behave decently with women. And just you remember that in here I am in command; and I shall invite whoever I please to come in here. I'm going to ask her in. She may say 'No', of course, but I think she'd be delighted to come in here for a better view of the Gorge. You know very well that I'll be on my best behaviour with her. I may be old, Tim, but I can see that she is a Lady, a Lady of distinction and aristocratic background—yes, on second thoughts I'll take back what I said about her looking like a buxom wench. I'll be a proper gentleman towards her, I will. Anyway, I'm only going to offer her the driver's mate's seat to give her a good view—that's all."

"Oh, is it?" said Mr. Blencow. "Well, I shan't be in your way, so I hope the two of you enjoy yourselves. Only don't blame me if you get the sack. Someone might easy report you, Tom, for improper behaviour while on duty. I only mean that as a friendly warning, mind you. I'm only saying: 'Don't be rash'. I wouldn't take a risk like that if I were in your place."

"Don't you worry, Tim," said Mr. Ruddock. "I'm going to be very careful. Hello!" (He reached for the brake handle). "Here we are at Bass Lake." The train was rounding a curve; a few hundred yards ahead were level crossing gates, open for the train to pass, and beyond them the two platforms of the next station.

"I must go through to the passengers," said Mr. Blencow. "See you later." As he went out he nodded to Mr. Beck.

"Come in, Nigel," called the Driver. And so, no sooner had Mr. Blencow left the cab than Mr. Beck went in. Mr. Blencow waited until the handful of new passengers at Bassenthwaite Lake Station had got in and the train was moving off again before beginning a round of inspecting passengers' tickets.

"Tickets please," he said, and looked round at Jim Sandy. "Well," he added a moment later, seeing the youth make no move to produce a ticket for inspection, "have you got a ticket?"

"Well, er, no, I'm sorry I haven't," said Jim rather awkwardly. "I got in at Cockermouth in rather a rush and I'm afraid I forgot about buying my ticket. I'll buy one at the other end, of course."

"Forgotten to buy your ticket?" said the Guard. "Where are you travelling to?"

"As far as Carlisle by this train."

"H'm, I <u>should</u> order you out of the train at the next stop, you know. It doesn't look too good, does it, to let a policeman get away with such a flagrant breaking of the rules?"

"My journey's important," said Jim quickly. "<u>Please</u> allow me to continue it. I shall certainly buy my ticket for this trip at the Booking Office at Carlisle when I get there. I'd be going there anyway to get myself a single to Euston."

"Oh, very well, you can do that then," said the Guard. "Is your name James Sandy, by the way?"

"Yes."

"I thought I recognized you. So you're a Police Cadet based at Cockermouth nowadays? You must be on leave, I suppose, and going away to visit relations in London?"

"Yes, I'm going down to stay with my mother who lives in London," said Jim. This half-truth seemed to Jim to be quite enough said about his travel plans, but he was relieved to find that the Guard had already left him to go on with his ticket inspection round. He looked at the grey water of Bassenthwaite Lake, now close beside the railway line, and beyond it to the vast mass of Skiddaw and its satellite hills which dominated the view to the further side of the lake; they were still well enshrouded by low clouds but the sky was beginning to look brighter, the cloud more broken. Its going to fair up soon, he thought; the rain must be nearly over.

Susan was quite entranced by the view through the left-hand windows. She forgot about Mrs. Beck, who was by now asleep beside her in the window seat (on the right-hand side of the train), as she noted with surprise the sudden appearance of the lake just beside the railway line moments after they had left the second station behind. Large bubbles showed on the smooth surface of the water as the rain poured down, but she could see that the sky was getting lighter. A solitary fisherman in a rowing boat was the only moving boat she could see on the wide, grey waters. Around there the water came right up to the embankment, within a few feet of the railway line, giving railway passengers a perfect view of the lake. It looks simply splendid, she thought. What must it be like on a fine, clear day? Susan was much too interested in watching the lake with its wooded shores and occasional rocky headlands to notice the Guard coming up to inspect her ticket.

"May I see your ticket, please, madam?" said a voice close beside her. Susan looked up with a start and saw the Guard.

"Oh! Yes, of course." What a very lucky thing it was that John had given her that ticket. Poor John, she thought, It's dreadful that he isn't here enjoying this nice trip with me. She took her purse out of a pocket of her jeans, took her ticket from it and handed it to the Guard.

"Thank you, ma'am," said the Guard politely. "Change at Carlisle for Euston." He punched a small triangle out of the edge of the little rectangle of card with his ticket-punch machine and handed it back to Susan, who noticed that he was now looking at the sleeping form of Mrs. Beck as if wondering whether he ought to wake her up.

"Don't wake Mrs. Beck," said Susan quickly. "She's only just gone to sleep and I believe she's very tired. I'm sure Mr. Beck will have her ticket with him."

"Yes, I expect he has," said the Guard. "Are you a stranger in these parts, ma'am?"

"Yes, I am, actually," said Susan, somewhat surprised that he seemed to want to stay to talk to her instead of getting on with inspecting the other passengers' tickets. "I'm on my way home at the end of a pleasant holiday."

"You've had some good weather on your holiday, likely, up to this morning?" said the Guard. "But the rain's stopped now, you see."

"Why, so it has. It was raining only a minute ago and I never noticed it stop, though I thought it looked like stopping with the sky getting lighter again." Susan noticed as she said this the way that the Guard was looking at her. She saw his lustful gaze directed with too much interest at the outline of her breasts through her blouse and saw how his gaze instantly shifted as she caught his eye.

"Do you think the storm is over?" she added, looking meaningfully into the Guard's eyes.

"Aye, I think so," He did not quite meet her look. "It'll likely be a hot, sunny afternoon."

"Oh. You don't think it will turn cooler after that thunderstorm?"

"I doubt it. It was only quite a little thunderstorm really."

"Quite a little thunderstorm?" Susan repeated his words to herself, remembering the fierceness with which the storm had broken. Well yes, now that she considered it, the storm <u>had</u> passed quickly. In a way, Susan was rather enjoying having the Guard talking to her, knowing that neither of them was really thinking about the weather in spite of the polite words they used; but she also hoped that he would very soon move on to someone else.

Mr. Blencow waved a hand to indicate the scenery through the carriage windows. The storm clouds were rapidly breaking up and had already lifted enough to reveal most of the Skiddaw massif, although the main peak was still hidden by a swirling grey veil of mist. High in the south-east (roughly ahead of the train) the sun was just breaking through the clouds. Patches of blue sky had appeared and a broad shaft of sunlight picked out bright shades of green and blue on the southern flanks of Skiddaw.

"Very pretty country it is around here. Don't you think so?" said Mr. Blencow.

"Yes, it's very beautiful," agreed Susan. Heavens! why doesn't he move on? she said to herself.

"Well, I hope you'll have an enjoyable trip. Good day to you, my Lady." The Guard left her and went on towards the back of the carriage.

What! thought Susan, He called me "my Lady". Mr. Beck must have told him who I am. She settled again to looking out of the window and saw that the train was just coming to the end of the lake. There was a bay seen briefly through the window where the water looked very shallow, a curving outline which cut into a very reedy, marshy looking bay. Susan noticed that the land thereabouts was so flat that, she thought, the lake must have once covered it in some past age. Again she had become too interested in the changing view to notice what other people in that carriage were doing, so it was not until several minutes later that she realised that Jim Sandy, the police cadet, had discovered a new, crafty way of looking at her without making it appear that he <u>was</u> looking at her.

Jim had made the discovery quite by accident. A few minutes earlier, in fact immediately after the Guard had left him, he had noticed the reflection in his ring stone. On the little finger of his left hand he was wearing a ring which had a large, plain stone set in it. The highly polished surface of this stone acted as a mirror under the right conditions and Jim suddenly noticed a fleeting image of the branches of trees in it; at that place small trees grew hard beside the line between an embankment and the edge of the lake. There was now a patch of clear sky over the lake in just the right place to increase the light enough to make the transient reflection in the stone sharp and clear for a second or so. Like a mirror, Jim thought, seeing the reflected branches and then reflections of the train windows as his hand moved slightly. Suddenly an idea flashed into his mind like a stroke of inspiration. A mirror lets you see things behind you without turning round, he said to himself, but it took him a few seconds to find the position he wanted; then: There she is! he thought, as a perfect reflection, very small but clear, of Susan's pretty face appeared in the ring stone as he held his left hand about six inches away from his left eye. He tried a few experiments and found that he could move his ring finger into a more natural and relaxed position but could still, with care, see that all-important reflection.

The short conversation with the Guard in which he had realised that he was travelling without a ticket had given him an embarrassing few moments, but he very soon forgot all about that as he gazed into his ring as if spellbound by the beautiful little reflection which he saw there. It was to be several hours later before he realised what a great stroke of luck it had been that he had forgotten to buy a ticket. The only risk he was concerned about now as he gazed into the ring was that Lady Dalmane might spot what he was doing and disapprove, but he thought this unlikely. It never entered his mind that the fact that he had not called at the Booking Office at Cockermouth would make it that much more difficult for his colleagues at the Police Station to find out where he had disappeared to if they should make enquiries there. Jim was, however, slightly bothered by a vague idea that there was something wrong or even immoral about the secretive way in which he was feasting his eyes on Lady Dalmane's beauty without her knowledge or consent, but he tried to reason this idea away for himself. I suppose it's dreadfully naughty of me to be doing this, he said to himself. After all, she is Lord Dalmane's wife so I really must stop this secretive looking at her. But he did not stop looking, at least not for longer than a few seconds. Instead, he let his thought run on in a slightly different vein. Bother it! Why shouldn't I look at her? She is just too tempting. Anyway, she's pretty unlikely to catch me at it.

In this belief, however, Jim was mistaken. The train was nearing Keswick when Susan happened to look forwards and noticed what he was doing. Her immediate reaction was one of considerable annoyance that any man, even if he was infatuated with her, should choose such a sneaky way of looking at her. She almost got up to give him a sharp warning to stop peeping at her in his ring stone, but then she hesitated. What was it that he had told her on that station platform? That his name was Jim Sandy, and that he was leaving the police and going up to London? Susan wondered what for, and why he was travelling alone, and why he was still wearing police uniform if he was leaving the force. Perhaps he had relations, aunt or uncle or cousins, or some of his more immediate family living in London, and was giving up a job hundreds of miles away from them to go back to where his family came from: in fact, to go home. Or was it for some other reason that he was making that long journey alone? Susan now realised for the first time that this lad in police cadet's uniform looked almost young enough to be still at school. But his furtive behaviour had revealed to her something deeper in his thoughts than mere physical lust for her. Poor lad, she said to herself, I suppose he's lonely, but I can see that he likes me. Well, why not? Why should I object to that? She looked again at him very carefully. Aha, she thought, He's looking secretly at me, but he doesn't know that I've spotted him doing it! I'll give him a little surprise just now. I'll have a word with him. She quickly stood up and walked up the gangway towards that front seat where sat her offending young admirer. Too late, Jim Sandy put both his hands between his knees and tried very hard to look as if he had never been doing anything but looking forwards along the line.

"Well, Master Sandy, is the reflection of me in that ring-stone really so much worth looking at?" she asked.

"Well . . . er . . ."

"Your name is Jim Sandy, isn't it?"

"Yes, it is," said Jim nervously.

"And do you really think that I look so attractive that you find it necessary to watch me by looking secretly at my reflection? Did you not consider that perhaps I would find it offensive to be peeped at in this way?"

"Oh . . . ah . . . Lady Dalmane, I'm very sorry, I really am. I didn't want to upset you." Jim was blushing as he managed awkwardly to say this, but Susan decided to spare his further blushes by changing her tone somewhat. She found that she had something of a liking for this infatuated young man and was keen to find out more about him. She smiled: almost, indeed, she laughed seeing that her questions had caused him a good deal of consternation.

"Upset me? No, of course you didn't upset me; but I do think that what you were doing with that ring was rather foolish. I don't particularly object to it, but another woman might well have found it very offensive behaviour and might have reprimanded you sharply."

"Yes, I suppose so," said Jim. "I apologize, Lady Dalmane, for doing it; it was foolish of me."

For a few seconds Susan looked at him but said nothing. She also saw the houses of a small town ahead, a town which seemed to be ringed all around with mountains and hills, but she hardly really noticed it. Then, unexpectedly, she crouched down close beside Jim, and said in a very quiet voice, hardly more than a whisper into his ear: "Are you travelling up to London in the 'Royal Scot'?"

"Yes," said Jim.

"Well, I am too," whispered Susan. "Look here, I'd like to have a private talk with you. If you can find an empty compartment in the 'Royal Scot' I'll come and sit beside you, and we'll have it just to ourselves while we talk." Having said this she got up and, without giving Jim a chance to answer, went straight back to her seat without another glance in his direction.

Half a minute later the train drew into Keswick station and stopped at a platform where there seemed to be quite a large number of people waiting to board it. The sun had come out again, and the light was glinting off the wet platforms with heartening brilliance. The confusion in Jim's feelings as he sat in his front seat was considerable, as his dominant emotions contradicted each other. On the one hand he was full of hurt pride at having been publicly shamed over this ridiculous ring reflection incident— publicly, because he knew that the Driver and Mr. Beck, who were both in the driver's cab, had seen Lady Dalmane come up to his seat to rebuke him. On the other hand, he was more than delighted—indeed privately he was almost ecstatic—over Lady Dalmane's final words, whispered in his ear. Over and over again he repeated to himself her words as if they were some sort of magical enchantment: "I'll come and sit beside you." Gosh, he thought, it's quite incredible! In a happy daydream he watched Mr. Beck get up just as they were coming in to Keswick station, and saw him return to his former seat. Then he saw the Driver get up and come through into the carriage. He heard Mr. Ruddock inviting Lady Dalmane to come through to take a seat beside him in the cab for the next part of the journey. Oh well, he thought, there's no need to envy him. I'll be sitting beside her in the next train!

★

A little earlier in the journey, at Bassenthwaite Lake Station, Mr. Beck had gone through to the driver's cab to talk with Mr. Ruddock. He told the Driver that he and his wife were leaving the area because of his wife's long illness, and that he himself had lately been off work because of sickness; but he also told Mr. Ruddock that he meant to continue in his own job as an engine driver when he had moved down to the South. Mr. Ruddock said that he was very sorry to hear that Mr. Beck was leaving and that, as between one driver and another, he would be greatly missed on the lines in and around the Lake District. Presently, however, Mr. Ruddock decided to change the subject.

"I hear from my Guard, Tim Blencow," he said, "that the other lady—the young lady who's sitting next to your wife—is called Lady Dalmane. Tim told me that you'd told him she was a Countess. What did you say her title was?"

"Countess of Saint Helens," said Mr. Beck.

"Yes, that was it. I suppose there's an Earl of Saint Helens too?"

"Yes, we met Lord and Lady Dalmane on the platform at Cockermouth."

"Did you indeed?" said Mr. Ruddock. "But isn't it very odd that Lady Dalmane has come on this train without her husband if they were <u>both</u> on the platform? Where has Lord Dalmane got to, if I'm not being too nosey in asking that?"

"Well, you'd hardly believe this, but I went for a short walk with him along the line and suddenly the police appeared and arrested him."

"Good heavens! Is Lord Dalmane a criminal on the run then?" asked Mr. Ruddock.

"No, of course he isn't. As far as I can see, it's all an absurd mistake. But you see, Tom, it's this murder hunt that's on at Cockermouth which has been responsible for this incident . . ."

Mr. Beck went on to describe in a little more detail the walk he had taken along the track with Lord Dalmane and the amazing circumstances of the Earl's arrest. He told Mr. Ruddock that, although he had never seen one of the posters of the Wanted Man, it was perfectly clear to him that what had happened was that the police had mistaken Lord Dalmane for their Wanted Man; and by now, no doubt, realised their mistake. "There's one of those Cockermouth policemen right here in this train," continued Mr. Beck, "this cadet, Jim Sandy, who's sitting just behind us now." He swung round for a moment and indicated the youth on the front seat who was staring into the stone of his ring. As soon as he saw the men in the cab turn round, Sandy instantly raised his eyes as if to look at the view straight ahead. But both men had understood what he was doing, and they smiled at each other knowingly.

"What's all this?" said Mr. Ruddock. "If this lad is a police cadet from Cockermouth and one of the party who came out to arrest Lord Dalmane, how does he come to be in my train? What's he doing—apart from looking at the reflection of Lady Dalmane in his ring?"

"Yes, I suppose he was having a sly look at Susan Dalmane," said Mr. Beck. "But, without going into details, what he's doing is going up to London by train. That's what he told me. His mother lives there."

"Oh, I see," said Mr. Ruddock slowly, evidently a little puzzled to hear this. "You mean, he's on leave? I thought you said . . . oh well, never mind that. And he does a little cautious flirting with Lady Dalmane meanwhile to amuse himself and pass the time?"

"Looking at her reflection isn't exactly flirting, is it?"

"Perhaps not, but you know, Lady Dalmane seems to have a lot of male admirers on this train," said Mr. Ruddock with a grin.

"What do you mean by 'a lot'?"

"Well, there's me for one: I think she's fantastically beautiful. And then there's this boy here who is clearly heavily infatuated;

and then there's Tim Blencow. I could see that he's another who's infatuated with her—in spite of all his banter to me about how I should watch my step."

"Oh? What was that about?" asked Mr. Beck with interest.

"It's this, Nigel. I told Tim that I meant to ask her to come in here and sit beside me—so that she can admire the view better, of course."

"And so that you can 'admire the view' better too, eh, you dirty old man! Yes, she has a fine bust, well worth admiring!" Mr. Beck broke into a spontaneous laugh at the pun he had made.

"Ah! Is that really so funny? Anyway, if she agrees, I'll ask her to join me in the cab when we stop at Keswick."

"But we'll reach Keswick in a few minutes," said Mr. Beck, quickly becoming serious again. "Look here, Tom, you'll be crazy to try this. What if an inspector boards the train and catches you with a pretty young woman sitting beside you in here? You'd get the sack for certain. I wouldn't dream of taking such a risk myself although I grant you that she is very attractive."

"Well, it's a very rare thing, as you know, to have an inspector on a train on this line," said Mr. Ruddock. "I say it's a risk well worth taking: and on that point I've absolutely made up my mind."

"Oh, very well, then; I'll go back to my seat," said Mr. Beck, but at this point Mr. Ruddock nudged him, and the two men, half turning round, saw Susan leave her seat and come up to the front to speak to Jim Sandy, who had clearly been caught red-handed playing his little game with the reflection. Mr. Beck and Mr. Ruddock could not help hearing what was said, except for the words whispered in the boy's ear.

"You won't be wanting me here so I'll go now," said Mr. Beck a few moments later as the train was coming into Keswick, and as they saw Susan Dalmane return to her seat.

"It would be better," said Mr. Ruddock, "though it's been delightful talking to you. I hope we get a chance to meet again before too long, Nigel."

"Good-bye, Tom."

That woman has turned his head, I fear, Mr. Beck thought as he walked back to his seat. It's a crazy idea to ask her in there, but I hope no one reports him. He's a very decent fellow and deserves to get away with it.

CHAPTER EIGHT

Susan looked round as Mr. Ruddock opened the door leading from the cab into the front carriage. She had just been looking at the view southwards over the little town of Keswick which began where a church with a square tower stood in a large churchyard beside the line. Then they had run past some houses, some sidings, and a coal-yard, and so had come to a stop at Platform Two of Keswick Station.

Mr. Ruddock came straight up to Susan and made a respectful little bow to her, taking off his cap with his right hand. The bow was really no more than a slight forward inclination of his head, and was executed with just the correct degree of chivalry, not ostentatiously, so that one might almost have thought that it had been well rehearsed.

"My Lady," he said, "I should like, if I may, to offer you a seat in the driver's cab so that you may enjoy the view better."

"Oh, how kind of you," said Susan. "Thank you very much, Driver. I should love to sit there!"

"You see, ma'am, there's the finest scenery on this line in the next section between here and Penrith, as I always think; but you can't really see it properly except with an unhindered view from the front. You'll be a stranger to these parts, ma'am, I expect? Are you on holiday?"

"Yes, we're just coming to the end of a holiday. My husband and I have never visited the Lake District before. We live in Dorset."

"Your husband, ma'am?" enquired Mr. Ruddock politely.

"My husband, the Earl of Saint Helens, was unfortunately unable to come with me on this journey; he's going to follow on a later train."

"That *is* unfortunate, ma'am, as this is such a beautiful run from here, as you'll see. Your husband, the Earl, met a friend, did he, and decided to stay behind?"

"No," said Susan, "it was not quite like that, but there was someone he had to talk to."

"I see." Mr. Ruddock noticed that Mr. Blencow, who had managed to catch his eye, was making faces at him. "Excuse me, ma'am, but it's time to start the train. Would you like to come with me?"

Mr. Ruddock knew that the other passengers in that carriage (there were plenty of them now) were all watching him and Susan as he lead the way up the gangway to the front; all except Jim Sandy, who felt so shamed after the ring incident that he dared not look round; but Susan gave him an encouraging smile as she walked past. Mr. Ruddock was very much enjoying all the attention which he knew he was attracting around himself and Susan. He held the door of the cab open for her, pointed to the extra seat on the right which was like a stool surmounted by a maroon-red cushion-like top, and politely stood aside as she took her seat there. Then he looked out of his window, saw the Guard wave his green flag (By gum, he thought, that fellow is green with envy; I can see it); and then, seating himself in the driving seat, he re-started the train.

Susan, as she sat down in the seat designed for the second man or the Guard, carefully adjusted the tension in the front of her blouse where it was tucked into her jeans so that it would not be stretched unnecessarily tightly across her bust, thereby attracting too much attention to the outlines of her large breasts. Gosh, it's a good thing I'm wearing these jeans and not a skirt today, she thought. It wouldn't be right for him to see too much bare leg up at the top. She glanced down for a second at her front and was satisfied that the outline of the brassière she was wearing underneath the blouse did not show through it; and then immediately, her mind being at ease about her personal appearance, she switched her attention to enjoying the view as the train left the platforms behind and came to a high bridge over a river. She was very much aware that it was not solely for her to look at the view that she had been invited to sit in that special seat; but also so that the Driver could look at her, which meant that even when she might appear to be entirely absorbed in watching the scenery she would be keeping a wary eye on the man who now sat close to her in the driver's seat. Susan had, like Mr. Ruddock, felt the eyes of the other passengers watching her as she had gone into the cab with the Driver. She was causing quite a stir: she knew this, but in her present buoyant mood she did not mind in the least. She knew that, in any case, the people in that carriage were more curious to know what was going on than envious of the privilege for which she had been singled out. The thought that the Driver might get into serious trouble because she had accepted his invitation never occurred to her and so, as they set off from Keswick, there was nothing to spoil her happiness. As for the obvious attention of Mr. Ruddock, she was happy that it should be so: always provided that he continued to behave impeccably. He will, though, I'm sure, she thought; he's a proper gentleman. She was certainly flattered and impressed by this man's bold but chivalrous manner towards her; and now she realised that she was no longer pining for her husband, as she certainly had been at the beginning of the train trip. She was even a little glad, privately, that he was not there.

"What a pretty river," she said as they slowly crossed the bridge just east of Keswick station. "My word, the view from here really is marvellous."

"It certainly is, ma'am," said Mr. Ruddock. "That's the River Greta. We see a good deal of it between here and Threlkeld, the next station, and we cross it several more times."

About a minute or two later they came to a place so spectacular in its dramatic beauty that Susan for a moment forgot everything but the view. The short run from Keswick Station had taken them into a very narrow valley, hemmed in on both sides by steep wooded slopes, a valley which Mr. Ruddock said was called the Greta Gorge. The train had just run through a short tunnel under a precipitous spur of high ground, and had emerged from this tunnel onto a sort of ledge in a wall on the left, at the foot of which ran the river, here quite wide, full of enormous rocks, and having some rapids and deep pools. Susan saw that the water divided around a small, tree covered island in midstream.

"Oh look, how lovely; if only we could stop for a moment," she said, half rising from her seat and involuntarily clapping her hands together.

"I'm afraid we can't do that," said the Driver, "but I'm taking the old train as slowly as is reasonable along here." Already they were again losing the river to view as it made a large loop away from the railway line.

"What are those buildings over there?" asked Susan.

"That's a little spot called Low Briery," said Mr. Ruddock. "Just a few houses down there on the flat ground in that river loop, and I believe there's an old mill there. And just here on our left" (he pointed through the left-hand cab window) "is the disused Briery Platform, which used to be a request halt."

"Oh. What a beautiful place it is," said Susan. There was just time for her to notice as they swept past it a very short platform to the left of the line; and then Susan saw a bridge coming up ahead.

"And here's that river again," she added as they crossed the bridge. "What magnificent scenery! My word, it's amazing to see how those trees manage to grow on such a precipitous slope." She was pointing to the steep north bank of the river, almost a cliff in places, which was completely covered by a wood in which it appeared that some of the trees had found very unlikely places for a root-hold amongst the screes.

Susan had for the moment completely forgotten that Police Cadet Jim Sandy was sitting just behind her on the other side of the glass partition. He was looking at her now with only half, or perhaps with less than half of his attention; with the remainder he was, like her, admiring the striking views in the Greta Gorge. Jim had travelled that way before on quite a number of occasions but, although the view seen through the windows was not new to him, he was enjoying seeing it all that morning as if it were for the first time. He had a vague idea that the brilliant sunshine which they were enjoying now that the storm had definitely passed had something to do with this element of extra enjoyment, and probably it had. The cloud overhead had now become well broken, leaving apertures of clear sky which had a wiped-clean look; the blue overhead and the colours down at ground level all looked surprisingly bright, and although this effect had in itself a decidedly cheering effect there was something else in Jim's subconscious which heartened him even more. He was not consciously aware of it, but the fact that he was doing just what he had hoped he could do when he had set off from home that morning encouraged him greatly. Furthermore, Jim felt that an extra zest was added to the excitement he was experiencing because his "escape" to London was to be in the company of the delightful Lady Dalmane all the way to London.

When a few minutes later the conspicuous signal-box on the end of the island platform at Threlkeld appeared around a bend, Susan never noticed how Mr. Ruddock was looking carefully ahead at the small group of people waiting there on the platform for the train; but there was no inspector amongst them. However, she was most amused a moment later to see the astonishment on some faces as they caught sight of a young woman in the cab sitting beside the Driver.

"They don't think I ought to be here with you!" she chuckled, turning to the Driver. "But maybe I shouldn't be really?"

"You'll be quite all right there, ma'am, if you care to stay," said Mr. Ruddock. In the back of his mind as he said this was the thought that if an inspector <u>did</u> get into his train at one of its stops he would be fairly trapped with Lady Dalmane sitting in his cab. Obviously this could happen so quickly that there might not be time to do anything about it; and anyway he could not very well ask Lady Dalmane to leave when he had invited her in as his guest—particularly as she had just told him how much she was enjoying the ride—so he would have to wait until <u>she</u> decided to go back to her seat in the carriage. I suppose I was a bit rash, after all, to have asked Lady Dalmane to sit in here, he said to himself as he drove the train out of Threlkeld station at the start of the stiff climb on the double-track section of the line up onto the high moorlands around Troutbeck. Anyway, he thought, she's enjoying the ride like anything with this good view from up in the front so I daresay it <u>was</u> worth taking the risk.

Susan was particularly delighted to see the sudden and dramatic changes in the landscape as the journey to Penrith progressed: first the very sudden transition at Threlkeld from the narrow, gorge-like valley of the Greta to a much wider, flat-bottomed valley with fields. Then, only two or three minutes later, as they left Threlkeld Station behind them, she saw that the railway line was leaving the fields of the valley bottom and climbing into a region of wide-open desolate moorland. When they came nearer to Penrith, Susan noticed that the scenery was changing again: the moorlands around the highest part of the line were giving way to a countryside of small fields separated by dry-stone walls, a country of low hills that was far from flat although the highest parts of the Lake District had been left behind. Here and there she saw ugly blemishes on this otherwise unspoilt country where there was a limestone quarry and, at one point, a lime works close beside the railway line. Soon the town of Penrith appeared ahead of them in the distance. Susan was surprised to recognize the once familiar shape of the houses of the town climbing up the wooded slopes of the little hill called Penrith Beacon.

"Penrith," she said. "I haven't seen this place for many years, but I recognize it well enough with that wooded hill rising behind it to the east: it looks just the same."

"So you've been here before?" said Mr. Ruddock.

"When I was a child we used to come here sometimes by train from London to stay with friends of my parents. But we never travelled on <u>this</u> line; not before today."

"How far are you travelling today, ma'am?"

"In this train, as far as Carlisle."

"And you're going on beyond Carlisle, are you?"

"Oh yes, I'm going up to London, and then on to Knebworth. We all are, actually: I mean, Mr. and Mrs. Beck and I. They got in with me at Cockermouth. You know Mr. Beck, I think?"

"Oh indeed, yes, I know Nigel. He's been a workmate of mine driving trains in this area for quite a few years, although I gather that he and his wife are leaving the area today. So you're bound for Knebworth? It's a long way to travel by rail in one day."

"Yes," said Susan, "but we're taking the 'Royal Scot' when we get in to Carlisle."

"That's right, ma'am," said Mr. Ruddock. "It's the 11.57 from Carlisle, and an excellent fast express to London it is too."

"And then, I believe, we have to take a local train from King's Cross to get to Knebworth," said Susan. "I expect you might be able to give me some advice about the times of those trains, Mr. Ruddock" (she had asked the driver earlier what his name was), "as you're a train driver yourself."

"So you want the times of the local services from King's Cross for Knebworth? Well, the 'Royal Scot' gets into Euston at 5.15. Then you'll have to allow time to cross Central London in the evening rush hour."

"I know," said Susan. "It sounds rather formidable, but we'll have to do that. But we should get to King's Cross by Underground by a quarter to six, I should think—if the 'Royal Scot' gets in punctually."

"Yes, you should certainly manage that in half an hour, or maybe less. So you might be able to get the 5.50 to Stevenage. And I think the next one after that is the 6.10, if you miss the earlier one."

"Half a minute, I'd better write those times down. Oh bother, I'll have to go back into the carriage to get my pen and some paper out of my knapsack."

"No need, ma'am," said Mr. Ruddock, smiling. He dipped his right hand into his jacket pocket (while he continued to hold the dead-man's handle in his left) and took out a diary which he handed to Susan. "There are some blank pages at the back of that if you'd like to tear one out and write on it. There's a pencil in the diary." He was delighted at his own resourcefulness and quick thinking in being able to produce so promptly writing materials for Lady Dalmane to make notes on. Susan thanked him and wrote down the train times from King's Cross when Mr. Ruddock had repeated them for her.

In her first view of Penrith and its Beacon Susan had glimpsed the place in the distance, still some three or four miles away; but about a minute after she had written: "Dep King's Cross 5.50 & 6.10p.m." on that blank page she had detached from Mr. Ruddock's diary, she saw another railway line curving to meet the one they were now running on, and houses ahead as well as sidings, railway signals, a signal-box, and other signs that they were approaching a junction of some note.

"This is Penrith?" she said.

"Yes, ma'am, we're just coming to the junction with the main line to Euston, the line over Shap Fell—the way you'll be going in the 'Royal Scot'." He put out his hand for the brake lever as he spoke and began to slow the train down for the stop at Penrith Station, which they saw a little way ahead of them when the train had run through the points of the junction.

"I say, there's quite a crowd of people waiting on this platform," said Susan a few moments later as the train was drawing to a standstill along a side platform of Penrith station, a rather dark and dismal place, shut in by a grimy sandstone wall immediately to the left, and covered over by a roof. Mr. Ruddock looked for a moment to his right at the crowd of faces, mostly women, who were waiting to get into his train. He noticed no inspector there in that cursory glance, and was in any case losing belief and interest in Mr. Beck's idea that an inspector might board the train somewhere along the route. The train had stopped and Mr. Ruddock was looking ahead again when the door of a waiting room opened and a man in railway uniform slipped out into the crowd on the platform. Neither Susan nor Mr. Ruddock noticed this man as he pushed through the crowd and entered the rear carriage of the train. But Mr. Beck had seen him and recognized him as he stepped nimbly into the train. Oh heavens, he thought, it's Inspector Dryden! Now Tom'll be in real trouble, and Lady Dalmane could even be ordered off the train. He's trapped now, having her in there. But maybe I could slip up to the cab now and warn Tom of what's happened without being seen by Dryden. He could see that the two in the cab were chatting together happily, obviously blissfully unaware of the new dangerous situation posed by the presence of the Inspector in the train. Mr. Beck glanced behind for a moment. Oh damn, he said to himself, it's no good; he's seen her. As he turned he caught the Ticket Inspector's eye, where he stood in the gangway between the two carriages. Mr. Beck saw the Inspector nod to him, point a finger for an instant straight at Lady Dalmane where she sat in the driver's cab, and grin maliciously. Mr. Beck frowned, but returned Mr. Dryden a recognizing nod of his head; but already Mr. Dryden was walking smartly back into the rear carriage, apparently not having noticed Mr. Beck's answering nod. That's done it, he thought sadly. I can't do anything more to save him from old Dryden now.

He looked round again. The Inspector was beginning a round of inspecting passengers' tickets and would, no doubt, be working his way forwards along the train until he ended up by the driver's cab, when he would go in and admonish Mr. Ruddock for breaking a Rule by allowing a passenger to ride with him in the cab. The worst of it was that Mr. Beck knew Inspector Dryden well enough to suspect strongly that he would not allow his old friend, Tom, to get away with just a caution, or even a severe reprimand; he would want to threaten him with dismissal for his blunder.

Mr. Beck did not much like the Inspector with the thin, reddish hair and gold-rimmed spectacles; but then he did not know Mr. Dryden as well as some of his other railway colleagues whom he had been used to seeing more often. He knew that Mr. Dryden was a bachelor and reckoned that probably he must be in his forties; in fact, much the same age as himself, and that he must be a lonely man.

The buzzer sounded as Mr. Blencow gave the signal for starting the train (he could use either the buzzer in his compartment to do this, or his green flag, or a whistle). Of course, thought Mr. Beck as the train began to move again, I could get Tim to go in there to tell him what's happened and to get Lady Dalmane out before he comes in. He looked round for a moment at his wife and saw that Mrs. Beck was fast asleep, her mouth slightly open, probably with a gentle noise of sleeping breathing coming from it, but that could not be heard above the sound of the train. She won't wake easily, he thought. He stood up, and: Oh, curse it, he said to himself, now that Tim's talking to him, so I can't tell him. He sat down again uneasily, feeling that he still ought to do something to warn Tom of his danger, but not knowing what he could do. Evidently the Ticket Inspector and the Guard had decided that they were going to do the whole round of passenger ticket inspecting together, which meant that Mr. Beck found himself in a frustrated situation.

Jim Sandy was in a chastened frame of mind as he sat quietly in his front passenger seat just behind Susan's new seat in the cab; yet he was jubilant too. Although she was now sitting only a few feet away from him, the glass partition in between them made Jim feel that she might as well have been sitting as far away as her former seat beside Mrs. Beck; and anyway, the view of the back of her head was not really very exciting. Yet his infatuation for this pretty woman remained burning within him, the fire of it occasionally fanned by glimpses of her face and head in profile when she turned to speak to Mr. Ruddock. He was also looking at the view through the windows but only enjoying it in a rather absent-minded way as his mind was busy with eager anticipation of the next stage of the journey, when she would come to him (if he could find an empty compartment) and they would have a private talk. Jim saw a crowd of people waiting to join the train on the platform at Penrith when they stopped there, but he was no more interested in these people than were Mr. Ruddock and Susan in the cab. His imagination was happily occupied in constructing hundreds of scenes of himself in intimate conversation with Lady Dalmane in a compartment of the 'Royal Scot' by themselves, and he was not, therefore, at all concerned about what anyone else in the train might be doing.

★

"It's been a really beautiful run through to Penrith from Keswick, seen from in here," said Susan as the train left Penrith. "And the bit beside Bassenthwaite Lake too; that was lovely, although we couldn't see things properly then because of the cloud and the rain. I wish it wasn't over so quickly. I'd like to see it all over again, if only I could."

"I wish I could drive you over it a second time, ma'am," said Mr. Ruddock. "I'm so glad you've enjoyed it. But the journey is not exactly over yet, you know. We've about another eighteen miles to go to reach Carlisle."

"I meant, I wish the journey along the branch line through the Lake District could have lasted longer," explained Susan. "I know there's this run along the main line to finish with, and it's very nice country around here too."

"It is; but not so spectacular as the Keswick to Penrith part of the run, is it?"

Very soon after leaving Penrith, Mr. Ruddock had the little two-car diesel train running at a really fast pace along the mostly straight and easily graded part of the West Coast Main Line to the north of Penrith Station. Susan found that although the views were no longer as magnificent as they had been, there was still much in the pleasant, pastoral landscape to hold her attention, so there was not much talking between her and Mr. Ruddock. Suddenly both she and the Driver turned their heads simultaneously.

"Eh?" said Mr. Ruddock.

"What?" said Susan.

They had heard someone tapping gently on the door behind them and had turned to see that it was Mr. Beck. He pointed backwards into the carriage as he said in a loud whisper, his mouth close to the glass: "Inspector Dryden is here! Lady Dalmane must get out of there—quickly!" Then he hurried back to his seat.

Damn! said Mr. Ruddock to himself. He knew at once that that very disaster about which both Mr. Beck and Tim Blencow had warned him was even now befalling him. He saw the Inspector standing now at the rear end of the leading carriage while he took a passenger's ticket and looked at it, but he noticed Mr. Dryden glance for a moment straight at him, and saw that there was a half-smile on his face: no more than a slight curling upwards of the ends of his thin lips, but Mr. Ruddock saw the malice in that smile.

"My Lady," said he, "if you wouldn't mind . . ." He broke off seeing that Lady Dalmane understood and had already stood up to leave her seat in the cab.

"I understand," she said. "I'm going now. I do hope you're not going to get into trouble, Mr. Ruddock, as you've been very kind to me. I'm sorry this has happened; but thank you, and good-bye for now. Perhaps I'll see you again for a word at Carlisle Station." They both glanced backwards for a second towards Mr. Dryden, who was pretending to be busy inspecting passengers' tickets while he kept looking at the two in the cab.

"Good-bye for now, ma'am," said Mr. Ruddock. Yes, he thought, perhaps it would be as well to have another word with her when we reach the platforms of Carlisle.

Susan knew that she must be out of the cab before the Inspector walked in, but she had very much wanted to say a brief word of thanks first for all the enjoyment her ride in the cab had afforded her. Now, as she walked back to her former seat she was wondering what was about to happen.

"Is Mr. Ruddock going to get into trouble because I've been in there?" she said in a voice little more than a whisper to Mr. Beck as she sat down once more in the seat opposite to his.

"I'm afraid so," said Mr. Beck, also very quietly. He turned his head sharply. Yes, Mr. Dryden was not yet standing close enough to them to overhear what they said if they spoke quietly. "Lady Dalmane," he continued, "I <u>had</u> to warn you and Tom Ruddock that the Inspector was here. He got in at Penrith, and I think he saw straight away that you were in the driver's cab. But it would have been very embarrassing for you if he'd walked in while you were still sitting in the Guard's Seat, and told you to clear out, and started talking about Regulations being broken, and all that sort of thing."

"Yes. Thank you very much, Mr. Beck, but it's been all my fault really if there's any trouble over this. I shouldn't have accepted when he asked me to go in there with him."

"'Sh!'" whispered Mr. Beck. The Inspector and the Guard, one looking at tickets on the left-hand side of the gangway, one at tickets on the right, had nearly drawn level with the seats where Mr. and Mrs. Beck and Susan Dalmane were sitting. Mr. Beck was glad that they (all the passengers from Cockermouth in that front carriage) were all on the right-hand side of the train which Mr. Blencow was taking as they would be passed over on this round of ticket inspection, Mr. Blencow having done a previous round at Bassenthwaite Lake. Mr. Blencow was now a little way ahead of Mr. Dryden and he winked at Mr. Beck as he walked past his seat. But just then Mr. Dryden looked at his watch, glanced out of a window, and spoke to the Guard.

"Will you go on with the ticket inspection from here, Mr. Blencow, please? I've just got to go into the cab to have a word with the Driver."

"But—but I don't think he likes to have anyone distracting him with talking while he's driving," said Mr. Blencow, who was desperately trying to think of something he could say to stop the Inspector going into the cab. He knew that this remark was a dismal failure in that respect even as he said it, but could think of nothing better.

"Oh, doesn't he?" said the Inspector sarcasticly. "Funny you should say that, Mr. Blencow, when he's just spent some time talking with a <u>certain passenger</u> in the cab." (He looked straight at Susan as he said this, but Susan looked away and pretended to know nothing about it.)

"But—" began Mr. Blencow.

"No! Time presses on." Mr. Dryden was already walking up the carriage to the front. "I must talk to Mr. Ruddock <u>now</u>." His hand was turning the handle of the door into the driver's cab.

Mr. Blencow had to give up his attempt to thwart the Inspector's immediate purpose so he went on with the ticket round.

"Good morning, Mr. Dryden," said Mr. Ruddock. "It's a nice day now, isn't it? Did you have a severe thunderstorm in Penrith an hour or so ago?"

But Mr. Dryden said nothing about the weather in reply. "Good morning, Mr. Ruddock," said he, and then paused for several seconds as if he were deep in thought. Mr. Ruddock made no move to offer him the Guard's Seat, so recently vacated by Susan, to sit down on.

"There was a woman passenger in here, Ruddock," continued the Inspector a moment later. "I saw her sitting here in the cab until a few minutes ago."

"Yes, that was Lady Dalmane, the Countess of Saint Helens."

"It doesn't matter who she was. How she came to be in the cab is what I want to know."

"I invited her to come in."

"You _invited_ her, Ruddock?" said the Inspector as if Mr. Ruddock had casually confessed to some dreadful crime.

"Yes."

"Now, look here, Tom Ruddock, you must know that by doing that you were contravening regulations. I don't see that there can be any excuse for you. But did you give the Lady any hint that she was in breach of the Board's bye-laws by being in here?"

"No, of course I didn't. I wanted her to enjoy her train ride, and naturally that wouldn't have been possible if she'd known that by being in here she was technically in the wrong."

"_Technically_, eh? I don't know about that," said Mr. Dryden, and there was another short pause as he drew a notebook out of a pocket. The conversation was turning out to be so much as Mr. Ruddock had anticipated that it almost seemed like a play in which they were both repeating their well-learned lines. He was, however, continuing to watch the line ahead with as much concentration, more or less, as if he had not been in conversation at all; at the moment he had his eye on a brilliant point of green light, a signal a long way ahead at the end of a straight stretch of the railway line.

"Well, Mr. Ruddock," said Mr. Dryden presently, "I take the view that this is a very grave matter, particularly as I've no doubt that you couldn't concentrate as well as you should on driving the train while some, or perhaps most, of your attention was being distracted towards an attractive young woman at your side. In view of this, I shall not turn a blind eye to this offence. If I did, I'd be failing in my duty to administer discipline to erring railway employees where it is due. You should learn to put a sense of duty first, Mr. Ruddock—"

"Oh, for heaven's sake, cut out the sermon, Dryden!" snapped Mr. Ruddock. "I know I've done wrong—been 'erring' as you put it—so if you've come in here to hand out a punishment, do, please, get on with it." He had not meant to interrupt the Inspector but had found his pompous manner of lecturing him unbearably irritating.

Mr. Dryden looked a little startled at the unexpected interruption to the smooth flow of his words of rebuke for Mr. Ruddock, who saw him raise his eyebrows slightly in surprise.

"But first," said Mr. Dryden after a few moments' hesitation (he laid considerable emphasis on the word "first"), "you must give me a few details of your employment history." He opened his notebook.

"All right, then," said Mr. Ruddock.

"Your age?"

"Sixty-five."

"Number of years service with the Railway?"

"Forty-seven years."

"And had you planned to retire soon?"

"I'd planned to retire after three more years," said Mr. Ruddock, who now knew what was coming next. Mr. Dryden was writing in his notebook.

"So, Mr. Ruddock, you had planned to have fifty glorious years of service and then to retire?" said Mr. Dryden, putting his pen away. "But alas, sir, you have blotted your copy-book. I fear that this may not now come to pass for you."

"What do you mean?" asked Mr. Ruddock, who knew very well what the Inspector meant.

"What do I mean?" said Mr. Dryden sharply. "Why, sir, I mean that I shall recommend to the Committee your immediate dismissal, having informed them of the details of this incident. I haven't the power to issue that dismissal notice myself, but you are to be suspended from your work as from midnight tonight. There is surplus manpower among the drivers, and we can manage without you, Mr. Ruddock, by re-organising the roster, for which I shall issue instructions today. I've no doubt that the Disciplinary Committee, when they meet next week, will endorse my opinion that you are not fit to continue in this responsible position, and give you formal notice in writing that you have been sacked. That's all I need tell you," (here he opened the door to the interior of the carriage) "except to remind you that you may continue your duties for the rest of today: but don't turn up for work tomorrow. Good-day to you, Mr. Ruddock."

This said, Mr. Dryden left the cab and returned down the train to the Guard's compartment in the rear carriage where Mr. Blencow was standing (the ticket round having been completed). The departure of the Inspector from the cab left Mr. Ruddock feeling stunned and horrified at what had befallen him, but he remained concentrating as calmly as he could on driving the train over the last four or five miles of the journey.

Jim Sandy from his seat just behind the cab had, of course, witnessed the whole incident, and it shocked him almost as much as it did Mr. Ruddock. He had heard every word spoken between the Inspector and the Driver, and considered that the Inspector's manner of delivering his reprimand and notice of suspension from duty had been thoroughly distasteful and unnecessarily cruel. When the man walked back down the gangway at the end of the interview, Jim knew that Mr. Ruddock was feeling very hurt by what had been said as well as very shocked at being suddenly told that he was to be suspended and probably sacked. It was beastly of him to say: "We can manage without you, Mr. Ruddock," he thought. That needn't have been said at all, even if it's true that there's surplus manpower among the drivers. And I bet Mr. Ruddock's feeling pretty upset at being spoken to in that nasty way by a chap obviously so many years younger than himself. What a good thing, though, that Lady Dalmane wasn't still in there when he came in. Of course it's jolly unfair that Mr. Ruddock is being made to take all the punishment, but I'm glad really, that he's let Lady Dalmane go free without even a caution for breaking the rules.

It was very true that Mr. Ruddock was feeling particularly hurt because his punisher, who had lectured him so pompously, he thought, before telling him that his dismissal was imminent, had been so much younger than himself. It was quite against the grain of his nature that younger folk should speak or act discourteously to their elders, even when the younger happened, as in this case, to be in a position of authority over the older. Mr. Ruddock found, though, that the full implications of his threatened dismissal—that he was out of his job as from tomorrow—were making a slower impression on his mind than his more immediate emotions: anger, hurt pride, and shock. As for the feeling of anger, he told himself that he could not help but feel bitter to some extent towards Mr. Dryden for the meanness apparent in his tone of voice and for the unnecessary severity of his punishment; but really he was angry with himself for not having heeded good advice. He had a sense too of having been publicly shamed, knowing that some of the passengers behind him had just witnessed the disastrous interview, even if most of them had not been able to hear the words. This made him impatient to get into Carlisle station, now only some four miles away, so that he could hurriedly slip away from the platforms before Lady Dalmane, or anyone else, had a chance to get a word in to him: the Inspector's punishment had made him change his mind about wanting to have a further word with Lady Dalmane. He began to turn over in his mind how he could best break the bad news to his wife; he hoped to find her out when he called at home shortly for a bite of lunch but Mrs. Ruddock would, of course, have to be told something of what had happened. Mr. Ruddock saw little possibility that the Disciplinary Committee, when they had heard Mr. Dryden's report on the incident, would agree to keep him on as a driver. He saw his career prematurely cut short, and saw more dimly that it had been his own foolishness that had brought this about.

CHAPTER NINE

When the diesel train reached the outskirts of the City of Carlisle Susan stood up and went forwards to have a brief word with Jim Sandy before picking up her knapsack off the luggage rack and preparing to get out.

"Jim," she said, "I <u>must</u> have a word with the Driver as soon as he steps out onto the platform. I expect you know very well, being up here, what's happened to him."

Jim nodded to show that he knew all about it.

"Right," continued Susan, "I said I'd have a talk with you in the 'Royal Scot', so don't hang about on the platform waiting for me while I'm finding out about poor Mr. Ruddock. Get straight into the 'Royal Scot' as soon as it arrives if I'm still busy talking to Mr. Ruddock—Platform Three, Mr. Beck says it goes from."

"Oh good, we don't have to cross the bridge if it's Number Three." Jim knew his way around Carlisle station well enough.

"That's right. You get in—"

"Oh bother! I'll have to go and buy a ticket first," interrupted Jim, suddenly remembering that he had travelled so far without having paid his fare. He also remembered at that moment that he had just had another lucky escape from a brush with authority in the form of the Ticket Inspector, Mr. Dryden. If Mr. Dryden had not decided to go into the cab when he had done so, leaving the rest of his ticket inspection round to the Guard, Jim would certainly have been caught by him travelling without a ticket, and what might have happened to him then he did not like to think: probably, though, he would have been ordered out.

"Yes, of course you must go and buy your ticket first," said Susan. "But you'll have time enough for that, I should think." She noticed that the train was running quite slowly now, through the points immediately to the south of the station; she could see the ends of the platforms and the roof canopies of the station a few hundred yards ahead. She looked at her watch.

"It's about four minutes after half past," she said. "I think we must be arriving about on time. Now, what was I saying before? Oh yes, you get straight into the 'Royal Scot' and look through the train to see if you can find an empty compartment somewhere. If you find one, I'll come and join you in it presently for a little private chat: not straight away, but probably when the train starts. You see, when I get in, I'll find myself a seat first in the same compartment as Mr. and Mrs. Beck, if I can, as I'd like to travel with them since they're going to Knebworth too. Then perhaps you'd care to join us later if there's a spare seat. But (she lowered her voice and put her head close to his for a moment) I've something important to say to you!"

"Oh, thank you very much, Lady Dalmane." Jim was both thrilled and very mystified to hear that Lady Dalmane had something important to tell him. She gave him a radiant smile as she turned to go.

"See you later, Jim!" she said as she went.

The train was now drawing to a halt near the middle of Platform One, a long platform on the outer edge of a large island of platforms. Aha, I've got him properly puzzled! thought Susan as she hurried back to her seat to pick up her knapsack and, if necessary, to help Mr. Beck to move his still sleeping wife. But I've got such a lovely surprise in store for that boy! He said he was leaving the police and running away to London, I think. Well, that's pretty daft, but he hasn't got a job, has he . . . ?

"Can you manage?" she asked Mr. Beck. He had decided to try to lift his wife out of the train without waking her, if that could be done, and to carry her across to Platform Three for the "Royal Scot".

"I can manage her all right," said Mr. Beck. "But you'd better get out ahead of me, Lady Dalmane."

"Thank you," she said. She grabbed her knapsack from off the luggage rack and stepped down onto the platform through the door which Mr. Beck had already opened. She looked at once towards the driver's cab. Mr. Ruddock had not yet left his seat, so Susan decided to wait close by his door to catch him when he came out. It's amazing, she thought as she walked smartly up the platform, how he sat there so calmly after that Inspector had gone, driving us just as if nothing had happened! I can hardly believe that he's going to get the sack because of me. But that mustn't happen! She put her knapsack down on the ground when she was adjacent to the door of the driver's cab of the diesel multiple-unit, and glanced behind her briefly. She saw Jim Sandy emerge from the train and immediately head off at a run for the footbridge, on his way to the Booking Office; and she also saw the Becks. Mrs. Beck had woken up on being lifted, awkwardly, but carefully, out of the train.

"Put me down, Nigel!" Susan heard her say crossly. "I _can_ walk, you know!"

"Yes, my dear," said Mr. Beck, and then: "Have you got a through ticket to London, Lady Dalmane?" he called out. "If you're busy I could run round to the Booking Office and get you one." He seemed to know that Susan meant to wait on the platform until she had interviewed Mr. Ruddock.

"Thanks very much, Mr. Beck, but I've got a ticket," Susan shouted back. What a stroke of luck it was that John had insisted on handing her ticket to her! The thought reminded Susan of her husband and she wondered vaguely where he was, but was a little surprised to realise that she did not much care where he might be at that time.

Just then Mr. Ruddock stepped down from his cab. Mr. Blencow, the Guard, had again been in there for a word with Mr. Ruddock, who at once began to make a hasty bee-line for a Staff-only exit near the northern end of the platform; but Susan was ready and was too quick for him.

"Mr. Ruddock!"

"Yes, my Lady?" he said politely, as if he had never thought of trying to slip quietly away from Lady Dalmane.

"What happened, Mr. Ruddock? Do, please, tell me what the Inspector said to you," said Susan.

"He told me that I'm to be suspended from work as from tomorrow, ma'am."

"Does that mean that you're sacked?"

"Yes, ma'am, almost certainly it does," said Mr. Ruddock. "There's a Committee meeting, I know, next week, and he said he would recommend to the Committee my immediate dismissal. They're sure to do what he says, so that's me out of my job."

"Oh, Mr. Ruddock, but how dreadful! And this has all happened because of me!"

"I wouldn't quite say that, ma'am. I mean, it was all my own fault really." He felt as he said this that he was not being wholly truthful.

"No, Mr. Ruddock," said Susan, "if you were breaking a rule, you did it for me. I don't think I've ever before had such an enjoyable railway journey: it was simply <u>wonderful</u> seeing things from the cab! You've been very kind to me, Mr. Ruddock, and it upsets me a lot to think that you may be dismissed because of this. We mustn't <u>let</u> them sack you."

"Well, ma'am, there's not a lot we can do to prevent them sacking me, as I see things. Of course, as a union man, my fellow members of A.S.L.E.F. could be called on to take industrial action if they do sack me, but I doubt we couldn't get the Committee to change its mind that way if they vote for my dismissal; and it could be very embarrassing for me anyway, when it gets widely known what I've done."

"You think train drivers might go on strike to support your case for reinstatement?" asked Susan.

"Aye, they might easy do that, in this area at any rate, and likely enough our N.U.R. members, like Tim Blencow, my Guard, would join in if there was a strike. But I wouldn't <u>want</u> a strike at all over this, seeing as it was definitely my fault: I <u>knew</u> I was breaking a rule by having you in the cab, ma'am—but I'm glad you enjoyed your ride. I'm sure it was worth it for that."

Susan thought for a moment; and Mr. Ruddock, who was privately very much wanting to leave Lady Dalmane now and go off duty, looked at his watch.

"Now, look here, Mr. Ruddock," said Susan a moment later. "I've an idea of how I could help you. Let me write to your employers and plead directly with them—the Committee you mentioned—in the strongest terms to re-instate you at once. That way there need be no industrial action; and anyway it's the least I can do to repay your kindness."

"My Lady," said Mr. Ruddock, "I am quite overwhelmed by your kindness!" This was true enough: he had not expected Lady Dalmane to come down so firmly on his side against the Inspector with a plan of action; he had really expected no more than kind words from her.

"But I mean what I say," said Susan. "Do, please, let me help by writing a letter on your behalf."

"Thank you, ma'am, I should be deeply grateful for your influence," said Mr. Ruddock, "if you really mean to write to the Committee Chairman." He glanced again at his wrist-watch. "Don't forget the time, ma'am. It's now ten to twelve. The 'Royal

Scot' should be here in a minute—aye, I thought so; here it comes."
The voice of the Station Announcer was heard on all the platforms
booming out an important message:

"The train now approaching Platform Three is the 11.57 a.m.
to London Euston, the 'Royal Scot'. This train is the ten a.m. from
Glasgow Central."

"Quick!" said Susan, "write me down the address of the person
I ought to write to, and your own address, Mr. Ruddock." The
Driver again took out his diary which now lost another of its blank
pages as he tore one out. While Mr. Ruddock was writing down
the two addresses, Susan could hear the sounds of the approach of a
mighty steam engine hauling a heavy train, and presently she saw it
as it drew towards the northern ends of the station platforms: a great
red engine with a black smoke-box, funnel, and side-sheets at the
front end; however, the red parts of the engine were so grimy that
Susan could hardly be sure that the colour was indeed red. On its
front end was a large headboard with the legend: **"THE ROYAL
SCOT"** together with a picture of a lion rampant. There was little
time to spare.

"Here you are, ma'am," said Mr. Ruddock, handing Susan the
paper with the addresses written on it. Susan looked at it briefly.

"Good," she said. "So you live here in Carlisle? Well, I'll fix
it for you if I possibly can." She glanced across to Platform Three
where the express train, the "Royal Scot", with thirteen carriages
behind the engine and tender, was about to come to a halt. She
could not, from where she was standing, see Jim Sandy, who at
that moment came running onto the platform off the footbridge on
his way back from the Booking Office, and in a tearing hurry to
get into the train as soon as it stopped to be in with a good chance
of finding an empty compartment; but there was quite a crowd
waiting to board the express for London. Susan and Mr. Ruddock
then shook each other's hands and said their Good-byes. At the last
moment she surprised Mr. Ruddock very much by giving him a

parting kiss on the cheek; then she turned and ran for her train, suddenly uncertain of the number of minutes it was supposed to wait there. She saw no sign of any of the others, Mr. and Mrs. Beck and Jim Sandy, and realised that they were already on board the train.

Mr. Ruddock remained where he was for a little longer, feeling a little stunned by the latest turn of events. He saw Susan step inside one of the middle carriages of the express with just over four minutes to go until the departure time. Well, he thought, that's good; it wouldn't have done for her to miss her train. But, my word, a kiss from her! Oh, that makes up for a lot! Suddenly he felt a strange reluctance to leave the station platforms until the "Royal Scot" had gone out. The time reached 11.57; someone on the platform blew a whistle, the Guard of the "Royal Scot" waved his green flag and stepped into his guard's van, and the express began to move. Mr. Ruddock watched the big "Duchess" Class engine almost with envy—he had read the name "Duchess of Sutherland" on the engine, and now he felt suddenly bored by always having to drive the small diesel-units nowadays—and he listened with a happy, professional ear to the slow puffs of smoke and the hissing of steam as the powerful locomotive slowly drew its heavy rake of carriages southwards out from Platform Three.

About a minute later the last carriage of the express was receding from his view as it came to the Blackwell Road Bridge; the "Royal Scot" was well on its way. What a splendid woman she is! thought Mr. Ruddock wistfully. I wonder whether I shall ever see her again? And with that thought a wave of something that was almost sadness came over him and for a few seconds he felt a certain hotness in his old eyes, and did not see things quite as clearly as usual (he had good eyesight, of course, as an engine-driver, and only had to wear glasses for reading). He had not until that moment realised that Lady Dalmane with her enchanting beauty had cast something of a spell over him. Well, I suppose I'd better be off now, he said to himself. He was due back on duty in an hour's time at one o'clock after his lunch break; and at 1.53 he had a train to drive back to Keswick, Cockermouth, and Workington.

"Hello, there, Tom! She's gone, eh?" said a cheerful voice just behind him which made Mr. Ruddock start.

"Gosh, Tim, you did give me a start, creeping up like that," said Mr. Ruddock, suddenly recognizing Tim Blencow, the Guard. "Yes, the 'Royal Scot's' gone, and Lady Dalmane with it."

"Ah, she's a lovely woman, isn't she?" said Mr. Blencow. "But, you know, I'm awfully sorry about old Dryden suspending you because of her."

"Yes, that's bad, but it could be worse. What do you know, Tim, Lady Dalmane says she's going to help me: going to write a letter to the Committee pleading with them not to dismiss me."

The two railwaymen were chatting as they strolled along together through the station, now heading for the exit to the Square and the streets outside. They parted temporarily as they each went their own way in the street.

"Are you coming for a pint at 'The Bull', Tom?" asked Mr. Blencow. This was a little pub in the city centre, in a street off the busy English Street; it was Mr. Blencow's favourite place for a lunch-time drink on the days when he was on the 10.8 from Cockermouth.

"Not just yet," said Mr. Ruddock. "I'm going home for some lunch now; might look in at 'The Bull' around quarter to one."

"Okay. See you there; or else on the 1.53. So long!" Mr. Blencow turned left into English Street, the city's main shopping street, while Mr. Ruddock turned right into Botchergate, which lead into London Road, the main road to Penrith, a very busy thoroughfare. A few minutes walk down London Road brought Mr. Ruddock to a very small street which opened off the main road to the right, towards the railway lines, an alley called Railway Terrace; a row of drab, identical houses on the left was the Terrace itself, houses originally built by the Railway Company for railway employees. Mr. Ruddock reached his own front door, tried it, and found it locked (as he had hoped to find it). She's out, he said to himself as he drew his front door key out of a trouser pocket and fitted it into the lock.

The first thing he noticed when he had opened the door was a piece of paper with a message written on it lying on the hall carpet, just inside the door, where he could not have failed to see it. He picked it up and smiled as he read the message:

"I won't be in at lunch-time, Tom. Your lunch is ready in the oven. M."

"Good!" he said aloud. "She _is_ out. But this evening I'll have to tell Margit what's happened." (His wife's name was Margaret, but he usually called her "Margit"). The smile left his face at the thought of the confession to be made.

★

It was between five and ten minutes past twelve when Mr. Ruddock came home. But it was about half an hour later when the Booking Office at Carlisle station had a telephone call from the Police Station at Cockermouth.

Sergeant Koppel had forgotten all about Cadet Sandy when he left the Chief Inspector's office at the end of Lord Dalmane's interview. Almost immediately afterwards a telephone call had come as a result of which the Sergeant had been so busy all morning that the thought that Jim Sandy was missing had never entered his head for the next two hours. It was nearly half past twelve when the Sergeant came back into the Station having been out all the time since half past ten investigating an "incident" (a reported burglary) with a colleague, Constable Nickley. Sergeant Koppel, who was now briefly off duty, was just thinking of going out to get something to eat when he suddenly remembered that Cadet Sandy was missing.

Damn! he said to himself. That dratted boy's never turned up. We'll have to have a search for him soon if he doesn't show up here. Let me see, he went to the station . . . yes, that must be it. He got on that train and went off to Keswick or Penrith for a lark. Well, I'll give him a piece of my mind for going off like that without leave . . .

The Sergeant rang up the railway station, in his mind cursing Jim Sandy for spoiling his lunch break by going missing without explanation. He presently learned to his surprise, after some delay, that the Booking Office at Cockermouth had never seen any young man in police cadet's uniform that morning. But the Sergeant pressed ahead with his enquiries, thinking that he might have travelled without a ticket; an idea which was confirmed for him a little later when the porter came to the telephone and reported that he had seen Cadet Sandy step aboard the 10.8 train. But I can't tell how far he went by that train, thought Sergeant Koppel. Then he rang up Keswick station and enquired whether the man who collected the tickets there had seen a fair-haired youth in police uniform get off the morning train to Carlisle: it seemed to the Sergeant that Keswick was by far the likeliest place to which Cadet Sandy would have taken off; but the staff at Keswick assured him that the lad had not been seen, and advised him to ring Penrith. The Sergeant rang Penrith station and received the same sort of reply from there. Then, becoming increasingly annoyed, he tried Carlisle station, where he reckoned that someone on the staff must have seen Cadet Sandy (he was discounting, for the present time, the idea that Jim might have got off the train at one of the smaller stations.) It took several minutes of enquiring, from one official to another, and learning nothing, before his call was put through to the Booking Office; and now, at last, he learned that at about a quarter to twelve that morning a police cadet, a tall, fair-haired young man, had indeed bought a ticket: to London Euston, of all unlikely places.

"Do you remember the number on the shoulder of his uniform?" he asked.

"Yes," said the Booking Clerk, "I believe it was a hundred and six."

"Thank you very much." The Sergeant put the receiver down. So it _is_ Jim Sandy, he thought. But gone to London! Whatever in the world does that lad think he's doing? He thought hard for a minute or two, wondering what to do next. "I'll have to put a stop to this nonsense," he muttered under his breath. "Gone to London, indeed, during working hours, without permission!" But I must find out, he thought, whether he intends now to come back and face discipline, or not. He took the telephone off its bracket again and dialled for the operator. "Could you give me the number of the B.T.C. Police Department at Euston station in London, please?" he said when the operator answered. One surprise deserves another, he thought.

CHAPTER TEN

Jim Sandy had a tremendous feeling of satisfaction and pure pleasure as the "Royal Scot" to London began the three-hundred mile journey from Carlisle by pulling out of the station slowly. He was indeed so delighted at the way things were turning out that he almost wanted to jump for joy or to laugh out loud; but he contented himself with a broad, satisfied smile. He had so far achieved everything that he had hoped to achieve when he had left home that morning, hoping that this was to be the day he would go up to London in the train; and indeed it seemed that his plans were going like clockwork. No one had appeared either at Cockermouth station or at Carlisle to prevent him from going any further, and now here he was in a corner seat of an empty compartment in the "Royal Scot", well and truly bound for London. To crown the luck of that morning, there had been his incredibly fortunate meeting with Lady Dalmane, and the knowledge that she was, as she had said, going to come and sit with him and talk to him. His feeling of eager anticipation would have been almost unbearably powerful, had not the distraction of the pleasant train journey, which was now beginning, been on hand to divert some of his feeling of ecstatic happiness into the pleasurable occupation of watching the passing scenery through the window.

At the moment of departure, at 11.57 punctually, the train began to move so gently and so smoothly that the precise moment of the start was hardly noticeable, and in fact Jim failed to notice it. He had just heard a whistle blown sharply for their departure by someone on the platform. Jim had been looking out of his window across two empty centre roads towards another long express passenger train which was standing at the main southbound platform (Number Four) opposite to the "Royal Scot"; but when he heard the whistle he turned to look the other way, to his right, at the people standing on Platform Three, waiting to see them off. Looking that way through two sets of windows (the corridor was on that side of the carriage), he noticed that those people, all waving their arms and shouting Good-byes to their friends and relatives in the train, appeared to be gliding slowly backwards; the train had begun to move but there had been no hint of a jerk, and Jim had not felt the motion until that moment. Suddenly he noticed and recognized a figure in railwayman's uniform, a peaked black cap on his head, standing well back from the platform edge: Mr. Ruddock was watching the departure of the "Royal Scot" from the station. Oh bother, thought Jim, I've forgotten to deliver Sergeant Koppel's message to him, which I was going to do when we got to Carlisle. Still, it doesn't really matter. Someone else is sure to tell him that the Cockermouth Police want to interview him.

Jim saw the ends of the platforms and turned again to look the other way, through the window beside his seat. Gosh, what a lot of rails there are here, he thought, and what a lot of points and crossovers. They were still moving very slowly, gliding through the maze of points outside the station. When will she be coming in here? he wondered. Any minute now? Gosh, I hope so. But what can she want to talk about with me? After all I don't really know her yet, and she doesn't know me. People, mostly carrying heavy-looking suitcases and baggage, kept continually going past the door of his compartment, and Jim Sandy was very much afraid that at any moment, before Lady Dalmane had had time to find him, someone else would come in and spoil the privacy with Lady Dalmane to which he was looking forward. Once or twice someone stopped outside the compartment and put a hand on the door, meaning to come in, and then thought better of it and walked on, no doubt trying to locate an empty compartment as Jim himself had just done. *If only I could lock them all out, and then let Lady Dalmane in when she comes*, he thought. But this he could not do.

The next moment he turned his head sharply as he heard the door pulled open.

"You can't come in here; all those seats are reserved," he found himself saying to an oldish-looking man who was standing in the doorway, looking at the empty seats. The man was dressed in a smart townish suit, and silvery-grey hair showed under the trilby hat on his head; behind him in the corridor stood his wife, a diminutive figure with fuzzy grey hair. A large suitcase had already been parked on the floor of the compartment.

"I don't see any Reserved Seat tickets on any of these seats," observed the man dryly.

"But they're all taken: they're my friends seats, all of them," said Jim, thinking quickly. "They're just along the corridor somewhere—in the Restaurant Car probably."

The man scowled at him, turned and muttered something to his wife, picked up the suitcase, and retreated into the corridor without another word, pushing the door sharply shut behind him. On the instant Jim was on his feet. He went over to stand beside the door to keep a watch on the movements of the people in the corridor, suddenly determined that no one else, other than Lady Dalmane, would even try to enter that compartment. It was at that moment of infinite importance to Jim to keep his compartment empty, ready for Lady Dalmane; he felt that he was prepared even to use force if necessary to turn people away and to tell whatever little lies might seem to him to be needed. After all, it had not been easy for him to find that empty compartment in a second-class carriage. He had got in somewhere near the middle of the train, and had immediately begun walking along the corridor towards the rear end of the train, looking at all the compartments he passed in trying to spot an empty one. He had been thinking of giving up the search when he had found what he wanted at last in the tenth carriage of the express (counting from the front); and by this time it was evident to him that the train was fairly crowded with passengers.

A minute went by while Jim stood by the door, and already there seemed to be fewer people passing up and down the corridor, looking for seats. The train was only picking up speed very slowly; Jim saw that they were running past the sidings in the southern outskirts of the city. Another minute went by and there was still no sign of Lady Dalmane, but Jim decided that it was safe for him to sit down again in his corner seat, thinking that by now the influx of new passengers all seemed to have found themselves seats somewhere. Why doesn't she come, he thought, or did she mean she'd come to sit with me later on in the journey? He remembered that Lady Dalmane had said something about seeing him in the "Royal Scot" "presently" and "when the train starts". Well, we certainly <u>have</u> started now, he thought. But it'll take quite some time, of course, for her to find where I am if she got in somewhere near the other end. He felt as if he had already been waiting for a long time for Lady Dalmane to appear at the door when he sat down in his corner seat for the second time although, in fact, it was only some five minutes since the train had started from Carlisle, and some seven minutes since he had found his empty compartment.

Jim looked at the view from his window, ready at any moment to turn his head if he heard anyone stop outside the door. The red brick houses of the outer suburbs of Carlisle were coming to an end on that side and instead there were green fields beside the railway line and, just a little way off, the small River Petteril; the railway followed its valley most of the way to Penrith. The weather was fine now and the wind light and southerly, blowing the smoke from the engine mostly backwards over the train, but occasionally Jim saw clouds of smoke hanging over the river meadows like morning mists, or sometimes it was not the smoke itself which he saw but only its shadows on the ground. The day was becoming hot; the sunshine was rather hazy although the sky was now cloudless, and the shadows of trees in the midday summer sun were very short but rather indistinct, giving little shade from the heat for grazing farm animals.

Would Lady Dalmane come to him or would she not? Perhaps she'd changed her mind, thought Jim. Perhaps she had decided to have lunch first in the Restaurant Car and then to come to him—a steward had gone past in the corridor calling from compartment to compartment an invitation to passengers to take their seats for lunch in the Restaurant Car. Jim was too occupied with thinking about Lady Dalmane either to feel hungry yet for lunch or to pay more than scant attention to the lineside scenery. It was, at least, very pleasant to fantasise about her while waiting hopefully for her to turn up. He held the picture of that incredibly beautiful face in his mind, and knew that he was longing for her to be really there with him in the flesh: the imagination was good, but it was not good enough for him. But, he thought, what is it about her I find so uniquely attractive? Is there <u>really</u> something special, something unusual about her face? Surely there can't be. But Jim had, after all, seen and admired many other attractive girls and women, and he knew that this woman <u>was</u> in some way different from any other he had yet seen, because she affected him differently. He thought of her lips. They were big lips, beautifully proportioned, and delightfully pink with lipstick. He imagined her planting a long, luscious kiss on his lips with those lovely lips of hers. This afforded Jim a rare bliss (he thought) even with the action entirely constructed in his mind; the fact that he knew very well that this was something that was not really going to happen did not spoil the enjoyment of the fantasy at all. He pictured her eyes in his mind's eye. Incredible eyes they were: surprisingly dark, sparkling, and seductive. Although he had seen very little indeed of Lady Dalmane at close quarters, he found that he could recall perfectly a mental picture of her eyes as he had seen them smiling at him when she had bent down to whisper to him in the other train. Well, at any rate, he thought, he had <u>not</u> seen before a girl or a young woman with such dark eyes, eyes which surely could be called "black"; and he was certainly finding it very exciting to think about them. Then it occurred to him that although her eyes and hair were so dark, her skin was certainly "white": fair skin with no hint of colour that would suggest a foreign origin.

He was so held by his delightful fantasies that he did not now really notice anything that he saw through the window. And she looks so young, he thought. She hardly looks any older than me, although I expect she must be . . . what? Eighteen? Twenty? Twenty-five? No, she <u>can't</u> be as old as that. But what a <u>marvellous</u> figure she has, whatever her age may be. She's beautifully busty . . . but her boobs are not too big . . . or too small!

The next moment his fantasies came to a sudden end as he turned his head sharply on hearing a gentle tap and the sound of the door being opened. The fantasy had become reality: there in the partly opened doorway stood Susan Dalmane, smiling at him. Jim had been so busy seeing mental pictures of her that he had not heard her approach until she had knocked and opened the door. In that very first instant of seeing her, Jim noted how true to life had been the pictures in his mind. And her face <u>does</u> look almost as young as a schoolgirl's, he thought.

"May I come in?" asked Susan.

"Please do, Lady Dalmane," said Jim, standing up as he spoke and hoping that he did not look as hot and agitated as he suddenly felt.

"Thank you," said Susan as she walked across the compartment and seated herself in the corner seat opposite Jim's. She motioned to him to sit down. "I've come because there's something I'd like to ask you," she continued, looking keenly at Jim. "Indeed not just one thing but several things, and one in particular. You see, I've a proposal to put to you which, I think, could be much to your advantage—it was just a little idea which occurred to me when we met in that other train." She paused a moment.

"Yes, I see, Lady Dalmane," said Jim nervously.

Susan laughed. "You don't 'see' at all—you don't know what I'm talking about! Naturally you don't, until I explain my idea—later."

Why not now? thought Jim. He felt a burning sensation on his cheeks and knew that he had blushed when Susan had laughed. So she found it amusing, or perhaps even silly, that I said "I see" when it was obvious to her that I didn't understand, he thought. But at least nothing more had been said yet about that reflection in his ring, and that was an encouraging point.

For a few seconds neither spoke. Susan was thinking: I can't tell him about it yet. First I must sum up his character with questions to find out if he's really the right person for the job. She looked into Jim's face as if she were reading certain traits of his character in what she saw there, but she found that the interpretation of his expression eluded her beyond a certain point. He's shy, I can see that, she said to herself; and indeed Jim was feeling very shy and awkward and could not meet her eyes—those eyes which he had just been thinking of as "incredible"—with his eyes, so he turned his gaze slightly aside to look out of the window. It makes him feel awkward when I look straight at him, said Susan to herself. Yes, he's shy, but very infatuated with me. But does he look honest? Does he look reliable? Does he look like a hard worker? I really don't know, but I suppose he <u>does</u> look like a good, honest sort. She was, however, too kind and considerate to let the young man feel awkward while she looked at him for longer than a few seconds. She smiled pleasantly and glanced at the view. It was obvious that Jim Sandy was feeling shy and more than a little frightened of her, so clearly the first thing she had to do was to get him to thaw a little towards her. Bearing this in mind, Susan knew the right sort of conversation to set up.

"Well," she said with a wave of her hand at the passing scenery, "how are you enjoying the trip?"

"I'm enjoying it very much, thank you, my Lady," said Jim. "It's very pleasant country around here."

"Yes, isn't it?" said Susan. "Look here: my name's Susan, so I think you'd better call me 'Susan', not 'my Lady' or 'Lady Dalmane'. We'll get on better that way."

"Yes, all right."

"And have you been this way before, Jim—this main line over Shap to Crewe and London?"

"No."

"I have, though," said Susan. "Mind you, it was many years ago when I last travelled on this line, when I was a little girl."

"Oh yes, er . . . and has it changed much since then?" Jim had to do some frantically quick thinking here to find something more to say in order to keep the conversation flowing.

"Well, no, I don't think it's really changed all that much— except that Carlisle seems a much bigger city nowadays than the place I remembered from my childhood. Mind you, the journey from Cockermouth in the other train was over completely unknown ground for me. How about you? I expect you live in Cockermouth, Jim?"

"Yes, I do," said Jim; "and I've travelled between Cockermouth and Penrith and Carlisle quite often on the local trains."

"Oh, so you know that line well. It's really pretty country that it goes through, I noticed, especially along that Greta Gorge. Of course, I had a really marvellous view of things sitting up in the cab."

"Yes, it must have been really good," said Jim. He thought it a little odd that she should mention her regulation-breaking ride in the cab, but as she had said nothing about Mr. Ruddock he also would say nothing about him. There was another short lull in the conversation. Well, thought Susan, he's quite good on making conversation in spite of his shyness, and he's beginning to forget that shyness anyway. Now, the next thing is to find out what he's up to: <u>why</u> he's making this train trip too. She and Jim were both looking out of the window at views of the fertile lands of the Petteril Valley; at least Jim <u>appeared</u> to be concentrating on looking at the view, but Susan caught a sneaky, sideways glance at herself, a momentary glimpse at the pleasures of her face which Jim had managed more by looking out of the corners of his eyes than by turning his head. Poor lad, she thought, he's longing to stare at me but doesn't dare do it! However, she fixed his attention again with a look.

"So you're going up to London," she said, "and I think you said you were leaving the Police at Cockermouth. Did you mean you were off on leave for a holiday, or have you left the Police for good?"

"I <u>have</u> left the Police Force altogether," said Jim.

"Didn't you like the work?"

"Well, er, no, I didn't really like it," said Jim awkwardly. I wish she wouldn't ask such awkward questions! he thought.

"Oh yes," said Susan thoughtfully, "but I was wondering what exactly you hope to achieve by going up to London . . . I hope you don't mind me being so inquisitive, but are you, perhaps, <u>running away</u> to London? Do I guess right?" She looked him straight in the eye.

"Yes, you do; I <u>am</u> running away." Jim suddenly found that it was something of a relief to tell the truth instead of trying to conceal it. "At least, father knows that I'm going to London, but they don't know at work yet—at the Cockermouth Police Station— I'll have to ring up and tell them where I am, of course. But I never told them this morning that I was going: I just slipped away when the Sergeant and the other two arrested your husband, so, you see, it <u>is</u> running away, I suppose."

Susan was listening to him in astonishment. He paused a moment, uncertain whether he should tell her any more.

"Go on," said Susan quietly.

"Well, the thing is," continued Jim, "that I really hated it, being a police cadet. Most of the things they made me do were really loathsome."

"Like what?" said Susan.

"Well, like spending hours on the beat each day—just walking about the streets accompanied by a constable—but not really doing anything. And having drill in the yard most mornings before going on the beat—standing to attention and all that sort of thing. And several times I've been scolded for not turning up punctually for work. I found it all very hateful."

A slight hint of a frown appeared on Susan's face as she listened to Jim telling her these things; they seemed to her very shallow reasons for hating the work of a police cadet. However, she knew that he really did mean what he said and that he was telling her, in effect, that he found that he had made a great mistake in joining the police. Of course the thought also passed through her mind at that time that Jim was being silly by leaving before he had had time to progress beyond the basic training of a cadet to more interesting work and promotion to the rank of constable. She did not answer him straight away when he finished speaking, but remained for several seconds looking thoughtful, her eyes looking now not at him but towards the floor of the carriage. I suppose he really <u>does</u> hate being a police cadet, she said to herself.

"So you're running away to London, Jim," she continued presently. "But why London? Surely you must realise that it's a huge, unfriendly place? I suppose you have some members of your family there—an aunt or an uncle you could stay with?"

"Not an aunt or an uncle; but my mother lives there, and I'm going to stay with her."

"Your mother lives in London?" said Susan wonderingly. "But your father lives in Cockermouth, doesn't he?—you said you'd told him that you were going to London."

Jim nodded.

"You mean, your parents have separated?"

Jim nodded his head again, but did not say anything; he was a little upset by Lady Dalmane's very searching, personal questions and was uncertain how much he ought to let her know in his answers. Was it really sensible, he wondered, to tell this woman intimate details of his family life? He remembered that he hardly knew her at all, even if he did feel that he was passionately in love with her.

"Look here," said Susan kindly, "I know you think I'm being nosey in asking you these personal questions, but I'd like to help you—I would, really; so it would help me to know a little about your background. Do you mind telling me these things? Answer honestly, Jim." She could see that Jim was wrestling with misgivings in his mind as to how much it would be safe for him to say, and hoped that by speaking kindly to him he would at least tell her frankly whether he objected to answering her questions, or not. Then she saw a smile appear on his face as he answered her.

"No, I don't mind at all, honestly. Thank you, Susan, for saying you'll help."

Susan smiled herself. "Well, why not, eh? But about your parents, Jim—are they divorced?"

"Not yet. They're trying to get a divorce, though. You see, mother's gone to live with another man in London."

"Since when?"

"Oh, just since last winter. It was just after Christmas when mother finally left home to go to live in this other chap's house."

"Where exactly is it?"

"Somewhere in Ealing in West London. But you see, Susan, mum already knew this man very well and they were . . . well, er, more or less living together already at home—I mean in father's house in Cockermouth and, well, that arrangement really wouldn't work, you see."

"I do see," said Susan, leaning forward slightly in her seat and listening seriously to what Jim was saying. "Life at home under those circumstances must have become very unpleasant. But let's not talk about that side of it now. What's worrying me is that here you are sitting in this train with me on your way to your mother's house in London—but your mother won't be expecting you presumably? Or did you write to tell her what you meant to do?"

"Oh no, I didn't. She doesn't know I'm coming. It's only that I don't know anyone else in London and, well, when I get there I'll have to stay somewhere, won't I?"

"Yes, of course you will," said Susan. "But have you ever been in London before? Will you be able to find your way about town?"

"I don't know. I've never been there before."

"But you have at least got your mother's address, I hope?" said Susan.

"Yes, I've got that," said Jim. He put his left hand into an inner pocket of his police tunic, took out his wallet, and withdrew from it a folded sheet of paper with something written in pencil on it.

"May I see it?" asked Susan. She took the piece of paper from Jim. "Gosh, I've no idea where that is." She read out the address: "'Ninety-Six Lakeland Avenue, Ealing, London, West Five'. I know whereabouts in London Ealing is from when I used to live in London before I met my husband, John. I was living in a nice house with a big garden in Hatch End, near Harrow, well out in suburbia and quite near the country—but that's all by the way. I don't know where Lakeland Avenue is any more than you do, and yet you're reckoning to find your way there somehow. You haven't got a street map of that part of London in a pocket by any chance?"

"No, I haven't; but I thought I could buy one when I get there."

"Yes, I suppose you could. Talking of buying things, have you brought much money with you?"

"Oh yes, plenty," said Jim happily. "See, I've still got ten pounds left after buying my train tickets." He had just pushed the address paper back into his wallet, and now showed Susan two crisp new five pound notes which remained stored in another compartment, nearly three pounds having been spent on his train fare from Cockermouth to London.

But Susan shook her head. "Oh dear," she said, "I'm afraid ten pounds won't get you very far in London. You don't know how expensive it is just to live there." She stopped talking for a moment and looked thoughtful before continuing. "Jim."

"Yes?"

"You know, I can't help thinking that your best plan might be to go straight back home to Cockermouth, though I know that's a hard thing to say."

"Go back? But I can't do that now that I'm in the 'Royal Scot' to London." Jim was suddenly horrified at the idea of returning home before he had even reached London, although the conversation with Susan had raised serious doubts in his mind about the wisdom of his escapade.

"You could, though," said Susan. "This train must stop somewhere before Euston, I suppose: Crewe, probably, and perhaps Preston, but I can't remember at all where the stops are. But you could get back to Cockermouth today, I expect, by taking a train to Carlisle from somewhere—say from Crewe—and then taking the local diesel from Carlisle."

"But I can't," said Jim. "I really <u>can't</u> do that, because, you see, I've sent a lot of my luggage on in advance to mother's address: I forgot to tell you that. So I expect she <u>will</u> be vaguely expecting me to come—sometime—though I never wrote a letter to explain."

"Why didn't you?"

"Well, in case I couldn't get to her on the day I'd said—if I'd put a date in a letter."

"Jim, I'm sorry to say this, but your plan is quite crazy—at least as far as hunting for a job is concerned, because you don't know anyone in London, apart from your mother—that's right, isn't it?"

"It is."

Susan had been speaking to Jim gently, in a tone as re-assuring as possible but she saw a look of mild shock on his face as she continued:

"You probably wouldn't find a job anyway; but if you did, I'm sure you'd feel terribly lonely and isolated for a long time in London; and if you were to find nothing to do there—which is more than likely—then I think you'd feel lonelier than ever."

"What do you think I should do then?" asked Jim doubtfully.

Susan smiled a little mischievously but for a second or two gave him no answer. She knew very well what she wanted to say to Jim to answer his point but she preferred to beat about the bush a little first to raise a feeling of suspense.

"Well, Jim," she said, "let me point out first that if you <u>do</u> press ahead with this plan there'll be great difficulties in store for you in London. Let's try to see clearly what the problems are. We'd do well to decide now what to do about such things as accommodation— would you stay for long with your mother?—about finding your way around London, about money, and so on."

"Yes, I agree with that," said Jim. "Now's the time to plan while you're here to advise me." He caught Susan's eye as he said this, and for a moment grinned at her almost mischievously while she smiled back at him. He had noticed with appreciation Susan's use of the word "we" instead of "you", and found that this small detail of the conversation excited him by its implication of more intimacy. Jim's mood had been undergoing some very rapid changes while he had been talking with Susan, changes which corresponded to the various overtones and moods implicit in the remarks which Susan had made: thus at first his happy infatuation had been overshadowed by his shyness and nervousness, then he had felt almost resentful at the more awkward questions and shocked at the idea of giving up his escapade to return home; and finally he felt simply very happy on hearing Susan say "we". Susan, for her part, had been surprised to find how agreeable it was talking with this confused but very good-looking young man (for she thought that way of him). If she were adopting a rather motherly tone towards him—and she knew that she was—it was all to the good: that was what he really needed at the moment. It seemed to her that Mrs. Sandy, Jim's real mother in London, was not going to be much use to him as a refuge to run away to in the big city; and in fact she had no intention of letting him go there on his own. I'll go with him when he visits him mum—briefly, she thought. He doesn't really want <u>her</u>—after what he's told me about her I'm sure he can't—but <u>I</u> can be 'mum' for him. That's what he's really wanting. As for telling Jim that he ought to go straight back to Cockermouth: that, she had thought, was something she had to say, but she had really wanted an indignant "No!" as his answer, and had now received just such an answer. She did not know, or had forgotten, that the southbound "Royal Scot" was scheduled to run non-stop from Carlisle to Euston. Had she known this it would, of course, have made nonsense of her suggestion that Jim could have travelled back to Cockermouth that day as, with the scheduled arrival time at Euston being five-fifteen p.m. this would have been an impossibility.

"So you're happy for me to advise you, Jim," said Susan several minutes later. "Well then, I think it would be a good plan for you to come and stay with me tonight, or perhaps for a few nights if you like. I'm sure Great Aunt Alice will be able to find room for you at Knebworth and, you know, you'd never be able to find your way to an unknown address in Ealing, miles from Central London, on your own. What do you think?"

"I'd be simply delighted to come with you, Susan—if you really think it would be all right," said Jim, his eyes sparkling. The effect on him of this totally unexpected, generous offer was, indeed, electric: a sudden inner radiance of joy came to him at the thought that this pretty Lady Susan Dalmane would not, after all, be saying Good-bye to him when they reached London. Nor was he only thrilled by the offer, but he was extremely relieved at the thought that he would not now have to try to cope with finding his way somehow across many unknown miles of Greater London to look for his mother's house in Lakeland Avenue, Ealing. Furthermore, he had known in his heart all along that he had not really relished the idea of meeting his mother in this way, unannounced, at the house of her lover. Of course, there was that box of his belongings there, but now that hardly seemed to matter: perhaps Lady Dalmane would even come with him when he called there to see his mother.

"It'll be all right, Jim, if you'd like to come," said Susan. "Great Aunt Alice lives alone in a big house in Knebworth, so there are always plenty of spare rooms and anyway, if there's time, I'll telephone to her when we get into Euston to explain about you. But she won't mind putting you up too while we stay there—my Great Aunt Alice is a very generous lady who likes meeting people."

"Well, thank you very much for inviting me."

"All right." Susan chuckled as she added: "I knew you weren't very happy about your idea of setting off on your own to try to find that address in Ealing. Well, come on with me to Knebworth instead. I'll tell you what, Jim: you'll have to go to your mother's house sometime because of your things being there (we suppose), so perhaps I could come there with you on Saturday when I'm on my way home from Knebworth: we live at Rhodes Castle, which is near Sherborne in Dorset. John and I have to come home via London, going by train, so we could leave you there if you'd care to stay with us at Lady Knebworth's house—that's my Great Aunt Alice."

"Fine," said Jim. "Thank you very much."

"Look," said Susan a moment later. "We must be nearly back at Penrith. That hill over there is the one behind the town, isn't it? Yes, look, you can see the houses of Penrith ahead of us on the hillside under the Beacon." She had stood up, as her seat was facing the wrong way, and was pointing ahead to the houses of Penrith which the train was rapidly approaching. Jim nodded. He could see the outskirts of the town, now about half a mile ahead, without moving from his seat, but was feeling far too excited by Susan's invitation to take much interest in what he now saw from the window.

CHAPTER ELEVEN

Mrs. Beck was asleep again. She had boarded the "Royal Scot" in a bad-tempered mood, but once a seat had been found for her she had soon resumed her drugged sleep. She sat in a corner seat opposite her husband who, in effect, had the compartment to himself and was much enjoying his solitude. Lady Dalmane had come in there with the Becks and had reserved for herself a corner seat on the corridor side of the compartment, but soon after the start she had gone off saying that she meant to have a talk with Cadet Sandy. Mr. Beck had settled down comfortably in his forward-facing window seat to enjoy the trip to the full for as long as he was uninterrupted by anyone else who might come in. He knew of many landmarks to look out for in almost every mile, and in some regions, in every <u>yard</u> of the three-hundred mile journey, but his mind was to some extent taken up in wondering what it was that Lady Dalmane clearly had in her mind to talk about with Jim Sandy. He assumed that as they could hardly yet know each other, Lady Dalmane must for some reason of her own be curious to know something about this youth's home background. He reflected again on the craziness of Jim Sandy's scheme of deserting the Cockermouth Police in the wild hope of finding a job in London with nothing arranged except that he knew his mother's address and meant to stay there.

The express train rattled through Penrith Station at a good speed, probably around fifty miles an hour, or faster. The buildings and platforms seemed to be passed in a flash as, slightly swaying on the long curve of the track, the "Royal Scot" clattered noisily through the points of the junction where the branch line went off on its way to Keswick, Cockermouth and Workington. Jim and Susan were both looking out and saw the place where the Keswick branch curved sharply away from the main line.

"There's the Cockermouth line," said Susan.

"Yes, now we're really on our way," said Jim with a grin.

"Over Shap to Lancaster—and then on towards London and the South."

A moment later they both saw for an instant the broad River Eamont, the boundary between the old counties of Cumberland and Westmorland, as the train swept over the viaduct above it into Westmorland. It seemed to Jim to be like passing an important landmark on the journey up to London, which was now to be extended to Knebworth. He asked Susan where Knebworth was and how they were going to get there, and she explained briefly where it was and said that it would be about another thirty miles on a local train from King's Cross. To be going with Susan Dalmane to her Great Aunt's house in Knebworth made the expedition seem to Jim more than ever like a carefree holiday. His colleagues back at home at the Cockermouth Police Station were completely forgotten; Jim was thinking not of where he had come from but of the unknown destination to which he was bound and feeling that good adventure lay ahead.

Susan was in no hurry to return to her other seat in the compartment with the Becks. She was quietly considering a problem in the back of her mind in between talking with Jim Sandy about quite inconsequential things. She had spoken to him almost as soon as she had come into his compartment about a proposal which she meant to put to him presently—when she had been able to probe certain aspects of his character—and was now considering whether it would be wise to put that proposal. *He'll have forgotten by now that I said I had a proposal to put to him which could be much to his advantage,* she thought. This was quite true. Jim Sandy, happily enjoying Susan's company and the view through the window of slowly changing country as the train climbed the easy gradients towards Shap Summit, had forgotten that Lady Dalmane had come into his compartment to tell him something special. When the express reached the wide open moorland country around Shap Summit Susan herself became forgetful of the fact that she had come to see Jim Sandy for a particular reason. The views up there that day were too magnificent to be ignored or overlooked in heated conversation on other topics. The light was very bright although the midday summer heat rendered the air hazy so that the distant views were obscured or indistinct; nevertheless, for a minute or so at the summit a spectacular view of jagged blue peaks of the high mountains of the Lake District was revealed to westward, and then hidden behind a new shoulder of the moorlands. They saw that large, puffy clouds were hanging over those distant peaks, the remnants of the morning thunderstorm around Cockermouth, for they were looking back in that direction.

Susan and Jim, fascinated by the superlative views over the wide, bleak Shap uplands, were content to watch mostly in silence as the train raced down the south side of the incline at a tremendous pace.

"We're coming to Tebay," said Susan presently, seeing the course of another railway line, the branch from Tebay to Kirkby Stephen, come into sight across the upper valley of the Lune, and almost at the same moment hearing a loud roaring noise as the driver of the "Royal Scot" made a full brake application to slow down in order to take the junction and curve at a safe speed. But a little later they were still travelling very fast as, with a great swirling rush of air, the platforms and buildings of Tebay Station came into sight and were immediately left behind. Jim and Susan, both looking out intently from their window, could not know that it took several minutes before the dust raised from the platforms by the rapid passage of their express began to settle down again. They saw the River Lune where the line crossed it just south of Tebay and noticed how its channel had shrunk between wide, stony banks, showing that little water was coming down in the spell of dry weather (it had been mainly dry for over a month). There did not appear to be any signs that it had rained at all there that morning. Then the train was making its way down the Lune Gorge for the next few minutes with breathtaking views of those lonely hills, the Howgills, rising steeply up from the eastern side of the narrow valley. Susan did not think again of that idea which she had been turning over in her mind until after the train had passed Low Gill, where the railway leaves the Lune Gorge, when it suddenly flashed back into her mind. Yes, she thought, I'll offer it to him. Let him come to Rhodes Castle, if he wants a job, at least to give it a try.

"Well, Jim," she said, "let's get back to the subject of a job for you. Do you remember, I said when I came in here that I had a proposal to put to you which might be to your advantage?"

"Yes, I remember you saying that."

"Jim, I wonder if you'd like to try working for us. We have a position vacant at Rhodes Castle which might suit you very well." Susan said this almost casually, but she saw the look of joyful astonishment on Jim's face as she said it and knew at once that he would eagerly accept <u>any</u> job at Rhodes Castle so that he could remain near her.

"I say, have you really got a job for me? It sounds most interesting!"

"Yes, I think you would find it interesting work: we have a vacancy for a Guide at Rhodes Castle—you know, someone to be a guide for the visitors we admit into our grounds. And as well as being the Guide, you'd be a junior assistant to the chap in charge of our security, a Major Ambrose. Are you interested?"

"Very!" said Jim boldly. "Yes, it sounds like just the sort of job I was thinking of."

"Well, seriously, Jim," said Susan, "I believe it would be a better job for you than anything you could find on your own in London. I wasn't at all happy about letting you go off on your own wandering about the capital and probably finding no employment. And what's more, I think you would be the very person for this job. You see, we have the grounds open to the public most days in the summer, and where there are crowds of course there's always petty crime. It's police work really, where I expect your training would come in useful. You know the sort of thing I mean: we need someone to mingle with the crowds and watch people to spot the pickpockets, to discourage vandalism, and generally to see that people don't misbehave themselves. Do you think you could do that?"

"I believe I'd love to if you'll allow me to give it a try. What about the Guide part of the job?"

"As Guide of Rhodes Castle you'd have to organise guided tours of our gardens and probably of the Castle itself too—we're thinking of opening some rooms to the public. And you'd often have to be in charge of several guided tours in one day. It may sound complicated but we could soon show you how to do it. Of course, on many days outside the summer season there are no coach loads of visitors and so there might be no need for guided tours, but you'd still have to be on hand to show people around, to watch them vigilantly, and to answer their questions."

Jim found this totally unexpected news of a good job at Rhodes Castle so exciting that it was hard for him to fully comprehend that perhaps here was a chance to settle down in a steady job (well paid, no doubt, working for an Earl and a Countess). And it would be a bonus to be working at the home of the lovely Lady Dalmane so that, hopefully, he would see her from time to time.

"Would I live in?" he asked.

"Oh yes, you'd have to, with your home being in the Lake District, hundreds of miles away. And your mother's house in Ealing would also be too far away, mind you, for you to visit her often."

"I wouldn't mind that," said Jim quietly. "And you don't want to interview me for the job?"

"There'll be no need for a <u>formal</u> interview for this job although, really, I've interviewed you already, in a way, and found you suitable. Luckily for you, the job hasn't been advertised yet, so there are no other applicants for you to compete against. Of course, my husband doesn't know about this yet, but I hope he'll catch us up tonight at Great Aunt Alice's house in Knebworth, and I'll be able to tell him about it then. John must, of course, give his approval of your appointment to our staff before you can say that we've given you the job—but he will approve, I know, if <u>I</u> do, so I wouldn't worry about that. And you'd find out soon enough whether or not you like the work; and we can find out easily whether we think you're suited to it." Susan was experiencing considerable doubts at the back of her mind as to the wisdom of appointing a new recruit to the Castle staff, as it were, behind her husband's back, so that he could only be told about it later, but she tried to tell herself that these doubts didn't matter. Anyway, I'm <u>not</u> appointing him, she thought, I'm only going to let him come for a trial period in the job first.

"That sounds fine," said Jim. "How soon can I come to see what the job'll be like?"

"You can come on Saturday of this week. You see, we've agreed, haven't we, that you're coming with me to Knebworth tonight?" (Jim nodded his agreement). "Well, you stay at Knebworth with us, and when we go home on Saturday you can come with us. There should be plenty of time to find out where your mother lives on our way through London, so we'll call there and make some arrangement for having your luggage brought on to Dorset. Then we'll all go home to Rhodes Castle together, and we'll get Major Ambrose to show you the ropes in the new job and you can give it a try for a few days—or longer. All right? Shall we call it settled that we'll at least do that, and perhaps you could stay if you like the work?"

"Very good, we'll call it settled," said Jim, trying not to sound as eager as he felt. "Thank you very much indeed, Susan."

But Susan was not altogether happy about what she was doing although she gave Jim a radiant smile which looked happy enough. What if John were to say "No," she wondered, to her appointment of Jim to the Castle staff?—even if she were to insist that it was only for a trial period? It was all very well for her to say to Jim: "He will approve, I know," when, after all, he might refuse to rubber-stamp her choice of a candidate for the vacant position of Guide. And what about this idea of hers that he could simply stay with them at her Great Aunt Alice's house until she and her husband were ready to go home on Saturday? It was now only Tuesday. That would mean having him there for three whole days and four nights if they left early on Saturday morning for London and Dorset. Susan, going over these points in her mind, suddenly realised to her horror that she had made an arrangement that was not going to work. It might possibly be in order for her to bring Jim Sandy, an uninvited extra guest, to her Great Aunt's house for one night as an emergency measure—that probably would be all right if she could find time to telephone to Aunt Alice from London—but for more than one night? No, that certainly would not do. Oh bother! she said to herself. Well, I suppose he <u>will</u> have to go to his mother after all tomorrow morning and stay there until I pick him up on the way home on Saturday.

Susan did not voice any of these considerations, nor did she notice much of the country through which they were passing at that time. The "Royal Scot" was now travelling at around its usual top speed for the long downhill stretch of line towards the coast near Carnforth. Just then, with a noisy rattling over points, the express rushed through Oxenholme station, the junction for the Windermere line, but Susan hardly noticed it, although Jim did.

Presently their conversation was resumed. Susan told Jim more about her home, Rhodes Castle, and the new job which he would be coming to try. Jim was longing to find out for himself what Rhodes Castle and its grounds would be like, but he was even more interested in that day's destination, Knebworth. Susan told him that her Great Aunt's name was Lady Alice Langley-Radcliffe, Dowager Baroness Knebworth, a widow who liked to be called simply "Lady Knebworth" (other than by her family and close friends). She told Jim that her Great Aunt lived in a large house called Langley House which had a big and very lovely garden; it was, Susan explained, more or less in the country but very close to the old part of Knebworth village. Jim gathered that Lady Knebworth was a kind-hearted elderly lady, although her ideas about formal etiquette were old-fashioned and rather strict. He cared very little about all this. All that really mattered to him was that he would not have to say Good-bye to Susan at the end of the day, but would actually be sleeping in a room under the same roof as her. It was a thought which seemed almost too good to be true, and which he still found hard to believe.

A little later Susan ventured to change the subject and to introduce a new and more daring topic.

"Tell me, Jim," she said, "do you have a girlfriend—apart from me?" The words "apart from me" excited Jim wildly. So Susan already knows how I feel about her, he thought.

"Well no, I haven't really," he said.

"I was wondering, though, how you got on at school with girls—that is, if you went to a mixed school. Perhaps you went to a prep school for boys before you joined the police as a cadet."

"No, I was at a mixed school—the local Grammar School quite near home."

"When did you leave?"

"At the end of last summer term, with six 'O Levels'. It wasn't until nearer Christmas that I joined the Police."

But Susan was not interested in Jim Sandy's academic qualifications just then. "You were a shy boy at school, I've no doubt," she said. "But there were girls. Did you have any particular friends amongst them?"

Jim was looking rather bothered as he answered: "No, not really. But some of the girls—well, one or two of them—I liked very much. There was one girl in particular in the Upper Sixth with me in my last year . . . I'm sure all the boys in that class were crazy about her, and I . . . well, I suppose I was too."

"She was very pretty?" asked Susan. Jim saw a meaningful smile in her eyes as she said this.

"Yes, she certainly was. At least, that's what I thought at the time . . ." His voice trailed off into silence, but he was smiling at Susan and blushing slightly.

"Oh yes," said Susan, "but what I was getting at is this: were you so shy that you could never let the girls you liked know how you felt towards them? What about that girl you mentioned in the Upper Sixth? Did she know that you had a crush on her?"

The blush on Jim's face now began to look rather more obvious.

"No, I'm sure she couldn't have known anything about it. I never dared to say outright that I fancied her—and I don't think I even hinted at that in any way."

"H'm. So you were shy then. You know, you were shy enough at first with me, Jim, but I think that perhaps you're not so shy now."

"Ah, well . . . I don't know about that," said Jim awkwardly.

"Oh, but I think I do," said Susan. "You're a little bolder with me now, aren't you?" Susan was going to say more, but stopped suddenly. She had been on the point of adding: "With a little more encouragement from me we could really get to know each other," and then to suggest that as they were, for the moment, entirely on their own, he might like to kiss her. She felt that probably she would soon give him a little encouragement in that direction anyway in spite of knowing perfectly well that it was unwise to do so. He's longing to kiss me, she thought, and he'd be dreadfully disappointed if I just walked away from this compartment without letting him do it—and, what's more, I'd be disappointed too. I rather like him. Then the thought came to her that she had already gone too far by offering young Sandy a job at her own home; that even if they refrained from kissing now it would only be a matter of time at home before they did so. Susan in that moment had a flash of prophetic inspiration. She saw quite clearly that at some time in the future at home—probably before the year was out, but <u>some</u> time fairly soon—she and Jim would be looking for and finding opportunities to be in each other's company to enjoy exchanging mutually held feelings of love. What had started as no more than a burning infatuation on Jim's part, but was already drawing a surprising response on her part, would grow and grow. They would certainly kiss and caress one another at home, but would they do more? Would they really eventually behave as lovers if he were to remain for years under her roof? Would he some day manage to coax her to come into bed with him so that they could make love? Heavens, that must never happen! she thought. John's my husband, but if I get too friendly with this lad I'd be unfaithful to my husband—no, I certainly can't do that. However, she felt quite at ease in her mind about explaining to her husband that she had taken on this former police cadet as their Guide and Junior Security Assistant. John was the kindest and most understanding of husbands, and the presence of this boy at home would not make him feel jealous: of that she felt sure. But I don't see why we shouldn't have a few minutes' fun together <u>now</u>, she thought. After all, a compartment to ourselves in an express train is an ideal opportunity for a quick kiss and a cuddle . . .

"Susan?" said Jim.

She came suddenly out of her daydream and saw that he was looking at her wonderingly. "Sorry," she said. "What was I saying? I think I've been rather lost in my thoughts just now."

"You were saying that you think I'm a little bolder towards you now."

"Why, yes indeed, and so you are. Do you know, Jim, there are some of your thoughts that I can read like a book! I don't think you realise how much you gave away about your fantasies when I caught you having a sly look at me reflected in your ring-stone. That was a very shy way of beginning, wasn't it? But now, you see, you *are* bolder: you're talking quite openly and frankly with me."

"Maybe," said Jim.

"But yes," said Susan. "And, of course, I don't know what form your private fantasies about me take, and I don't really want to know if you don't want to tell me. But since the time when I came in here to talk to you it's been as easy as easy for me to read the meaning of the look in your eyes whenever you looked at me. And you may have been too shy on other occasions to know the right things to say to a girl to begin to make friends with her; or if you did know what you wanted to say, I expect you never could bring yourself to say it."

"Too true," murmured Jim.

"Well, then, Jim, let this time be different! I hope I've said it all for you, all that need be said by way of breaking the ice, as it were." Susan at this point leant forwards in her seat and, with her face now several inches nearer Jim's face, continued in a rather lower voice: "Come now, why not enjoy yourself with me for a few minutes?" She stood up for a moment, took hold of both of Jim's hands, and kissed him lightly on the cheek.

Jim was so surprised by this totally unexpected action on Susan's part that for a moment even the exquisite pleasure aroused for him by the touch of her lips on his skin quite passed him by: he was simply too startled to notice that moment of pleasure—at first. And then the very next moment he received a nasty shock. Susan had gone over to the door. For one dreadful moment he thought that she was leaving him, but she was not.

"What about the blinds?" said Susan. "Shall we have them down? We're alone in here, and there's no one in the corridor at the moment, but you never know. It'd be more private in here if we knew that anyone going past couldn't see what's going on in here."

"Yes, yes!" said Jim. "Pull them."

Susan pulled down the three blinds, one for the door (with a window in it), and one each for the other two windows on the corridor side. Then she turned to him with a radiant smile on her face as she said: "There you are. Now people <u>can't</u> peep in at us—if anyone should come past—and the other side won't matter so long as the train doesn't stop at a station, which I don't suppose it will."

They embraced and kissed for some three or four minutes, Susan now sitting right beside Jim, but when it was over Jim felt as if it had only just begun; and Susan too did not notice the passing minutes as she embraced her new lover. The regular rhythmic sound of the wheels on the rail joints together with the rapid motion of the train made a soothing background to their embracing but neither of them really noticed these signs of the train's progress; nor was it surprising that neither saw anything of the passing scenery during these few intimate minutes. The "Royal Scot" came to the small North Lancashire town of Carnforth, close to the coast, and passed through the station and junction; it was a place which Susan might well have recognized from her travels of many years earlier had she looked out of the window; but she was too busy to do this.

Jim, of course, was in the Seventh Heaven while he held Susan in his arms, ran his fingers gently through her hair, and planted kisses on both her cheeks and her lips. But he was not aware that he was in heaven. Only the delights of Susan's face and body filled all of his conscious senses. He was very much aware of the closeness of her enthralling dark eyes; they looked dreamy and soft but he saw an excited sparkle in them too. Jim had, of course, utterly forgotten that the lady he was embracing was the wife of Lord Dalmane, the Earl of Saint Helens. But had he remembered that Susan was Lady Dalmane, the Countess of Saint Helens, it would have meant nothing to him at that time: to him Susan was simply a very beautiful and highly desirable lady.

Presently Susan got up off her seat and raised the window blinds.

"Oh, look," she said, "there's the sea. We must have just passed Carnforth. You get this very brief glimpse of Morecambe Bay here, where the tide usually seems to be out, although it looks further in today than I remember seeing it before." She and Jim were looking for a moment through the corridor windows at a stretch of seaside sand close to the railway line and at the sea water which was not very far behind the sand. The train passed the level crossing at Hest Bank while Susan was speaking and then, still standing by the door and looking out, she noticed beside their main line the single track branch which curves away from Hest Bank to Morecambe.

Jim had not been attending properly to what Susan was saying and had not heard what she had just said about the tide. Also his eyes were hardly taking in what they saw of the brief vision of the seaside at Hest Bank and, having looked without interest for a second or so, his gaze automatically re-focused on Susan where she stood by the doorway. She seemed able to switch her interest very quickly from kisses to looking out of the windows at the view but Jim felt that he could not do this, nor did he want to. He was still revelling inwardly in the sensuous delights of the last few minutes, and he wanted that mood to go on for as long as possible.

The line of the coast curved away from the railway track and the sea shore became lost to view. Susan remained for a little longer standing by the door, looking out that way. "We're coming to Lancaster just now," she said, talking to herself rather than to Jim. "I wonder if we'll stop there. Probably not." She turned round and came back to Jim but did not sit down, standing instead by the window facing him. For a minute or two she watched in silence the country to the north of the suburbs of Lancaster, while Jim watched her and continued mentally to revel in the loving embrace which had so recently ended.

"Jim," asked Susan presently, "was that really your first time? I mean, the first time you've kissed a girl properly—not counting such occasions as being kissed by your mum or by a sister (if you've got one)?"

"Yes, it was my first time," said Jim, "and it was gorgeous, Sue, really fantastic! Thanks most awfully for allowing it! And thank you very much for my new job too."

"That's all right, Jim," said Susan, now smiling at him and not attending to the view through the window. She had noticed with approval that he had called her "Sue" this time, rather than "Susan". Well, why not, she said to herself. He's coming to live with us so he can call me "Sue"—after all, we've kissed so, whether it was wise or not, we've started a friendship that's bound to grow. "Mind you," she added, "you haven't <u>definitely</u> been given this job yet, but I've no doubt a quick-witted lad like you will manage fine in it after a day or two of training; so you can really count yourself already as the new Guide of Rhodes Castle, I suppose. I'm sure you'll enjoy being with us. Ah, there are houses out there now; it's the beginning of Lancaster."

Jim, glancing out of the window, saw roads serving an area of neat, suburban housing. "We're slowing down," he said. There was no doubt about it. They could tell by the noise of the brakes and the feeling of deceleration that the driver was making a brake application.

"But now that I think about it, I don't believe the 'Royal Scot' does stop at Lancaster," said Susan.

Jim put his head close to the glass of the window in an attempt to see more of the line ahead.

"It's a signal against us," he said. "A colour light signal. I just had a glimpse of a yellow light on a signal post ahead—there." They saw the signal as the window of their compartment passed it.

"So we may have to stop?" said Susan.

But the train did not stop there. It slowed down to about fifteen miles per hour which both Susan and Jim thought was a bonus because it gave them the opportunity to get a good look at the tidal River Lune as they crossed the great bridge over it before coming to the station. They saw narrow banks of tidal mud on either side of a channel of deep, murky water; and there was even time to notice that flecks of foam in the water were moving away from them upstream on a flood tide (their near-side window of observation was on the left-hand or <u>eastern</u> side of the train, from which they were looking at the river which flowed <u>west</u>). Jim now also stood up (Susan was still standing at the window) the better to try to see the next signal, his head close to the glass of the window. But by the time he sighted it, when the train had crossed the bridge, the appropriate semaphore arm of the signal had been raised for the passage of the "Royal Scot"; and as they passed through Lancaster Castle Station a few seconds later it was certain that they were putting on speed again.

"Well," said Susan when the station had disappeared behind them, "I'm going back now to sit with Mr. and Mrs. Beck again: I said I'd be back presently. Come and join us if you'd like to, Jim. Or perhaps you'd rather not risk losing your place in your empty compartment here?"

Jim thought for a moment before answering. Susan's hand was already on the door; she half opened it and looked round at him. Jim did not like the idea of going away from his empty compartment and thereby risking losing it (perhaps he would want to come back there later); but nor did he want to lose sight of Susan while his emotions felt so light and jovial after their recent adventure.

"I'll come with you," he said.

CHAPTER TWELVE

Susan and Jim came out together into the corridor. The monotonous rhythm of the train wheels on the rails was much louder out there than it had sounded inside the compartment; and it was especially loud as many of the windows were open as far as they would go for ventilation on that hot day. Strong draughts of warm and somewhat smoky air were blowing into the corridor through the many open ventilators as Susan and Jim began the long walk forwards through the train. They put their hands to the handrails of the windows to steady themselves against the swaying motion of the train as they walked, Susan leading the way; the express was rapidly regaining its former speed, and a considerable amount of vibration and swaying were perceptible in the corridor. The compartment to which they were heading, the one in which the Becks were sitting, was well forward in the train, in the third carriage from the engine, with only two First-Class carriages in between. Susan and Jim were coming from the tenth carriage of the thirteen-car train and had to pass through four intervening Second-Class carriages and the Restaurant Car and Kitchen Car, which were in the middle of the train.

They were reminded of the lunch they had not yet eaten almost as soon as they had left their compartment. A steward was coming towards them and passed them, calling out from door to door: "Last call for lunch. Take your seats for lunch now, please. Last call for lunch in the Restaurant Car." Susan looked at her watch.

"Gosh!" she said, "it's just after half past one, which is high time for some lunch. But we'll go on and find the others first."

They walked slowly on. They came to the Kitchen Car before the Restaurant Car and here, in the corridor, a pleasant cooking smell greeted them. Jim suddenly felt hungry. Up to that moment he had not had a thought in his head about food, although he had not had anything to eat since he had finished his breakfast at a quarter past eight; even when Susan had said that it was high time for some lunch he had not felt any great pangs of hunger.

"That smells good," said Susan. "Are you feeling hungry, Jim?"

"Yes, very."

"Well, then, come and have some of my picnic lunch. Luckily I've brought far more food with me than John and I could have eaten on our own, so I'll invite Mr. and Mrs. Beck to share it with me, and you too if you care to join us."

"Thanks very much."

They passed through the Restaurant Car where they saw passengers seated at neatly laid tables, waiting for the final serving of lunch, and walked on through two more carriages of Second-Class seating accommodation. However, such was the strength of Jim's infatuation for Susan Dalmane that he quickly forgot about food and found himself again happily daydreaming thoughts about her. This is my lucky day, he thought. It's almost like having a new start in life. First I'm invited to stay until Saturday where she's staying; then I get a job working at her home just as easily as anything could be; and then she lets me kiss her. Oh, it's really more than amazing! Then it suddenly occurred to Jim to doubt whether all these good things were really happening or whether it was all a dream. He followed Susan through the noisy connecting gangway between one carriage and the next one. The express train certainly <u>seemed</u> to him to be solid and real enough to judge by the noise and the feeling of the floor vibrating under his feet. He looked through the corridor windows of the next carriage not so much to admire the view as to re-assure himself that the landscape he saw really was somewhere far away from his home town of Cockermouth. He saw that it was indeed unfamiliar; and yet, in a way, it did look very similar to the country just outside Cockermouth to the east, where the railway line followed the Rudd Beck towards Embleton. They were a few miles south of Lancaster now, and Jim saw that the line ran through flattish country, but that there were hills not very far away. Close beside the railway line was a main road, the A6 trunk road; and Jim could see through the windows that there was a great deal of traffic on it.

Jim followed Susan from that carriage through the gangway into the next one. He had quite lost count by now of the number of carriages they had walked through and was content to follow Susan mechanically, busily pursuing his own thoughts. Is this all a dream? he wondered. Am I really asleep and in bed at home? Well, perhaps I am: it doesn't seem natural that so much good luck could really come my way all in one day. I suppose at any moment the dream will come to an end when I hear Dad come and thump on the bedroom door and say: "Come on, Jim! Breakfast! Look sharp, or you'll be late for work!" But no, that can't be right. I've <u>had</u> breakfast this morning, hours ago, at the usual time . . . or was that all part of the same dream . . . ?

"Here we are," said Susan, opening the door of the Becks' compartment and turning round to wait for Jim who was lagging behind her by several yards.

Jim felt himself suddenly jolted back into reality out of his daydream. A second or two later he was following Susan into the compartment where Mr. and Mrs. Beck were sitting opposite each other, Mr. Beck facing the engine, and Mrs. Beck, now awake, facing him; both were in window corner seats. In that instant Jim suddenly knew beyond all doubt that his experiences of that day were real and no dream. It was the presence of Susan, more than anything else, which re-assured him that he was not dreaming. However, the fact that he had held her in his arms and kissed her was not the vitally convincing factor in his mind—kissing a beautiful woman was just the sort of episode that might well have been a dream—rather, it was that he knew that he could never have made her up in his imagination in the first place. Unless he had really seen Lady Dalmane in his waking life there would have been no memory on which the dream image of her could have been based; and as Jim considered this point it seemed to him to be proof enough that he could not be dreaming. These thoughts passed quickly through his mind as he came into the compartment, said "Hello" to Mr. Beck, nodded to Mrs. Beck, and sat down, after Susan had sat down, in a corner seat on the corridor side opposite Susan.

Soon afterwards Susan, remembering the time, stood up again and reached for the luggage rack over her seat to take down from it her knapsack which she had left there when she had first come aboard the train at Carlisle.

"It's nearly twenty to two," she said, "so I expect you two (addressing the Becks) are ready for something to eat. Jim's going to share my picnic lunch with me, so I hope you two will as well. There's plenty for everybody here."

"I'd love some lunch," said Mrs. Beck.

"Thank you very much," said Mr. Beck.

Susan noticed that Mrs. Beck sounded far more cheerful than she had been while she had been waiting with her husband on the platform at Cockermouth; Susan put this down to the fact that Mrs. Beck must have been cheered up by noticing when she woke up how well their journey to the South was getting on.

The picnic lunch was a good meal with sandwiches, cake, and cheese and biscuits to eat, and a bottle of red wine and tea for drink. Susan had stocked up the yacht <u>Osprey</u> on the previous evening with more than enough supplies to make this final picnic of her holiday; but, in fact, she had been thinking of getting enough food for <u>two</u> picnic meals that day, lunch and a late tea, in case it should be very late by the time they reached Knebworth. Now, as John was not with her, and because she knew they were likely to reach her Great Aunt's house not later than eight o'clock, and probably earlier, in time for dinner, she had decided that all the food and drink should be consumed now, if possible, in this lunch picnic. All four of the travellers from Cockermouth liked the wine and enjoyed eating Susan's food, but Jim noticed that, as the picnic went on, Susan was talking less and less, and he often thought that he caught an oddly thoughtful expression, almost an unhappy look, on her face. Something was bothering her; Jim wondered what it was and whether it could have anything to do with him.

Susan was wondering whether her motherly impulses towards Jim Sandy had lead her to act unwisely. In spite of her long deliberations before mentioning the Guide job she now felt that she had, after all, made a serious mistake in giving it to Jim. She thought too that she had then made her mistake worse by encouraging him to kiss and touch her playfully. She reckoned that she had, in effect, actually <u>given</u> him the job since she had implied that in what she had told him, so that it would be hard indeed now to take it away from him. But she could not think of going back on her word and, indeed, had absolutely no desire to do so. Susan found it hard to dismiss these thoughts from her mind while she ate her share of the lunch picnic; indeed, from time to time, for the rest of her journey to Knebworth, she would find her thoughts coming back to these matters when she was not attending to anything else in particular. Of course she thought up many arguments to try to persuade herself that no harm would be done by the appointment of the new Guide either to her relationship with her husband or, indeed, to Jim himself; yet she remained doubtful of how the arrangement was likely to work out. Of course, he'll be given a room well away from our bedroom, she thought, and anyway, his infatuation will be bound to cool off, given time; and he won't see me often anyway when he's working. It'll all work out well enough presently, I'm sure.

Soon the "Royal Scot" came to Preston and Susan's mood of introspection was distracted when another signal check occurred, this time briefly stopping the train in the station. As had happened at Lancaster, slow running of the train gave the passengers an excellent opportunity to look at the river as the train moved slowly across the bridge over the tidal River Ribble. Susan and Jim, looking down at the dirty water of the river, could see that the tide looked higher than it had before: there was only a little mud to be seen at the edge of the tidal water. Susan filled up the plastic mugs from her knapsack with more wine, passed round more sandwiches, and the jolly picnic went on. Jim, in particular, thinking of the new job he would shortly be starting, was in an especially light-hearted mood; but so was Mr. Beck, and even Mrs. Beck was chatting happily with her husband.

"Well, Jim, I suppose this trip up to London in the 'Royal Scot' must seem rather like a holiday to you," said Mr. Beck.

"It does," said Jim, wondering that he should have guessed his feelings so accurately. "Yes, sitting here, watching things go past through the window gives a very holiday-like feeling to the day for me."

"You haven't been this way before?"

"No, I haven't; and everything being new makes it all the better, of course."

"No doubt it does," said Mr. Beck. "And it's nice to see everything looking so bright in the sun, isn't it? They probably didn't have that thunderstorm around here that we had this morning. But have you given any thought to what you're going to do in London, apart from staying with your mother?"

"No," said Jim shortly, and was suddenly silent, wishing that he had not told Mr. Beck why he was going up to London. He thought that he had better not tell Mr. Beck that the plan to go to his mother's address was already out of date, having been replaced by something far better. He glanced across at Susan, but got no help from her; she was eating a sandwich but there was a faraway look in her eyes and she did not seem to notice him at all.

Suddenly Jim remembered that it had been in his mind to ask Mr. Beck a question, and he now decided to put it.

"I say, Mr. Beck, you've been an engine-driver until quite lately, haven't you? You must have had some super times on the footplate. Won't you tell me something about what it's like to drive a steam engine? I'm rather envious of you, you know, for having been an engine-driver."

"Are you indeed?" said Mr. Beck. "But I still am an engine-driver although I haven't been working lately. I hope to go back to driving when we've moved down to Hertfordshire. Are you by any chance looking for a job on the railways now that you've run away from the police in Cockermouth?"

Jim looked again at Susan. This time he saw that she was smiling knowingly at him, and on the instant Jim changed his mind and decided to give Mr. Beck a little shock. He smiled back at Susan and said:

"Oh no, Mr. Beck, I have a job now."

"He's coming with me to work at Rhodes Castle," said Susan. Her doubts seemed to evaporate from her mind by saying this aloud.

Mr. Beck gasped with astonishment at hearing this news, and for a few seconds he made no answer. Then, finding his voice again, he continued.

"Then I say that you're a very lucky young man. Employment at Rhodes Castle, in the service of the Countess and Earl of Saint

Helens is, no doubt, not easily come by. This is your lucky day! As for envying me—don't you think that I might rather envy you?"

"I don't know, Mr. Beck. Perhaps you might."

"Perhaps I might, you say? Well, well, so you're not looking for a job on the railways." He went on to tell Jim something of his experiences as an engine-driver to answer his question, and the two were soon happily talking about railways and trains. Susan occasionally put a few words into the conversation, but Mrs. Beck did not say much.

By the time the train reached Warrington the lunch picnic was over, except for mugs of tea to finish with. Susan remembered that an aunt and uncle of her's, Baron and Baroness Padgate of Dallam, lived at Warrington in a big house called Dallam Hall, which was just outside the town to the south and close beside the main railway line. She told the others something about her Uncle Geoffrey and Aunt Nora, Lord and Lady Padgate of Dallam, and remembered that she and John had a standing invitation from them to visit Dallam Hall sometime.

"We'll be seeing Dallam Hall in a few minutes," she said as they were passing through Bank Quay Station in Warrington. "I must write to Aunt Nora to invite them to come and stay at Rhodes Castle, so I daresay you'll be meeting them, Jim; they're very nice people. But it's our turn to stay with them first, really; you see, we last saw them when they came to our wedding in April of this year." Good heavens! thought Jim. So Susan's only been married a few months! But I suppose I'll be meeting this Aunt Nora and Uncle Geoffrey sometime at Rhodes Castle.

Susan pointed out Dallam Hall when they came to it soon after the train had crossed the bridge over the Manchester Ship Canal.

"There it is," she said. "That great house in the Park is Dallam Hall. Uncle Geoffrey must be at home; there's his personal standard on the flagstaff." The others saw an unattractive house of red sandstone, a many turreted, rambling building standing in a spacious park which extended from the foot of the railway embankment.

They finished their mugs of tea; then Susan collected all the mugs and the waste paper and packed them back into the knapsack. Soon after that, before the train reached Crewe, she fell asleep. It was hardly surprising that by that time she was feeling somewhat sleepy, having been up and busy since before dawn, around half past four that morning. The express slowed down to pass through Crewe, but there was no stop, and Susan was not woken up by the slowing down. She slept very quietly, her hands in her lap, and her head only slightly bent forwards. Jim could really only tell by her closed eyes that she was asleep; her breathing was so quiet that Jim could not hear it at all above the many noises of the moving train. He felt more than ever attracted to her now, he thought, as he looked at her lost in sleep. Although her eyes were closed it was almost as if there were a gentle smile on her pretty face; her mouth was not open, but her luscious lips were not quite closed, and looked to him quite entrancing. And to think that those lips have kissed me, he thought, and that I've kissed them. Oh, she is so, <u>so</u> beautiful!

Susan woke up about an hour and a quarter later when the "Royal Scot" was again slowing down, this time at the approach to Rugby. She opened her eyes and looked a little surprised to realise that she had been asleep.

"Hello, Jim," she said sleepily, seeing him watching her. She looked out of the window for a moment at a prospect of houses, factories, railway lines, and goods wagons and carriages in sidings.

"Where are we?" she asked, looking at Mr. Beck.

"Rugby," said Mr. Beck. "We're just coming to Rugby Midland Station."

"Oh yes," said Susan a little later as they came to the platforms of the station and passed slowly through, "so it is. There's the name on the platforms but I recognize the place anyway." She looked at her watch. "I say, it's four o'clock; I've had quite a long sleep. What about going along to the Restaurant Car soon for some tea, eh, Jim? I've nothing more in the knapsack. Would you be joining us for afternoon tea, Mr. Beck?"

"Yes, thank you, Lady Dalmane, but not just yet. I was thinking of going along to the Guard's Van and perhaps staying there for a while for a chat if the Guard turns out to be someone I know; but I'll come along to the Restaurant Car presently, if you like."

"And Mrs. Beck?" Susan looked doubtfully towards Mrs. Beck, whose eyes were again closed.

"Norma's asleep again," said Mr. Beck. "I think we'll quietly leave her where she is until we get near Euston, unless she wakes up first." He got up and went out into the corridor.

"We'd better not go just yet," said Susan. "We'll wait for that steward to come round announcing that they're serving afternoon tea—or has that already happened while I was asleep?"

"No, he hasn't been round yet," said Jim.

They amused themselves by looking at the view through the window for a while. The train had passed the junction where the line to Northampton via Long Buckby came off the main line, but they could see that line from the window; after the junction east of Rugby the course of the Northampton line runs close alongside the main line for a few miles before turning away in a more easterly direction. Then came the long darkness of Kilsby Tunnel, only broken momentarily at intervals by the ventilation shafts, which were like wells of pale, smoky daylight. Then it was out again into the afternoon sunlight. Very soon after the tunnel the brand new motorway, the M1, not yet opened to public traffic but looking quite ready for it, lay close beside the railway line and ran parallel with it for several miles around Weedon and Welton. Jim and Susan both thought it odd to look at the wide dual-carriageway road deserted except for a few contractor's vehicles here and there.

The steward, whom they had met earlier in the journey, again appeared in the corridor, calling out from door to door: "Afternoon tea now being served." Jim and Susan left the compartment and made their way back along the corridors to the Restaurant Car, admiring as they walked some good views of the Grand Union Canal, on which they saw cruising many small boats, mostly barges converted to pleasure craft. The sight of those small boats reminded Susan of how, early that morning, she had still been at sea in the Osprey with John: it had certainly been a memorable holiday. The Restaurant Car, when they came there, was almost empty, and it did not fill up very much while they were there, much to Jim's pleasure as he felt that he could enjoy Susan's presence far better without crowds of other people. Susan ordered Afternoon Tea for two; it consisted of a pot of tea and toasted teacakes for three shillings each. They sat down at an empty table and began to enjoy a leisurely tea while they watched the progress of the express through the arable country around Blisworth and from there onwards towards Wolverton. Mr. Beck did not join them there until they had nearly finished their tea; he said when he arrived that the Guard had turned out to be an old acquaintance of his, a Mr. Nick Welton, so he had stayed for a long chat in the Van. Mr. Beck paid for his own tea, and so Susan presently paid a bill for six shillings for herself and Jim; then they went back to their compartment.

The "Royal Scot" was now moving very fast indeed, but there were still some fifty miles to go to Euston (they were between Wolverton and Bletchley when they left their seats in the Restaurant Car). However, it seemed to Susan, who was now in country she knew fairly well, that they were approaching London with astonishing rapidity: it seemed to take hardly any time at all before the Chilterns appeared around Tring, and hardly any more time until the train flashed through the suburban station at Hemel Hempstead. Susan knew that she would very soon be seeing Watford and then the outskirts of London itself. She had earlier told Jim that she had lived for a time before she was married at Hatch End in Middlesex, while she had been a nursing student at a London hospital; and that before that she had lived at home, which was somewhere in the north-east of Essex (near Harwich) with her parents who were, Jim was astonished to hear, none other than Lord and Lady Ardell, the Marquis and Marchioness of Walton. When the "Royal Scot" reached the last pleasant stretch of open country around Hatch End, between Watford and Harrow, Susan told Jim that her former address, where she had lodged as a student, lay only some two or three miles away out of sight to the east.

The "Royal Scot", still travelling at around a steady eighty miles per hour, then hurried through mile after mile of the dreary suburbs of Greater London: Harrow, Kenton, Wembley, and Willesden. The train slowed down to pass Willesden Junction, and a few minutes after that, as they passed Kilburn High Road station and approached Primrose Hill Tunnel, Susan stood up, took down her knapsack off the luggage rack, and told Jim that it was time to leave the compartment and to queue up to be ready to get out at the nearest door: they were nearly in to Euston, she said. Jim had just been thinking how very dull London looked, seen from the train, and now he followed her willingly through the door into the corridor. Mrs. Beck had woken again of her own accord and seemed quite happy to see that they were at last in London; and Susan was now following the Becks forwards along the corridor. But Jim was by now, in spite of being with Susan, suddenly experiencing awful qualms, almost feelings of fear, at what he was doing. He had to remind himself sharply that he was not (thank heavens!) staying in the huge, unfriendly capital, where he knew no one except his mother, but was travelling on with Susan to Knebworth.

The "Royal Scot" pulled into one of the long arrival platforms at Euston station at twenty minutes past five, only five minutes late. With a great squealing of brakes from underneath the floor the train stopped. Jim stepped down onto the platform immediately behind Susan. He knew that he must at all costs keep close to her; the platform was very crowded with people who all seemed to be in a great hurry, and Jim knew that it would be easy to lose sight of her in that crush of hurrying folk if he happened to get separated from her side. His first impression of Euston Station was not of a very dirty or ugly place, but simply of a very unfriendly one.

Neither Jim nor Susan noticed a policeman pushing his way through the crowds towards them, a tall officer with the three white stripes of a sergeant on his tunic shoulder. Mr. and Mrs. Beck were some way ahead of them, nearing the ticket barrier. Jim had not walked more than twenty yards when he was startled to feel a strong hand press down on the collar of his police cadet's tunic. He twisted his head round, alarm showing in his eyes.

"Police Cadet One Hundred and Six, Cumberland Constabulary: you come along with me, my lad," said the policeman in a stern voice.

CHAPTER THIRTEEN

Sergeant Koppel drove the police car through the arch from the police station yard and out, turning right, onto Cockermouth's Main Street. In the passenger seat beside him sat Lord Dalmane, feeling decidedly cheerful again now that he was once more on the move. The car turned right again where the main road bridge crossed the River Derwent.

"How far is it to Carlisle?" asked Lord Dalmane a moment later; he had not seen the signpost by the bridge.

"About twenty-five miles," said the Sergeant, "so it won't take very long to get there."

On the back seat of the car was a nearly empty briefcase. Sergeant Koppel was on his way to the main police station in Carlisle to pick up there a large bundle of evidence and other matter on sheets of typing paper, which he meant to pack into the briefcase for bringing back to Murder Enquiry Headquarters at Cockermouth; and he wanted to talk to the officers at Carlisle as well while he was there. But he would drive first to the railway station to set Lord Dalmane down to wait for his train so that he could then be free, without any passenger waiting for a lift, to take as much time as was necessary on his police business in the city. But for the moment the Sergeant was not thinking at all about the murder hunt and, like Lord Dalmane, was in a light-hearted, cheerful mood. The two men were soon chatting away happily like old friends.

When they reached Carlisle, after a quick and uneventful journey along the main road, Sergeant Koppel turned the car into Courthouse Square outside Citadel Station. He and Lord Dalmane were still deep in interesting conversation which Lord Dalmane was loth to break off; the Sergeant was telling him something about the special skills which police drivers have to learn, and the special techniques which sometimes have to be employed in a high-speed chase. Sergeant Koppel was feeling almost glad of the morning's bungling mistake (although he had found it shaming enough being in the Chief Inspector's Office when the mistake had come out); but he was particularly pleased to know that Lord Dalmane harboured no animosity towards him on account of that mistake and that they were parting as good friends.

The Sergeant pulled up his car in front of the station and opened the passenger door for the Earl to step out. Lord Dalmane thanked him for the lift, and they said their Good-byes and shook hands heartily; and then they parted, Lord Dalmane walking into the station, while Sergeant Koppel drove away in the police car, thinking as he went on his way to the city's main police station what a gracious and magnanimous man the Earl of Saint Helens was: he had never said another word about being inconvenienced by the mistaken arrest although he doubtlessly had had his day severely disrupted.

Once again Lord Dalmane had too much time on his hands; it was not quite half past three and so he had about an hour and a half to wait until his train was due to depart. But now that he had got away from Cockermouth he thought of himself as being well on his way up to London in pursuit of his wife, and his mood of cheerfulness remained with him. He went first to the Booking Office and booked himself a First-Class Single to London Euston; but it was only as he was putting his ticket into the ticket compartment of his wallet that he remembered, on finding a ticket already in there, that he had bought himself and Susan through tickets from Cockermouth that morning. Damn! he said to himself. I'd forgotten all about those other tickets. Jolly good thing, though, that I gave Sue her's. My word, she must be getting somewhere near London by now. I'll never catch her up before Knebworth, but it doesn't matter. Now, what am I to do with this ticket I've just bought? I'll have to use it, I suppose, and waste the other one, or, no—couldn't I get the clerk to give me my money back for this one, and travel with the Cockermouth to London one and pay the difference?—there'll be a bit extra to pay, I suppose. He considered the problem for moment or two, and then decided in a typically generous-minded way to do nothing more about it; to simply keep the Cockermouth to Euston ticket as an unused souvenir of the morning train journey that he had missed.

He divided the time waiting at the station between sitting in the Refreshment Room on Platform Four and walking about the station looking at things. He had tea in the Refreshment Room as slowly as he could and read the famous Latin inscription carved on the Gothic-style stone mantelpiece: DEUS NOBIS HAEC OTIA FECIT, and its translation below it on a little framed notice: "God has given us these Places of Rest." Well, fancy that! said Lord Dalmane to himself as he read it.

When the "Mid-Day Scot" came in, Lord Dalmane was waiting on the platform for it. He stepped thankfully into a First-Class carriage near the front of the train and found himself a seat in an empty compartment without difficulty. The train left Carlisle punctually at four minutes to five. Lord Dalmane's trip up to London was fast, comfortable, and altogether unremarkable, but he found it a pleasant enough journey nevertheless. The weather had been improving all day slowly since the thunderstorm had cleared away; Susan and the others had found themselves in unbroken sunshine from east of Keswick on the 10.8 train to Carlisle, but back in Cockermouth it had never really fully come out sunny after the storm. Now, however, from Carlisle onwards the "Mid-Day Scot" of that day, the 30th June, was travelling in the full sunshine of the late afternoon and early summer evening.

Presently the steward came round announcing that Dinner was being served in the Restaurant Car. Lord Dalmane went along there and ate an excellent meal for ten shillings—a reasonable price to expect for a three-course dinner in those days. Later, having returned to his still empty compartment (there were not many First-Class passengers in the train) he settled himself again comfortably in his former seat and presently fell asleep.

When he woke he found that it was nearly half past nine and noticed that the sun had just set. It had disappeared below the north-western horizon which Lord Dalmane could not see from his seat as the train was travelling south-eastwards, and his seat was facing the engine on the left-hand or eastern side of the train; but looking south-west through the corridor windows he saw that there was still plenty of reddish daylight left in the sky. It was now perfectly clear and the sunset colours faded only very slowly that evening; a few thin lines of white cloud, now lit up a dull red in the glow of the sunset, were the only signs of cloud anywhere in the sky. The train passed through Watford, a blaze of street lights, and then came to the last piece of open countryside before London, where Lord Dalmane watched through the corridor window the black silhouettes of lineside trees against the still livid afterglow of the sunset. There was little light now, and no colour except the deep red of a band of sky close along the horizon: and all the outlines of things against that surprising light were staringly black. Minutes later hundreds of lights appeared everywhere, the suburbs of Hatch End and Harrow, the beginning of London, and Lord Dalmane knew that this part of his journey was nearly over.

The train arrived at Euston only a minute late; Lord Dalmane looked at his watch before he stepped down onto the platform. He wondered whether he would be in time for the last local train from King's Cross, and decided to go along there at once by Northern Line Tube; if it was too late in the day to get to Knebworth by train he would take a taxi from King's Cross. He knew that it was only about thirty miles to Knebworth, and was not in the least bothered by the thought of a taxi fare there, having plenty of money with him. But before going down to the Underground station he decided to telephone immediately to Lady Knebworth at Langley House from a call box (he had the number written in his diary).

The journey by Underground from Euston to King's Cross was quickly accomplished (it is only one station along by Northern Line), and Lord Dalmane came out onto the platforms of King's Cross station at ten minutes to eleven. He soon discovered that he had just missed a Knebworth train by five minutes, but as there was another at 11.15 p.m. he was not bothered: he had long ago made up his mind to the fact that he was sure to arrive eventually at Langley House, Knebworth, sometime long after midnight. It was, in fact, a quarter past twelve when he arrived at Knebworth station and rang for a taxi to take him to Langley House.

CHAPTER FOURTEEN

Jim Sandy was startled to find himself suddenly stopped in his tracks on the platform, but when he looked round and saw the policeman he immediately guessed that they had somehow found out at Cockermouth Police Station that he had gone up to London by train.

"But . . . but what's it all about?" he faltered.

"Your name is James Sandy, isn't it?" said the policeman. "And you've come from Cockermouth in Cumberland?"

"Yes, I am Jim Sandy, and I've come from Cockermouth."

The policeman now looked at Susan who (much to Jim's relief) had stopped and was standing by his side.

"Are you accompanying this youth, madam?" asked the Sergeant politely.

"Yes," said Susan. "I'm acting as his guardian for the time being."

"Very good, madam, you can come along with us, then. Now then, Cadet Sandy, you must come with me to my office."

"Are you arresting me?" asked Jim nervously.

"No, not yet. But if you don't do as I tell you, I'll have to put you under arrest. All right? You'd better co-operate, hadn't you, and then you can go on where you will, if they're not asking for your immediate return to Cockermouth."

"I've got to ring them up, I suppose?"

"Just so. Your Sergeant Koppel has been on the telephone to me about you, and he said that you were to ring him up as soon as you arrived at Euston. He'll be giving you a rocket, no doubt, for running off without permission. You can use the telephone in my office; and you, madam, could take a seat in the office, if you'd like to, until we've done the telephoning."

"Thank you," said Susan.

As they walked towards the ticket barrier, now left behind the main crush of people leaving the "Royal Scot", Jim saw Susan wave an arm to someone. She was pointing and waving Good-bye. Jim saw then that Mr. and Mrs. Beck had already passed through the barrier, in a hurry, no doubt, to get to King's Cross for the next train to Knebworth. He saw them both wave their hands and a moment later disappear in the crowds, walking towards the entrance of the Underground Station. We'll miss the next train, said Jim to himself. At least, Susan probably will, but I—perhaps I'll be ordered to take the next train back to the North. Oh dear, oh dear! Well, it's my own fault, of course, if they make me go back . . .

The Sergeant was one of the railway policemen of the British Transport Commission; in those days the B.T.C. police were quite separate from the regular forces, and were based at the country's main railway stations. There was a room in the old Euston Station which the railway police used as their office, and it was for this room that they were making.

"I was waving the Becks on," said Susan when they had gone through the ticket barrier. "Telling them not to wait for us. They seemed to understand. Now, Jim, I'm going to wait for you while you ring up Cockermouth."

"Oh, thank you most awfully," said Jim. "But I was going to ring up anyway, you know, as you'd reminded me that I'd have to."

"Well, it's five twenty-five now. Mr. Ruddock said there was a five-fifty or a six-ten train that we could catch for Knebworth, so I suppose we could try for the six-ten—we're almost sure to be too late for the five-fifty. Perhaps there's a six-fifty if we miss the six-ten, but I don't know about that; we'd have to see about it at King's Cross, if necessary."

"But don't you think," began Jim nervously, with a glance towards the policeman who was striding along some yards ahead of them, "that I may be ordered to go straight back to Cockermouth?"

"Well, perhaps your Sergeant may want you to go straight back, and in that case you'll certainly have to go, and that, I'm afraid, would have to mean that I can't give you our Guide job after all. And if that does happen, you know that you've really only got yourself to blame."

"I know," said Jim wretchedly. By now both he and Susan were wondering where on earth they were being taken to on this long walk through the station.

"All the same," said Susan, "I should think that if you apologise properly for what you've done, and if necessary say that you have another job lined up so that you don't need to come back to your old job in the police, then, I should think, perhaps you'd be allowed to stay away."

A moment later they saw that the railway policeman had opened a certain door, and was holding it for them to go inside.

"Go on, Jim, you first," said Susan.

Jim entered that room, a small, dingey place, rather dark as the window was small (and badly in need of cleaning), with a sinking heart, believing nothing but that he was about to be ordered to go back to Cockermouth. But he felt so nervous all of a sudden at the thought of the things his Sergeant might be about to say to him that there was an uncharacteristic weakness in his legs and almost a feeling of lightness in his head. Oh dear, he thought, this is very like going into the Head Master's study knowing that it's going to be a caning! He glanced at Susan but got no re-assuring smile back in reply.

"Go ahead," said the railway policeman, handing the telephone receiver to Jim, who unwillingly took it. Come! he said to himself crisply, he can't kill me.

"Hello, Sergeant Koppel. I'm very sorry I ran off this morning without saying where I was going. I'm really very sorry about it, sir, if it's caused you a lot of trouble."

"Are you sorry, indeed?" said Sergeant Koppel. "You jolly well should be anyhow. Do you know, you've caused me a great deal of worry today, until I eventually found out that you'd taken a train to London? Let me tell you, Jim, that I consider what you've done to be absolutely disgraceful behaviour, for which you deserve to be dismissed from the Force immediately."

"Yes, sir, I have behaved disgracefully," said Jim meekly. "I'm sorry, sir."

"I'm assuming, Jim, when I say you deserve immediate dismissal, that you weren't trying to dismiss yourself: that you will want to come back to us now that you've realised the folly and stupidity of your escapade. Why ever did you want to go up to London anyway? Weren't you happy working with us?"

"It wasn't that, sir, but I came to look for a job."

"To look for a job in London? Are you mad, boy?"

"No, sir," said Jim as calmly as he could. In a moment's very brief pause he flashed a glance towards the armchair where Susan was sitting, hoping for an encouraging nod of her head, or some other helpful sign from her; but Susan seemed to be far away in her own thoughts. "I have, in fact, found myself a new job already, sir," he continued.

"You've found yourself a new job already?" repeated Sergeant Koppel slowly. Jim could tell from his voice that it hardly sounded as if what he had just said was credible to his Sergeant. "In London?"

"Well, no, sir, not actually in London. At a place out in the country in Dorset. You see, I met someone in the train who happened to offer me a very good job . . ." He paused and looked again at Susan, desperately wanting some sign from her that would mean that he was saying the right sort of things. This time she had come out of her apparent daydream and was looking at him; He caught a slight, a very slight, nod of her head.

"Yes, go on," said Sergeant Koppel. "You met someone in the train who offered you a job?"

"Yes, sir; so I agreed to take this job because I believe it will suit me very well. That's the truth, sir, honestly." Jim decided then not to tell his Sergeant what the job was unless that question were specifically asked.

"Oh, is it? Well, it all sounds most astonishing to me. Do I take it from what you're saying, Jim, that you don't want to come back to your job here because you're saying you've found a new, better one?"

"That's right, sir."

"Are you quite sure about this, Jim? When I said you deserve to be sacked immediately, I meant it, but I <u>didn't</u> mean that we actually propose to bar your way if you want to come back. You've said you're sorry, and I'll accept that; and as this incident hasn't been reported to the Chief Constable we could, as it were, brush it under the carpet. You can come back to your work as a Cadet here— you know, I've been very pleased with your progress until today— and you could consider yourself pardoned if you're coming back this evening or tomorrow to go on with your police training as if nothing had happened."

"That's very kind of you, sir, but there's this other job: you see—"

"You propose to accept this other work, whatever it is, do you, and leave us? Well, do so if you must, Jim; it's all the same to me. But <u>are</u> you sure that you want to leave the Police to change your job? Are you?"

Jim looked once more at Susan. This was a moment of critical decision for him. Sergeant Koppel's offer to take him back fully pardoned was so kindly meant that it was hard for him to say: "No, thank you," to it. Jim had thought that the new job as the Guide of Rhodes Castle was his, all fully decided on, and as good as confirmed. Now, however, a moment of wavering doubt came to him. Oughtn't I really to go back? he said to himself. But he looked at Susan, caught her eye, and saw just a hint of a smile on her face, and instantly said "No!" to himself. It was hardly a hint from her, but he dimly understood that Susan was trying not to influence his decision in any way by word or gesture from the armchair where she was sitting in a corner of that little room.

"Well, Jim? You're in some doubt about it, are you?" said Sergeant Koppel's voice, after a pause.

"No, sir," said Jim resolutely. "I'm in no doubt at all. I want to resign from the Police Force immediately, sir, so that I can take up my new position."

"I see. Then you must write a formal letter of resignation, without delay, to the Chief Constable. And I shall expect a note from you as well, by way of a formal apology and to confirm that your intention is not to come back. And there's another thing."

"Yes, sir?"

"As you're not coming back, I must take back the pardon. There's two weeks' pay which should have been due to you, Jim, but that will now be forfeit as a penalty for leaving your job in an irresponsible manner and without authorisation."

"Very good, sir," said Jim.

"And don't forget to write to me. Good-bye, Jim."

"Good-bye, sir." He hung up the receiver. The docking of a fortnight's pay did not affect him (he had expected some punitive measure against him) but he was rather hurt by the fact that Sergeant Koppel had changed his tone towards the end of the conversation and had taken back his pardon; at the same time he fully understood why the Sergeant had found it necessary to speak as he had done. He looked up at the railway policeman who had stood quietly by watching him gravely while he had been speaking on the telephone; now the policeman opened the door of his little office for them, and Susan stood up to go.

"Good evening to you, madam," said the policeman politely, touching his helmet as they walked out onto the station concourse again.

"Well, that's taken less than ten minutes," said Susan when they were outside the police office again. "So we'll try for the six-ten train. We should have plenty of time to get to King's Cross for it."

After that neither Susan nor Jim said anything more as they walked back towards the entrance of the Underground Station.

It was as if Susan and Jim had come to an unspoken agreement that they would not discuss the outcome of Jim's talk on the telephone with Sergeant Koppel at least until they were sitting comfortably in a train to Knebworth. The crowds of evening rush-hour travellers did not trouble them much as most people were heading for the northbound tube platforms to travel <u>away</u> from the central region of London, rather than towards the centre. Susan and Jim were lucky at the Tube station platform. A train to Morden via Bank came out of the tunnel about thirty seconds after they had arrived on the platform. After that it was only a journey of about a minute or two before the tube train doors opened at King's Cross Northern Line Tube station.

"Ten to six," said Susan. "We're O.K. for the six-ten train."

The rest of the journey to Knebworth was uneventful. They discovered which platform on the suburban side of King's Cross Station the six-ten to Stevenage left from, boarded it, and found seats in a compartment with two other passengers. The train was, of course, full of commuters leaving London. Susan knew straight away, before they even boarded it, that it would be hopeless to expect to find an empty compartment in this train, which was Second-Class only (she usually travelled First-Class by train); so she and Jim were content to travel in a shared compartment and to talk only of inconsequential matters, again not discussing Jim's recent telephone conversation with Sergeant Koppel.

The train arrived at Knebworth at ten minutes past seven. Susan and Jim stepped down onto the platform, handed over their tickets at the barrier, and walked out to the road outside the front of the station.

"Hello!" Jim was startled by Susan's sudden shout. Who was she waving to? A moment later he saw that two people walking slowly towards them along the road were Mr. and Mrs. Beck.

CHAPTER FIFTEEN

"Hello, Lady Dalmane," said Mr. Beck. "Hello, Jim. So we meet again."

"Well, this is a surprise to meet again here," said Susan. "I thought you said you were going to stay tonight at your aunt's house in Knebworth before going on to your parents tomorrow."

"That was the plan. But we've just been to Aunt Annie's house—it's Number Four, Datchworth New Road, on the other side of the Great North Road—and found the house empty and locked up. She's away."

"So we'll have to try to get to Tolmers—where Nigel's parents live—tonight if we can," said Mrs. Beck. "We need a train to Stevenage first."

"Well, you've just missed one," said Jim. "We've just got off the six-ten, but it went on straight away, before we'd even walked out of the station."

"Damn! said Mr. Beck. "Blast it! Now we're sure to have to wait another hour for the next one—unless there happens to be a six-fifty from King's Cross. You didn't think to look that up on the Departures Notice at King's Cross, did you, Lady Dalmane? We didn't look at it because we were in too much of a hurry."

"I didn't," said Susan. "But you caught the five-fifty?"

"Yes, we did. But, you see, the tiresome thing is that now we're at the wrong station for getting to Tolmers."

"Where is Tolmers?" asked Jim.

"Just south of Hertford, but it's hardly surprising if you haven't heard of it. Tolmers is hardly a place at all: just a house or two—more like a name for a little region of the countryside, I suppose. It's about six miles south of Hertford."

"So it's quite a long way from here?" asked Susan.

"Yes, indeed. And I said we'd come to the wrong station for Tolmers because to get there by train from here you've got to change at Stevenage and take another train via the Hertford North line. Cuffley is the station nearest to Tolmers."

"Ah, I know where it is now," said Susan. "You could have travelled from King's Cross direct to Cuffley on a Hertford North train if only you'd known that you were going to find that your Aunt was away. I thought I knew this part of Hertfordshire fairly well, having stayed at Langley House with Great Aunt Alice before, but I haven't heard of a place called Tolmers; but Cuffley—there used to be some beautiful country around there, I remember."

"I hope to find that the country is still unspoilt," began Mr. Beck. "Eh, what's up, Norma?" He turned round to see that his wife was scowling furiously. She had just given him a sharp dig in the side with her elbow.

"How much longer are you going to stand there chattering, Nigel?" she said. "Come on, let's go."

"Go? But how can we go, Norma?"

"Well, we could get a bus to Tolmers, couldn't we, rather than wait here ages for the next damn train?"

Mr. Beck sighed audibly and looked around for a moment before answering his wife. They were all still standing on the pavement just outside the entrance to Knebworth Station.

"Norma, my dear," he said, "I honestly don't think we'd do any better by bus than we would by train. You see, it's so late in the day." (It was about twenty minutes past seven, as Mr. Beck saw by a glance at his wristwatch). "If we took a bus we'd have to change at Hertford and—"

"Then we'd better look for a hotel, a guest-house, or a bed-and-breakfast at Stevenage," interrupted Mrs. Beck. "We'll have to damn well wait here for the next train after all."

"Listen," said Susan. "I'll tell you what: why don't you two come with me and Jim to Langley House? I'm sure it'll be all right for you to stay a night when I've explained about you to Great Aunt Alice."

"Now that's a very kind offer, Lady Dalmane," said Mr. Beck. "Why shouldn't we stay at Langley House, Norma, if it _is_ all right with Lady Knebworth?"

"But we don't know this woman, Lady Knebworth," said Mrs. Beck, giving vent to her feelings of annoyance at what seemed to her a stupid plan. "She doesn't know anything about _us_—so how can it be all right for us to go to her house? I think we should say 'No' to this idea. Come on, Nigel. Let's get back to the station at once for the next train to Stevenage." She made as if to pull her husband towards the station entrance by his jacket, but Mr. Beck stood his ground.

"Oh, look here, Norma. I'm all for accepting Lady Dalmane's splendid offer. It would be very much easier than going off to Tolmers now either by train or bus; and I doubt we wouldn't be able to complete the journey this evening either way. And as it's about twenty miles away by road, I should think, we can't be taking a taxi either, or walking there. It doesn't matter that we don't know Lady Knebworth, and she doesn't know us—does it, Lady Dalmane?"

"No, of course it doesn't. Look here, I'd better ring up Great Aunt Alice now; there's a phone box just around the corner, I saw, so it won't take more than a few minutes. I really meant to ring her up from London, but perhaps it's just as well that I didn't."

Susan went off to the telephone kiosk while the others stayed where they were, mostly in silence, except that Mrs. Beck continued to grumble about the new arrangement of having to stay with Lady Knebworth instead of with her husband's parents, whom she knew, and whose house at Tolmers she had visited before. Beneath her façade of complaint she did not, in fact, mind very much the thought of staying a night as the guest of a complete stranger, but Mr. Beck knew that she was "in one of her moods;" she was feeling querulous and using this issue as an excuse to do a bit of moaning and grumbling. He did not much mind that, but it shamed him to think that Lady Dalmane must see Norma's response to her generous offer as ungrateful and sulky.

About five minutes later Susan appeared again, looking distinctly cheerful.

"It's all fixed up. Come along, everybody, and I'll lead the way to Langley House. Aunt Alice says you'll all be very welcome tonight."

Mr. Beck and Jim Sandy thanked her again, but there was a moment of silence while Susan and Nigel Beck looked at Norma Beck.

"Well, Norma?" said her husband quietly. She was frowning and looking past her feet at the pavement sulkily. "Come, Norma, dear: Lady Dalmane and Lady Knebworth are offering us a <u>free</u> night's accommodation, remember."

"Oh, very well! We'll come with you, Susan. Is it far to this Langley House?"

"No," said Susan. "At least, it's about a mile from here. We walk up to Old Knebworth and turn off this road from the station just before we get to Knebworth House, the other big house in the village. I believe you're feeling rather tired, Mrs. Beck, but do you think you could manage to walk that far?"

"I suppose so," said Mrs. Beck. "Lead on, Susan, and bring us to this place. I can see it'll <u>have</u> to be all right."

Mr. Beck felt a great desire to hit his wife. He was shocked at her rude way of answering Lady Dalmane, yet he sensed that Lady Dalmane seemed to understand that Norma's depression made her act in this dreadful way when she felt tired or irritated. Mr. Beck, however, controlled his temper perfectly, merely saying to himself: I'm ashamed of you, Norma! Susan lead the way, and they set off on the walk to Langley House. After a minute of walking they had reached the end of the houses of the new village.

Knebworth is a place which is in effect two separate villages about a mile apart. The newer community is clustered around the railway station, just off the Great North Road, and is usually called just "Knebworth" on maps, as it is on the road signs; but the old village is called Old Knebworth to distinguish it from the newer, separate Knebworth. The road which leads westwards from the station towards Old Knebworth goes uphill at a gentle gradient as one leaves behind the newer houses around the railway station. Old Knebworth used to be a delightfully pretty, unspoilt village amidst the pleasant Hertfordshire countryside. Nowadays festivals of pop music and the like are sometimes held here for several days at a time, but these events were (mercifully) unknown there in the late fifties. A more permanent intrusion into the peacefulness of this part of rural Hertfordshire today is the new motorway which is crossed by a bridge taking the old road over it; but the advent of the motorway here also lay still in the future in those days. However, apart from the intrusion of the motorway into the scene, little has substantially changed.

Jim Sandy, as he walked beside Susan, had just been asking her why part of Knebworth was called "Old", and she had explained to him how the village had come to be in two parts a mile apart. Then, referring to that telephone conversation in the police office at Euston, she added her opinion that Jim had made the right decision by saying a firm "No" to Sergeant Koppel's offer to re-instate him at Cockermouth.

It was now a perfect summer evening and the excitement of walking in a strange place on such a glorious evening, together with the joy of being with the woman he adored, moved young Sandy greatly. After that telephone conversation his mood had remained somewhat subdued until now, when he again began to feel unrestrainedly happy, especially because it was now clear that Susan had approved of the way he had spoken with Sergeant Koppel. One small irritation, which did not mar his pleasure, was the sun: it was now getting fairly late in the evening (towards half-past seven), and as the sky was now perfectly cloudless the sun was getting low; and as the direction of the road happened to lie rather north of west, the brilliant circle of the sun was almost directly ahead of them, and was tending to bother not only Jim's eyes, but those of the others also.

Mr. Beck was walking in silence up the hill beside his wife. His momentary feeling of anger had completely dissipated when old and happy memories had most unexpectedly come flooding into his mind. He suddenly remembered that he had walked up that hill once before, long ago, when he had been still a boy at school. He had forgotten all about it until now when something— or perhaps the total rural scene of the road sloping upwards through the fields—had triggered the old memory in his mind. The last time that Mr. Beck had walked up that road, as it now came back to him, had been a day thirty years ago when he had been the fourteen-year old Nigel Beck, going to a school scout camp with his school pals. The camp had been held in, of all places, the garden of Langley House, the very place to which he was now walking; it had been held there by permission of the owner, the late Baron Langley-Radcliffe of Knebworth, an old boy of the school which Nigel Beck then attended. He had, in fact, been there to a scout camp on at least three occasions, as he now remembered; Lord Knebworth had been in the habit of regularly allowing the scout troop of his old school to have "weekend camps" in his spacious grounds. One, in particular, of those three occasions came back to Mr. Beck's recollection with poignant nostalgia: it had been, he believed, a very similar beautiful mid-summer evening when he and the other scouts and their scoutmaster had arrived at Knebworth by train from London, just as Mr. Beck had now done again. These memories were too sweet for him to talk about for the moment (for he had greatly enjoyed his young days as a boy scout), so he was walking along in silence, admiring again the once-familiar views, and quite forgetting his wife, who was sullenly stumping along by his side.

Presently the travellers from Cockermouth saw a little cluster of old houses and big gardens a little way ahead, the village for which they had been aiming. Here, however, Susan, who was leading the way, turned off the main road into the narrow opening of an unsurfaced country lane on their left. She explained to the others that they would approach Langley House in this way, from the back, as a short cut instead of going round to the drive gate and up the main drive (a much longer walk). On their right now was an area of rough grass, and about fifty yards back from the lane and parallel with it a high wall, the wall of the garden of Langley House. From the further side of it the branches of trees hung over, and on the inside of it they caught glimpses of the roof and chimneys of a large house.

"Why," said Mr. Beck, putting his daydreams into words, "I do believe this wall here is the garden wall of Langley House."

"It is," said Susan. "So you've been here before, have you?"

"Yes, I've been here before: to this house and its garden, I mean, but I'd forgotten all about it until we began to walk up the hill from the station."

"But you must have been to Knebworth before when you've come to see your aunt—or have you never visited her before here?"

"Oh yes, I've visited Aunt Annie before; but, you see, Datchworth New Road, where she lives, is on the other side of the <u>new</u> part of Knebworth. It's a curious thing, I suppose, that whenever I've come to stay at my aunt's house—and I haven't been down to this part of the country for years—whenever I've been there, I've never found the time or opportunity to come up to Old Knebworth. I believe it must be all of thirty years since I was last here, when we used to come to school scout camps in Lord Knebworth's garden, just on the other side of this wall."

"Good heavens! said Susan. "Thirty years is a long time when you come back to a place you haven't seen in all that time. No doubt lots of old memories will come back to you, Mr. Beck, when we go through into that garden in just a moment."

"They will," said Mr. Beck, "and they are coming back already; walking along the road to Old Knebworth from the station has already recalled a lot for me."

"Here we are," said Susan. "Our short cut goes through that door you see there in the wall; it takes us straight into the garden."

"I remember it," said Mr. Beck.

Susan lead the way along a little path across the rough grass, a path which branched off from the lane and ran straight to a green-painted closed wooden door in the garden wall (the lane went on and gave access to the back drive and the tradesman's entrance to the house, Susan explained). They came to the door and for a moment they all wondered whether it would be locked, but Susan put her hand to the door-knob and turned it, and the door opened. Jim, looking through the narrow doorway as it opened, caught a glimpse of the sparkle of water and, glancing upwards for a moment, noticed that the top of the high, smooth wall was well protected against the invasion of tresspassers by having plenty of pieces of broken glass set into it to act as a barrier like barbed wire.

"I say," he said as he followed Susan through the doorway, "what a beautiful garden!" Mrs. Beck and then Mr. Beck followed him into the garden, Mr. Beck pausing for a moment to close the door.

Half a minute later, as they were walking across an area of rough grass close to a little lake on their way to the lawn and the house, Mr. Beck stopped short. A look of delighted amazement was on his face.

"Well! he said. "But this is the very place where we had those scout camps when I was still at school—our tents were pitched just here on this patch of grass. How I remember it all now! I don't believe this lovely garden has changed a bit in all these years."

"But it <u>must</u> have changed," said Mrs. Beck. "The trees, at least, must have grown a bit, and some of them may have been cut down. I had no idea that you'd been here before, Nigel, but I really don't see what's so specially lovely about it. You only say that because it brings back happy memories, you know."

"Well, it does, and I say it <u>is</u> a lovely garden, still beautifully looked after, as it used to be. And of course the trees have grown a bit, but <u>overall</u> it still looks much the same." He was looking at a little wood which came down to the further edge of a long, narrow, ornamental lake. There were willow trees by the water's edge, and a number of branches leaned well out over the water, some trailing leaves into it. The other trees in the wood were all deciduous except for one tall Scot's pine, which stood rather by itself in a clearing. The rough grass on which they were standing went down to the brink of the water, and extended to their right up to one end of the lake, but a smoothly mown lawn on their left stretched from the lake, sloping gently upwards, to the place where the main drive ended in a wide sweep alongside the front of the house. The lawn reached as far as the other end of the lake (by the road) and went some way round that shallow bay until it met the wood. The lake, like the house behind it which was narrow and rectangular, had a south-west to north-east axis; and the southern corner of the front of the house was behind the backs of the travellers as they looked admiringly at the lake.

Mr. Beck looked all around him for a minute or so, and then: "What a lovely smell of smoke!" he exclaimed, at the same moment first noticing a small fire which had burned very low on a blackened patch of grass behind them. The pleasant smell of wood smoke rose into the still air. Mr. Beck sniffed at it again happily, and it seemed to him then that there could be no more pleasing smell in the world than wood smoke.

"Ah! How it all comes back to me," he said. "The delectable smell of that wood smoke somehow brings all those dear old memories to life again. I do believe this fire could be on the very spot where we used to have our camp fires—it could almost <u>be</u> our old camp fire!"

"Oh, rot!" muttered Mrs. Beck savagely. "You and your 'dear old memories', indeed! What's so special about the smell of wood smoke, then?"

"But it is a very pleasant, fragrant smell," said Susan. "I quite agree with you, Mr. Beck. I don't wonder it helps to revive fond memories."

"Indeed it does," said Mr. Beck, ignoring his wife's question. "I remember waking up one summer morning in a tent which must have been pitched just about here, where I'm standing. When the door flap was pulled back we could look out at the lake, because the tents had been pitched to face it. It was a lovely morning, probably late May or early June, and I must have looked out quite early, around six maybe, and seen a light mist rising off the water, and so I knew that it was going to turn out a nice day—which, I seem to remember, it did."

"Look here," said Susan. "I'm sorry to interrupt you, Mr. Beck, but we must remember the time. I said we'd arrive around eight, and it's five to eight now. We'd better amble on in the direction of the front door—yes, that's the porch over there, by the drive—and we can go on talking as we go. Where's Jim?" She looked round and for a moment could not see where Jim Sandy had gone to.

"Here," called Jim's voice, and Susan saw that he had gone back to the south-western point of the lake, where the path by which they had arrived from the door in the wall passed close to the edge of the water.

"Come on, then," said Susan. "It's time for us to meet our hostess. You can look around the garden later or tomorrow."

Jim, feeling a little bored by the conversation of the others, had gone back to the point of the lake by the path and then round to the other side, where the willows overhung the water; but he returned as soon as he heard Susan call for him.

"I met the gardener in the wood over there, and he wanted to chuck me out for trespassing," he said with a grin, "until I told him that I was here as Lady Knebworth's guest and that I'd come with Lady Dalmane."

"That's lucky for you, Jim," said Susan. "Hello, Mr. Potter. What a beautiful evening it is." The gardener, hearing that an important guest had arrived in the garden, had come up to greet her. He was an oldish-looking man who wore an unbuttoned old jacket over his open shirt. He had rather baggy trousers, tucked into his socks; and on his head was a very broad-brimmed hat. But Mr. Beck did not recognize him; although he was obviously old (in his seventies perhaps?), Mr. Beck was inclined to think that he had not been there thirty years ago at his scout camps.

"Good evening, ma'am," said Mr. Potter, the gardener, for a moment removing his hat to reveal receding silvery hair, and then replacing the hat on his head. "Aye, it's been a really grand day."

"It's nice to see that you're still working here, Mr. Potter," said Susan. "Are you keeping well?"

"Well enough, thank you, ma'am. Nowt to complain of. Now, this evening I've just been burning up a bit of wood trash from some branches that had blown down in the wood yonder." He threw a handful of twigs and dead leaves onto the fire and then picked up a large stick which was lying handy to use as a poker to stir up the dying red ashes. In a moment there were flames and the more pungent smell of fresh smoke rising into the air. "I'm going home now," he continued. "Finished work for the day. You're coming to stay with Lady Knebworth, are you, ma'am?"

"Yes, we all are," said Susan. "We must be going in now. Good-bye, Mr. Potter. It's been nice to meet you again."

The old gardener touched his hat by way of saying Good-bye, and stayed a little longer by his fire, while Susan lead her party on across a corner of the lawn, heading for the large stone porch on the front of Langley House.

Then, for the benefit of Mr. and Mrs. Beck, Susan repeated what she had told Jim before, warning them that Lady Knebworth had old-fashioned ideas of formal behaviour.

"There you are, Nigel, I <u>told</u> you we shouldn't have come here!" grumbled Mrs. Beck quietly to her husband. "Who wants to be bothered with good manners and formal etiquette, and all that sort of thing at a time like this, when we're tired? At least <u>I'm</u> tired—very tired."

But Susan had heard her. "I'm sorry that you're tired, Mrs. Beck," she said. "But don't worry too much about meeting my Great Aunt: she's shy with people she doesn't know, so we're likely to see little of her. And of course you'll be able to retire to bed early if you care to."

They had again stopped walking, and now Jim suddenly saw that Susan was looking disapprovingly at him, almost as if she were seeing him for the first time.

"How dreadful you look in that police uniform, Jim," she said. "I don't like the idea of presenting you wearing that, as I'd rather not explain why you're in police cadet's uniform. It's a pity we can't hide those clothes, or hide you."

"I could stay outside in the garden," said Jim, suddenly not at all wanting to meet Lady Knebworth.

"No good," said Susan. "You'll have to be introduced as she knows now that you're coming here for a meal and for tonight. There's nothing to be done about it now except that we'll have to explain the police uniform somehow if she asks about it."

"I could manage that," said Jim, wondering at the sudden fuss Susan was making over his uniform.

They sauntered on, talking as they went, and crossed the broad sweep of gravel in front of the house, and so approached the porch and the front door. A large black car was parked alongside the porch, but apart from that there was not a sign, looking in through any of the nearby ground-floor windows of the front of the house, that anybody was at home; yet Susan, having just spoken to her on the telephone, knew that her Great Aunt was in, and probably sitting in her little private sitting-room which was not one of the front rooms. However, now that it was time to ring the door-bell, Susan's mood changed dramatically. She had just been telling Mr. Beck about her late Great Uncle, Alfred Langley-Radcliffe who, it transpired, must have been the Lord Knebworth whom Mr. Beck had met at his school scout camps; but now for a moment she stopped feeling carefree and full of happy chatter, and suddenly found that she was feeling nervous, and desperately wishing that her husband was there to give her moral support. But as he was not there, she summoned up all the courage which she thought she could muster, and rang the front door-bell and heard the electric bell ring inside the house. During the few seconds between the ringing of the bell and hearing a sound of approaching steps in the hall, Susan looked nervously round at the others and tried to read the moods apparent on their faces. There was Mrs. Beck looking as glum and sulky as ever, as she had expected; but Mr. Beck, no doubt still wrapped up in his happy old memories, did not look in the least bothered. And there was Jim, standing just behind her, looking almost more frightened, she thought, than she felt herself. I wish he was wearing an ordinary suit, instead of those police things, she thought. And I wish I could get rid of Mrs. Beck altogether somehow. She seems so awfully moody and depressed, and irritable too. The way she spoke to me when I suggested that they come here for the night . . . what if she comes out with some appalling rudeness to Aunt Alice? Heavens, she looks as sullen as a thundercloud! I wish I could make her vanish into thin air rather than have to present her! No, that won't do: I've told Aunt Alice about Mr. and Mrs. Beck, and she said: 'Of course they can come'. But it's a funny thing that I don't feel brave at this moment when I've just been talking to Aunt Alice on the phone about a quarter of an hour ago. Ah, here comes someone to open the door . . . but what an extraordinary thing I'm doing! I'd never met any of these people I'm bringing to Aunt Alice before this morning, and I've already made a close friend of one of them . . .

A bolt was drawn back with a sharp click and the butler opened the front door.

CHAPTER SIXTEEN

Lady Alice Langley-Radcliffe, the Dowager Baroness Lady Knebworth, was standing by the fireplace of her drawing-room, a half empty glass of sherry in her hand. A minute earlier she had not been in that room at all; she had been sitting in an armchair watching an episode of a favourite serial on television while she ate a sandwich supper: a little table was right beside her chair, and on it was a supper tray with plates of different kinds of sandwiches, her sherry glass, and a little silver bell to summon a servant. But she had hurried through to the drawing-room to greet her guests in there on being told by her butler of their arrival. She was a very spry and healthy old lady who hardly looked as old as her age, which was eighty-four: she looked more like a lady in her seventies. Lady Knebworth had felt that it was right to dress up in her best evening outfit that day in order to welcome her Great Niece, Susan Dalmane, and her husband, John, the Earl of Saint Helens. When she had heard from Susan on the telephone that John Dalmane would only be arriving much later and that she was bringing some other guests instead for dinner and the night, she was not perturbed, neither did she think that her evening dress would no longer look appropriate because Lord Dalmane was not going to be there. She was a very tall lady and, in Jim Sandy's opinion, when he first glimpsed her, a rather grim-looking elderly lady. Her evening dress was long and two rows of pearls were hung round her neck, while from her ears hung heavy-looking ear-rings encrusted with jewels. Her hair was a steely-grey colour and seemed to be set in tight little curls in such a way as to add more emphasis to her height. Altogether, attired and made-up in that way, she appeared stately and dignified and might almost have passed for an elderly queen.

Jim was feeling so shy as he entered the hall of Langley House behind Susan that he almost wished that he had stayed behind in London after all. He felt certain that he had caught for a fleeting moment a very dirty look from the butler (an immaculately dressed man) when the latter had first glimpsed him at the opening of the front door. But the butler knew his business well enough and apart from that one look he ignored Jim utterly (as Jim himself thought). He doesn't approve of me coming here in my police cadet's uniform, he thought. He saw at once in the elegance of the hall that he had entered the house of a very rich old lady and, although what he saw around him was pleasing enough to the eye it was, nevertheless, with extreme reluctance that he followed Susan through the door into the drawing-room to be presented to Lady Knebworth. At that moment, in fact, he was wishing that he could have been swallowed up under the floorboards rather than meet Lady Knebworth face to face. But it was a little odd, although he did not know it, how quickly he plucked up courage once she had addressed him and given him the chance to speak to her. Another thought, apart from thinking that she looked grim, which came to him when he saw Lady Knebworth, was that here was someone totally different from Susan. But <u>how</u> was she so different? Was it just that she was so old, while Susan was so young? Jim was not sure about that. Long ago, however, he had ceased to think of Susan as a Countess or any kind of V.I.P. (he could not possibly be shy with her after that kissing in the train); but in this old Baroness he saw someone who <u>looked</u> far more like a titled lady than Susan did. The contrast between the two was indeed striking: Susan in her casual holiday clothes, Lady Knebworth in her very formal dress.

"Lovely to see you, my dear," said Lady Knebworth as Susan came into the drawing-room, followed by the others. "And so this is your party of travellers from Cockermouth? I'm sorry to hear that John couldn't come with you."

"Good evening, Aunt Alice," said Susan. "Yes, we've all arrived, except John, but I do hope we aren't too many for you."

"Not at all, my dear; not at all."

Then Susan introduced the others, beginning with Mr. Beck, then Mrs. Beck, and lastly Jim Sandy. Her moment of nervousness on the doorstep had passed and now she felt confidently in charge of her party of guests once more. Her confidence was helped by the fact that the sullen, glowering expression on Mrs. Beck's face seemed to have evaporated away, so that she looked simply pale and tired, and perhaps unwell, as she muttered an almost inaudible "How do you do?", and shook Lady Knebworth's hand in a limp handshake. Lady Knebworth noticed the weakness of this gesture, but turned at once to the third and youngest of her Great Niece's friends.

"And this is Mr. James Sandy," said Susan, introducing him.

"How do you do, Lady Knebworth?" said Jim, politely offering his right hand to shake.

"I'm pleased to meet you," said Lady Knebworth. "I see you are in the Police, a most worthy and excellent profession to follow."

"But I'm not in the Police any more. I left today to take up a new and better job."

"He's going to be my new servant at Rhodes Castle," said Susan helpfully, and Jim looked at her gratefully.

"Oh indeed, how very interesting for you, young man," said Lady Knebworth. "And what will you do at Rhodes Castle?"

"I'm going to be the Guide and a Junior Security Assistant."

"Ah! Well, you'll be very well looked after at Rhodes Castle by the Earl and Countess of Saint Helens, I've no doubt," said Lady Knebworth. "And now, you people would like something to drink after your long journey, I'm sure." Jim noticed an elegant glass decanter containing sherry on a low table in a corner of the room and four empty sherry glasses on it. "Will you have a sherry, Susan, or can I get you anything else?"

"I'd love a sherry, thank you," said Susan.

A footman, who had been standing unobtrusively near the sherry table (a small and elegant mahogony table) began to decant the sherry into the glasses. Mrs. Beck refused a drink but the other two each took a glass of sherry.

"Would you like a soft drink, Mrs. Beck?" asked Lady Knebworth kindly.

"No, thank you," whispered Mrs. Beck. Lady Knebworth looked suspiciously at her for a moment, seeing that there was something wrong with her. Could it be that Mrs. Beck was unwell? Her face had certainly become very pale in the last few minutes. Or perhaps it was only intense shyness which was making her act a little oddly? Lady Knebworth already felt a little anxious about Mrs. Beck, but she turned again to Susan, meaning to keep the conversation flowing.

"Have you had a good trip, my dear? You people have come a very long way today, I know, and I daresay you're all feeling a little tired."

"We've had a really lovely journey, thank you," said Susan. "We came up to London in the 'Royal Scot' and it didn't arrive late at Euston—or only slightly late—and the local train here ran punctually too, I believe."

"Oh, that's good. But tell me, Susan, did you meet these new friends of your's on the train, or was it before your journey started this morning that you met them?"

"I met all of them on the platform at Cockermouth station this morning before we set off."

"I see; but your good husband, John, my dear: I didn't quite follow what you said on the telephone when you told me he'd had to be left behind and that he'd arrive later. I hope nothing untoward has happened to him."

"Oh no, no; it's nothing like that," said Susan. She glanced quickly round at Jim's face before continuing, and saw that he was listening to her: a quiet smile was on his face. They were all standing round the hearth with their drinks in their hands, except Mrs. Beck, who had no glass to hold, and who was staring blankly at nothing and apparently far away from the conversation in her own thoughts. "I've no reason to suppose that anything untoward has happened to John," continued Susan. "What happened was this: there was someone at Cockermouth whom he had to go and see, and that meant that he had to stay there for a while. But he said I'd better carry on and take the morning train, and so I did; and John, I think, will be following on an afternoon train from Carlisle. I expect he'll ring up when he gets to London to say that he's well on his way, but I'm afraid he probably won't be able to get here until very late—perhaps even well after midnight. I <u>am</u> a little worried about that: I mean, will he be able to get into the house in the middle of the night?"

"Don't you worry about that, Susan, my dear," said Lady Knebworth soothingly. "When he arrives, whatever time it may be, I'm sure that James will let him in." (James was the butler). "He'll only have to ring the doorbell. I don't suppose he'll be too dreadfully late anyway."

Susan thanked her, and then Lady Knebworth said that they must all be hungry as it was already quite late for dinner, but that dinner would be ready for them soon, at around half past eight, she thought. "I hope you'll excuse me," she continued, "if instead of eating with you, I have mine off a tray in my sitting-room. I should think that perhaps if you're tired after your long journey you might prefer not to have the burden of having to make polite conversation with me during dinner, much as I should have liked talking with you."

"Oh, don't mind about that, Aunt Alice," said Susan. "If you'd rather eat alone we'll look after ourselves quite all right in the dining-room."

Just then Lady Knebworth was struck again by the strangely vacant expression on the face of her guest, Mrs. Beck, and by the whiteness of her face. Her hands were at her sides, her fists clenched, and her eyes were not staring out of the window (as one might have thought) but were not focused on anything.

"You look ill, young woman," said Lady Knebworth. "Do you feel unwell—Mrs. Beck?"

Mrs. Beck did not answer. They all looked at her. Susan thought that she detected a slight swaying tendency in her motionless standing.

"Norma! Do you hear me?" asked Mr. Beck.

"Mrs. Beck?" said Susan rather sharply. Still no response. A second or two passed.

"Quick!" said Susan. "Catch her!" as she herself lunged forwards and was just in time to prevent Mrs. Beck's head from crashing against the carpeted floor as she suddenly collapsed in a faint. In an instant Mr. Beck too was holding his wife's unconscious body, and Susan and he between them gently lowered her to lie in an armchair which the footman adroitly pushed into the right place for them. They all crowded round, except the footman, Charles, who hurried out of the room before Lady Knebworth had time to tell him to fetch some water.

"Is she all right?" asked Lady Knebworth shortly.

"Yes," said Susan, "her pulse is all right and she seems to be breathing normally." Susan had given up her idea of a nursing career when she had failed the examinations (this had been shortly before her marriage to John Dalmane); but she knew a good deal about basic first aid. She was kneeling beside Mrs. Beck and had taken her patient's left hand and was pressing two fingers of her right hand against the artery in the wrist to feel Mrs. Beck's heartbeats. "She's fainted; that's all. There's nothing wrong with her heart is there, Mr. Beck?"

"Oh no, not that I know of," said Mr. Beck anxiously. "Why? There isn't anything wrong with her pulse, is there?"

"No, it's fine," said Susan. She was timing it with the second-hand of her wrist-watch.

"I _am_ sorry about this, Lady Knebworth," said Mr. Beck, "but my wife does have a serious illness, and she has not been too well today. Probably she's walked too far this evening, coming here from the station."

"Oh, Mr. Beck, I'm sorry to hear about that," said Lady Knebworth. "But you needn't apologise because of this. If I'd only known that your wife was not well enough to walk up from the station I'd have had you picked up in the car. Ah, good man, Charles!" The footman came back into the room bearing a jug containing some cold water which, at a sign from his mistress, he handed to Susan. She slopped a little water over Mrs. Beck's head. Then they all watched Mrs. Beck's face; they saw her eyelids move and heard a low moaning sound come from her lips.

"She's coming round," said Susan.

"Fetch my smelling salts, Charles," said Lady Knebworth. "You know where I keep them?"

"Yes, ma'am." The footman hurried out of the room.

Mrs. Beck had regained consciousness but was looking extremely dazed. They helped her to lie back comfortably in the armchair.

"Now, Susan," said Lady Knebworth. "I suggest that we put Mrs. Beck to bed and let her lie there quietly. Do you think that would be best, Mr. Beck?"

"Yes, definitely," said Mr. Beck.

A minute or two later they were ready to move Mrs. Beck, after the smelling salts had been brought for her and she had inhaled, and had seemed to revive under the effect of the smelling salts. Mr.

Beck and Charles, the footman, carried her carefully between them, while Lady Knebworth lead the way, and Susan brought up the rear, leaving Jim for a few minutes on his own in the drawing-room. He sat himself down in an armchair and pondered over recent happenings.

Later that evening, with the time getting on for half past nine, Susan, Jim Sandy, and Mr. Beck were reclining in deck chairs in the garden, looking at the ornamental lake reflecting the after-sunset colours, and drinking cups of tea or coffee while they chatted happily together. They had eaten an excellent three-course dinner in Lady Knebworth's sumptuously furnished dining-room, with servants waiting on them, while Lady Knebworth herself had returned to her private sitting-room. As the guests tucked into their meal heartily there was nothing to make them guess that their arrival had caused Lady Knebworth any inconvenience, although by the time she got back to her chair in front of the television to resume her interrupted supper picnic most of the programme she had meant to watch was over. Mrs. Beck was in bed. She lay there on her back staring disconsolately at the ceiling and feeling generally ill and sorry for herself. When she had been helped to get into a bed in a spare room, a light meal had presently been brought to her on a tray, and she had eaten it. Lady Knebworth had clearly been upset that one of her guests had been ill on her arrival, and was now concerned that Mrs. Beck should be left as comfortable as possible. She had asked Susan whether she thought that she should send for her doctor to see Mrs. Beck, but this had been suggested more out of politeness than because she really believed that Mrs. Beck was ill enough to need to be examined by a doctor; but Susan had assured her that she believed that it was not necessary to send for the doctor. She borrowed a clinical thermometer to take Mrs. Beck's temperature, checked her pulse again, and satisfied herself that her patient was not seriously ill. She told her Great Aunt that

Mrs. Beck's faint had, she believed, been due to a combination of causes: her general poor state of health, tiredness, too little food eaten that day, and perhaps exhaustion caused by walking the mile from the railway station. However, it was a great relief to Susan to be able to leave that bedside presently to go with Mr. Beck (who had hung about, getting in her way) to join Jim Sandy for dinner in the dining-room. No one said so, but they were all feeling rather pleased and surprised that Lady Knebworth had decided not to stay with them for dinner. Mr. Beck too was rather pleased to realise that he would be without his wife's company for a few hours: he would be able to relate anecdotes from memories of his school scout camps without being interrupted by Norma's inevitable and annoying remarks.

It had been Mr. Beck's idea that as it was still so warm outside they should sit in the garden after dinner. Susan asked the servants to bring out garden chairs for them. They placed the chairs on the rough grass near the smouldering fire, which was revived to a cheerful blaze by the addition of a few handfuls of twigs and trash gathered from a circle of unburnt stuff around the fireplace. They settled down there as if sitting round a camp fire, and began to relax and enjoy themselves now that the cares of that day were over. The talk was mainly about Mr. Beck's memories of his school scouting days and the camps at Knebworth, although Susan told Mr. Beck something about her and her husband's background and about their home at Rhodes Castle. Mr. Beck told Susan that he was a native of Hertfordshire and that therefore his journey south had felt like coming home; he had been born in Hertford, he said, and had lived for some years as a child at Bengeo (which is a suburb of Hertford). He had moved to the North, he said, when British Railways had offered to move him to a driving job based on Carlisle, and he had accepted it. By that time, ten years ago, he was married, having met his wife, Norma, while he was still in Hertfordshire, and so they had moved together to a new home at Cockermouth in Cumberland. Mr. Beck said that he had enjoyed working in Cumberland and living on the edge of the Lake District, but that he had always felt in his heart as if he had been living in a kind of exile; but that his wife, with her tendency to depression had soon grown to hate living there (she had always been used to living in a large town), and that this and his own feeling of wanting to return to familiar ground had made them decide to return to the South.

Jim came up to them presently and threw a handful of small sticks into the fire. He had begun by sitting with Mr. Beck and Susan and listening to their talk, but had long ago finished his cup of tea and, beginning to be bored by their conversation, had gone off on his own, looking all around the garden.

"I'm sorry if we've been neglecting you a little, Jim," said Susan with a smile, "But, you see, we've been talking about the things that Mr. Beck remembers about this place."

"That's all right," said Jim. "I wanted to have a walk round anyway to look at things."

"It really is delightful, the smell of that smoke, and being out here so late in this quiet garden," said Susan. She looked at the fire as it crackled under the new fuel and the pungent smell of the smoke filled the still air. "It is almost like sitting beside a camp fire, isn't it? It gives me a most romantic feeling, just being here—you know what I mean, Mr. Beck?"

"Very well," said Mr. Beck. "Yes, it's an atmosphere that stirs up nostalgic memories—it's certainly romantic. What do you think, Jim?"

"I think it's very romantic," said Jim, with a grin at Susan.

"You would think that!" said Susan, and they all laughed. Jim knew why the other two and he himself had laughed, but thought that somewhat the wrong meaning was being attached to his remark. He had really been thinking of the whole of that evening scene there in the garden of Langley House when he had said: "it's very romantic," and not just of his "romantic" feelings towards Susan, in spite of his grin at her. He was well aware that there was beauty in nearly everything he saw, not in Susan alone. It was growing fairly dark now: the sunset colours were fading in the north-western sky and from the reflections seen in the mirror-like surface of the lake; yet what light and colour still remained uplifted his spirit. It was a natural beauty which, very much enhanced by Susan's presence, was "romantic" in his mind in that sense.

Presently Susan realised that in the gathering darkness they could now see little that was not shown them by the light of the flames and so she suggested that, as it was getting late, they should all retire to bed. She had for some time been feeling a little restless herself because she was thinking that John might ring up from London any time now, and so she thought that perhaps she ought to be back inside the house. The other two agreed with her suggestion, Mr. Beck adding that he felt very tired. They had been shown their rooms before dinner so now they picked up their deck-chairs and carried them back into the house, leaving the embers of the fire to burn out slowly on their own account. Susan then said Good-night briefly to Mr. Beck and to Jim, and was thinking of going to her room, when she heard the telephone ring in the drawing-room. John, she thought. It was her husband; a moment later Charles, the footman, appeared to ask her to come to the telephone. Susan thought that it was fortuitous that she had come into the hall just then (it was twenty minutes to eleven). She heard John's voice telling her that he had just reached Euston; that he hoped to get a train from King's Cross, but that he reckoned that he could not possibly arrive at Langley House before midnight. "I don't know, but I should think I'll probably get there some time between twelve and one," he said.

After that Susan went upstairs to her room, unpacked a few things from her knapsack, and began slowly to go to bed, telling herself that she must manage to stay awake to welcome her husband when he should arrive. I feel wide awake now anyhow, she thought, so I'll read for a while. Her watch showed her that it was only five past eleven so she thought that she would read until nearly midnight and then listen to the radio to keep herself awake. She read the novel which she had brought with her for a while, at first following the story keenly, but presently finding that her eyes seemed to be tired of reading, that the book seemed to be feeling almost too heavy for her hands to continue to hold it open, and realising at the same time that she was hardly following in her mind any longer what she was trying to read. She was becoming very sleepy; nevertheless she tried to continue to read the story. Suddenly she realised with a start that the book had dropped clean out of her hands without her knowing it. This won't do, she said to herself. I must have dozed off. She got out of bed and, without putting anything over her nightdress, walked barefoot across the room to the window (the room, which faced north-west, had had the sun on it for most of the evening and was still very warm). She drew back one curtain a little and looked out into the darkness of the warm summer night. It's six minutes to midnight, she said to herself. John'll be here soon. Susan put her head out of the open window and looked around, but could see nothing at all except some lights in the upper windows of the houses of Old Knebworth village, a quarter of a mile away; there was no moon, which seemed to make the night very dark. Then she remembered that it would be no use looking out there in the hope of seeing the headlights of a taxi bringing John from the station because the drive came up to the other side of the house, the front side which faced the ornamental lake. After half a minute or so of standing there with her head and shoulders exposed to the fresh air (which now felt pleasantly cool) she drew herself back into the room, allowed the curtain to fall back into place, and returned to bed. Her Great Aunt had thoughtfully placed a battery radio set on the bedside table in that spare room so that the Dalmanes could listen to it, so now Susan switched it on, being sure that she was keeping the volume well turned down so that no one else in the house would be disturbed by it. I'll listen to the news, she said to herself. She checked her watch by the time signal at midnight and then switched off the bedside light while she lay down comfortably in the double bed and listened to a man who was reading the midnight news bulletin on the radio. The news ended and a programme of music followed it, but Susan did not feel at all inclined to reach out her arm to switch off the transistor set. She lay very comfortably on her back in the dark and listened to some soothing music for five minutes . . . for ten minutes . . .

Susan woke with more of a start than she had woken the previous time, when the book had dropped out of her hands. She sat up in bed straight away. Reminded by a faint hissing noise from the radio set that it was still switched on, although transmission had ceased on the station to which the set was tuned, Susan switched on the pocket electric torch which she had brought with her and by its light hurriedly switched off the radio, wondering how long she had been wasting the battery. She flashed the torch onto her wrist-watch. Ten minutes to one. Thank goodness she had not slept for any longer, but perhaps John had already arrived at the house. She sat perfectly still for a minute or two while she listened very carefully for any sounds of people moving about the house, but all was quiet. Suddenly, however, for a second or two she saw light behind the curtains of her window. Was that the sound of a car pulling up by the front door round the other side of the house? She thought she had caught the sound of gravel scrunching under wheels, but could not be sure: if a motor car <u>had</u> just arrived its engine was certainly being driven very quietly. Susan remained sitting up in bed in the dark, her torch switched off, and listening. That must have been John arriving, she thought. That light I saw must have been the headlights of a taxi bringing him here, just as it turned off the road into the drive—yes, that's a car driving away now. Again that slight sound of wheels on gravel came momentarily to her ears, and for a fraction of a second just a glimmer of light seemed to fall on the window. Then again darkness and absolute silence. Susan listened. A minute passed, perhaps longer, and still she heard nothing. Was that John arriving, or wasn't it? she wondered. He must be in the house by now if it's him. I didn't hear the doorbell, of course, but Aunt Alice <u>said</u> the butler would let him in when he rang the bell. But what if James is asleep and hasn't heard the bell? What if . . . ? Suddenly the silence was broken when Susan realised that she could hear people coming quietly up the stairs; and she saw that a light had been switched on in the passage outside her door. The next moment she heard the butler's voice speaking in a hushed tone in the corridor, just outside the door: "That's her Ladyship, Susan's door, the first on the left of this corridor. Go in there, my Lord." Susan hurriedly switched on the bedside light.

The door opened and there at last was John Dalmane.

"John, darling, how lovely that you've got here at last," said Susan with great relief at seeing her husband again.

"Sue, my love!" said Lord Dalmane as he came straight over to the bed and kissed her. "Yes, my darling, here I am at last. I'd have been here sooner if only I hadn't had to wait so long for a taxi. I got to Knebworth station at twelve-fifteen and rang for a taxi, but I had to wait about half an hour before it turned up. The driver said that he had to come out from somewhere . . . Stevenage or Hitchin, I think, because of it being so late. But the main thing is that I've found you here, and now we're together again."

CHAPTER SEVENTEEN

The morning of the first of July (Wednesday) dawned fine but not altogether bright as there was high cloud across the sky. Jim Sandy woke soon after five and, feeling a little restless, went to the curtains, drew one aside, and looked out of the window. There before him on that side of the house lay the main lawn going down to the lake, grayish in the early morning light. Immediately in front of his window was the gravel of the drive, but further over to the right was part of the area of rough grass where they had sat on deck chairs in the late evening twilight. He looked up at the sky; he could see many patches of pale blue sky which showed through here and there in gaps in the general cover of thin white cirro-cumulus cloud. Jim could see that the grass of the lawn was wet with dew and this, together with the thinness and patchiness of the cloud, lead him to believe that there was a good chance that it was going to turn out another pleasant day with plenty of sunshine. Then he chuckled to himself as he remembered his happy situation. Yesterday he had woken up as usual in his bedroom in the house in Lorton Road, Cockermouth, where he lived with his father and his twin sisters, Carol and Victoria. Yesterday he had gone to work as usual, setting off at half past eight for the Police Station. Yesterday he had started his day's work with a very dull job at that card index until the Sergeant had told him to come with him in the car; but then had come that arrest of Lord Dalmane which had given him the chance he wanted to put into operation his wild plan to run away from the job at Cockermouth. And now today that plan had worked so well that it did not seem to have been a wild and silly idea after all: here he was hundreds of miles away from Cockermouth, and under the same roof as the gorgeous Lady Susan Dalmane. What, oh what, a stroke of luck it had been to meet her at the beginning of yesterday's travels! How fantastic she is! he said to himself. Oh, those dreamy, dark eyes—they haunt me, they fascinate me! Really I can't quite believe that I've been so incredibly lucky—beyond my wildest dreams of what running away might lead to. A job for me in Rhodes Castle, where Susan lives, and a living-in job too, at that! It's fantastic! Incredible! Amazing!

In a little while, beginning to feel cold, he climbed back into bed (he had been standing at the open window in only the pyjamas which he had been lent by Mr. Beck, who luckily had some spare clothes with him in his suitcase). Before leaving the window Jim re-pulled the curtain across it, although it was now broad daylight. He told himself that he ought to go to sleep again, but he soon found that he could sleep no more. There were too many exciting things to think about for sleep to have much of a further chance now that he was well rested, so presently he gave up the idea of trying to get back to sleep. He had a great deal to think over but his thoughts kept coming back especially to one important question: What is going to happen today? He had been told that breakfast would be between eight and nine o'clock in the dining-room, so he planned to get up in order to come in at about five minutes past eight; but it was about what might happen <u>after</u> that which kept him wondering. Susan had told him that she and her husband meant to stay on there with her Great Aunt Alice until Saturday, and only then to go home to Rhodes Castle. <u>That</u> would be all right, but Jim wondered what they would do about him in the meantime; presumably he would hardly be welcome to continue to stay at Langley House for a further three days and three nights. I'll probably have to go to stay with mum in Ealing until Saturday, he thought. Well, it doesn't matter. The great thing is that I've got this splendid job at Rhodes Castle. Then he remembered Lord Dalmane. I suppose he's turned up here during the night, he thought. That may mean that I'll have to talk to him, perhaps this morning. But Susan <u>did</u> say that she didn't think that he'd object to me working and living at Rhodes Castle. So, if he agrees to me coming, I shall—and it'll be fun, great fun, whatever the work may be like!

In their bedroom the Dalmanes were also awake long before they were ready to get up, exchanging stories of the previous day's adventures. Susan said that there was little to tell about her day of travelling and asked her husband for a full account of how his day had gone. So John Dalmane began at the beginning of the tale by telling of his walk along the railway line and of his arrest and questioning at the Police Station. He told of how quickly it had become apparent to the police that they had made a serious mistake in arresting him, and of how apologetic and kind to him they had been thereafter. He told Susan about his lift to Carlisle Station in the Sergeant's car and his journey up to London on the evening train, the misleadingly named "Mid-Day Scot". Susan then told him that Mr. Beck, having walked back to the station from the scene of John's arrest, had travelled, as he had planned to do, with his wife and herself first to Carlisle on the local train, and then on to London in the "Royal Scot". She told John that Mr. and Mrs. Beck were at the moment under the same roof with them, because Mr. Beck's aunt at Knebworth had turned out to be away from home; and that by the time the Becks had discovered this it had been too late in the day to go on to Mr. Beck's parents at Tolmers Hall. "They're going on there this morning, I believe," she said. She had as yet told her husband nothing at all about Jim Sandy, although she felt that it was now time for her to mention how it was that she had brought him with her away from Cockermouth; however, she now felt a strange reluctance, almost a shyness, to the thought of confessing to her husband that she had, without waiting to consult him, offered Jim the job of Guide of Rhodes Castle. But I <u>must</u> tell him about it now, and tell him that Jim's here, she thought. But there were a few minutes of silence in that bedroom while Susan thought about the best way to introduce the subject of Jim Sandy and the Guide job.

"John," she said presently.

"Yes, my dear?"

"Do you remember, there's that vacancy we have at home for someone to be our Guide and a junior security assistant?"

"Yes, my love, we do have such a position vacant. But what about it?" Lord Dalmane was slightly mystified by the change of subject.

"Why, yesterday I found the very person to fill that vacancy," said Susan. "So, having interviewed him informally, I told him I'd given him the job, including living-in at Rhodes Castle."

"Really? You found this person <u>yesterday</u>, my dear? But when did you manage that? I thought you'd spent most of the day after I'd left you travelling on various trains to get here. Or do you mean that you've found someone suitable for the job here in Knebworth? Or on the train?"

"No, John, I found him in Cockermouth. In fact he's that police cadet who was with Mr. Beck. You remember that when they arrested you there was a police cadet there who didn't go back to the police station, but instead walked back along the line with Mr. Beck to the railway station? Do you remember him, John?"

"Yes, Sue, I remember that there was a police cadet there although I didn't know that he'd gone to the railway station. But surely, my dear, you can't have offered <u>him</u> our job? I mean, he's got a job already, hasn't he?"

"No, he hasn't," said Susan. "He told me that he'd left the police and that he was looking for a job, so I thought that it would be all right to offer him the Guide job. His name's James Sandy, but people always call him just 'Jim', and he came on the train with us to Carlisle and then, as he was travelling south too, he was in the train to London with us as well."

"Well!" said Lord Dalmane in some astonishment. "That police cadet from Cockermouth, eh? But did you say that he'd <u>left</u> the police force?"

"Well, actually, John, he told me that he'd run away from the police in Cockermouth because he didn't like the work. And he said he was intending to go up to London to look for a new job: that's what he told me."

"He was running away from his job!" Lord Dalmane sounded very shocked. "And yet you offered him a job?"

"Yes, John, dear," said Susan quietly and resolutely. "You see, he <u>needed</u> me to help him, and so I did."

There was a short silence while Lord Dalmane thought over the startling news which his wife was divulging to him.

"Sue, my love," he said presently, "if you've taken on this lad, Jim Sandy, as a servant, what have you done with him? Where is he now?"

"Here," said Susan, smiling because the story was taking shape only gradually, keeping an element of suspense going.

"Here? You mean, he's lodging somewhere in Knebworth?"

"He's staying <u>here</u>, in this house," said Susan (Lord Dalmane gasped in surprise where he was lying on the other side of the bed). "Right now he's in that room just on the other side of the passage from our door! Well, darling, having engaged him for that job I just couldn't leave him to wander about on his own, could I?"

"Well, maybe you couldn't; but it staggers me all the same to think of that lad turning up here under the same roof as us! How old is he?"

"Eighteen."

"But he's run away from them," objected Lord Dalmane. "I don't care for that part of the story too much. Suggests irresponsibility to me."

"Oh no, John, he's not like that at all. I'm sure he's a most responsible lad. You wait till you meet him."

"Well, I hope you think his character is all right," said John, "if we're going to employ him. It's most important to be sure, you know, that a prospective employee is honest, reliable, a hard worker, and generally of good character. Do you think, my dear, that you've sounded him on all these points?"

"John, dear, I really think that you needn't worry about those things: yes, I've sounded Jim Sandy for good character carefully. I've talked to him enough, I think, to find out what he is really like, and you'll find he'll be a hard, conscientious worker <u>and</u> an honest one. Just you wait and see." Susan was anxious to justify herself before her husband over the hasty appointment of Jim Sandy to her staff—from motives on her part which were not, in truth, based very much on an assessment of good character, if John Dalmane could have known the true facts. Mercifully John doesn't know, and isn't going to know, that I've got something of an infatuation, almost, for that boy, and that he's got a whacking great infatuation for me! she thought.

"All right, my dear," said Lord Dalmane. "I take your point that you're happy about this lad's character; and so I shall, as you say, 'wait and see'. But I still feel a little uneasy about a job at Rhodes Castle being given to someone who has <u>run away</u>: run away from his former job and, presumably, from home. He may not settle down well with us, so far from his home. Don't you think, Sue, that presently he might want to run away from <u>us</u> to go back to his parents in Cockermouth?"

"No, I definitely don't think so, John," said Susan. "For one thing, he comes from a family with only one parent at home, his father, his mother having run off with another man to go and live together somewhere else. For another—"

"But, good heavens!" interrupted Lord Dalmane, "That's another member of this family who's run away from home! Does this tendency 'run in the family', as you might say?"

"John, dear, don't make silly jokes about it," said Susan, smiling; but her husband only laughed.

"Sorry, Sue, but I couldn't resist making that pun."

"Oh, very well! Now where was I? Oh, yes: you said that he might want to run away from us to go home, but I was telling you that he has no mother at home, only his father. Now, he's told me, plainly enough, that he doesn't fancy the idea of going to live with his mother, and I think he's quite right about that. True, he was indeed aiming to go there before I suggested that he should come to Rhodes Castle but, you see, he was only thinking of using his mother's house, which is in Ealing, in West London, as a temporary lodging place. Now, though, if he comes to us, he's not likely to want to run away there."

"Yes, that's probably true."

"Nor is he likely to want to run back to his father in Cockermouth," continued Susan, "because I firmly believe that he'll enjoy living-in at Rhodes Castle and working for us. And he's a lad who has ambition, and he's intelligent too. As Guide he could be in charge of people almost straight away—when he's learnt the basics of the job, which he'll learn quickly—and as an assistant to Major Ambrose in security matters he might well want to stay on and seek promotion presently to being in charge of security altogether: Ambrose will probably retire fairly soon, as you know." (Major Ambrose was Lord Dalmane's Estate Agent and Security Officer).

There was a little pause.

"Yes, my dear, there's certainly something in all that," said Lord Dalmane, after he had thought over what Susan had said.

"I think we'd be hard put to it to find a more suitable person for the job," said Susan. "Only think, John, he's had basic police training which should make him ideally suitable for dealing with people when we've got the grounds open to the public."

"Yes, I know; I should think that with that groundwork of police training that we assume he's had, he <u>should</u> be an ideal person for the job. But I must talk to him first, my dear, before we finally decide on anything."

Susan agreed that if there was time, depending on their plans for that day (although they had not yet made any definite plans), John should have a talk to Jim Sandy that very morning after breakfast so that they might be able to reach an agreed decision on whether to give him the job. However, Susan smiled happily, thinking that the matter of Jim's appointment to their staff was already as good as confirmed; she was confident that Jim would be able to manage an informal interview with her husband convincingly. There was silence now in that bedroom for quite a long while, nearly half an hour, as each pursued their own thoughts. Towards half past six John Dalmane had all but dropped off to sleep again, but Susan thought of a new and urgent problem in connection with Jim. She had been lying, thinking of nothing in particular for several minutes, while she looked hopefully at a patch of blue sky which she could see between the curtains (which they had left not quite pulled together), when she suddenly thought: What's to be done about Jim <u>today</u>? He can't stay here any more.

"John," she said quietly.

No answer.

"John! Are you awake?" A little louder this time.

Lord Dalmane suddenly moved in the bed as if rolling over onto his back, having been lying on his side, his head pressed into the pillows.

"Yes, dear?" he said sleepily.

"John, what are we going to do today?"

"Oh . . . well, perhaps we might go somewhere nice today—somewhere fairly near here, of course . . . and just the two of us."

"By car?"

"H'm . . . yes, we could hire a car, couldn't we, Sue, until Saturday morning. Unless . . ."

"Unless we go by train again?" said Susan. "I'll tell you what I was thinking, though, John. If we can hire a car here today, why shouldn't we motor to Soken Hall and call on my parents? I remember now that I told mother that we might do that at the end of the holiday, after Knebworth, and she said: 'Do come and see us if you've got time to'."

"I say, that's a good idea, Sue," said John. "Let's go there. It can't be too far to drive to Walton from here—if we can hire a car—and perhaps we could borrow a map from your aunt. I should think that we could get to Soken Hall by about lunch time if we were to start about ten, and then this afternoon we could go and look at boats at Walton Yacht Club and perhaps get afloat on the Backwaters ourselves. We'll have to leave Jim Sandy behind, of course, so that we can go just by ourselves. He can find somewhere else to stay, I suppose, until Saturday, so I should think there should be no problem there."

Susan, however, disagreed with this simple idea of John's and said that she thought that there <u>was</u> a problem over what they should do about Jim Sandy, although she agreed with the rest of his plan (Soken Hall was the home and seat of Susan's father, the Marquis of Walton; it was close to the village of Kirby-le-Soken, near Walton-on-the-Naze). Now that she was re-united with John, Susan did not want them to have to take Jim with them on a visit to her parents' home. On the other hand, she could not think of simply abandoning her new servant by putting him into a hotel or a guest house for the next three days, even if she were to pay the hotel bills herself. In the absence of the boy's mother she felt more than ever responsible for looking after him as a deputy mother: in her opinion he was quite young enough to need such motherly care and protection. So she and John discussed various possible plans. The best way out of the difficulty, they both thought, would be if the Becks were to take young Sandy off their hands until they returned to pick him up on that Saturday morning, but Susan was very doubtful of what that moody and depressed Mrs. Beck would say to such an idea. Susan thought that it really ought to be mainly Mr. Beck's decision whether or not Jim Sandy could go with them because it was to <u>his</u> parents' house that they would be heading. And, of course, they might well want to consult with the senior Becks before they committed themselves to taking Jim Sandy along as an extra guest. But if the Becks did not want to have any part in looking after Jim (which seemed likely enough, thought Susan) the most obvious alternative was to send him to his mother's address in London. Or they could cut their holiday short—After all, thought Susan, We've already finished the best part of it—and return home with Jim immediately ("if I like him after I've talked to him," said Lord Dalmane). Then Lord Dalmane suggested that if they adopted this last alternative they could leave Jim Sandy at Rhodes Castle while he and Susan went to Essex to stay a night at Soken Hall, but Susan would not hear of this.

"No," she said, "it would be cruel just to abandon him like that before he knows his way around Rhodes Castle while we go off and enjoy ourselves; and anyway it would be wasteful because that way <u>we'd</u> have to travel ever so much further—we must be much nearer Walton here than we are at home."

Susan and John argued gently over the various alternative plans for a while, but in the end they only decided to mention the problem to Mr. and Mrs. Beck to find out whether they would be willing to help. Time went slowly on, but Susan, who now felt wide awake, forced herself to remain lying quietly in bed until it was half past seven; then she prodded her husband (who had fallen asleep again) and stepped out of bed.

"It looks as if it's going to be another nice day," she said as she stood looking out of the window, having pulled back the curtains. The morning sunshine had by now broken through the thin covering of high cloud, and it was beginning to feel pleasantly warm.

★

Breakfast was a formal meal in the dining-room with their hostess, Lady Knebworth present at the table; and Mrs. Beck was also there with her husband. Susan was pleased to notice that Mrs. Beck seemed to have quite recovered from her illness of the previous evening and that now she was surprisingly cheerful. Mrs. Beck told Lady Knebworth that she and her husband were leaving shortly after breakfast to travel on by bus to Tolmers; she apologised profusely for the trouble she had caused by feeling ill on her arrival, and thanked Lady Knebworth for her kindness and hospitality.

Susan decided to settle the question of where and how Jim Sandy was to spend his time until they were ready to take him home.

"We're going on somewhere else today, John and I," she said to Jim. "But what about you? What would you like to do today?"

"I'll do whatever you suggest, Lady Dalmane," he answered with deliberate politeness after a moment's hesitation. His heart had sunk on hearing that Susan and John Dalmane were going off somewhere else. He knew that in that company he could not say that he would like to be allowed to remain with Susan; and anyway it was clear to him from what she had said that she no longer wanted his company—until, presumably, she should be going home with Lord Dalmane on the Saturday of that week. But Susan was pleased with his answer and succeeded in that moment in catching Mrs. Beck's eye, hoping that she would understand the hint and respond to it favourably.

"Why not let Jim come with us?" said Mrs. Beck. "Don't you think, Nigel, that it would be quite all right for him to come with us to stay with your old parents at Tolmers?" Susan looked very relieved at hearing this invitation made. How splendid that she's understood my hint so well, she thought.

"Quite all right, I'm sure," said Mr. Beck, "and we'd be delighted to have you, Jim. We folk from Cockermouth ought to stick together in these unfamiliar parts."

"I quite understand, Lady Dalmane, that you would rather not have anyone else with you and your husband while you enjoy what remains of your holiday," said Mrs. Beck. My word, thought Susan, she's a very different woman from the grumpy and depressed Mrs. Beck of yesterday!

"I think perhaps it would be better that way," she said thoughtfully, as if the idea were new to her.

"So what do you think about it, Jim?" asked Mrs. Beck.

"Oh, I'd love to come with you," said Jim. "Thank you very much." He said this cheerfully enough, managing to hide his real feeling of distress at the parting from Susan, so soon to be made. Oh well, it's only for a few days, he reminded himself.

Lord Dalmane was already thinking that his wife's choice of the ex-police cadet from Cockermouth was going to turn out a happy one for the job at Rhodes Castle. He was not saying much as he sat at the breakfast table because he was waiting for an opportunity to have a few words with Jim Sandy without his wife being present; and at the end of breakfast, when Susan rose from her chair and left the room after their hostess, he saw that such an opportunity had arisen. He was quickly impressed by Jim's mental alertness and obvious intelligence as shown in the way in which he answered his questions with apparent ease. Lord Dalmane wanted to know, of course, why the youth had decided to run away from the police, and Jim told him quite frankly and truthfully that he had found the high level of discipline in the force irksome, and that he preferred work in which he was more his own master. "In that way, sir, I think I'll be very happy to be your Guide at Rhodes Castle," he said, "because I'll be more or less in charge of myself, I suppose, as well as being in charge of the visitors, of course."

"Yes, you're quite right there," said Lord Dalmane. "I see that my wife has explained it all to you quite thoroughly. Yes, you will be for much of the time your own boss at work when you're being the Guide. You'll be working under Major Ambrose's instructions, as I think you already understand, but he'll only give you general guidance. You're going to be our only Guide, you see, at least at first—perhaps later we'll have to appoint a second Assistant Guide as well if we decide to open the Castle itself to the public—only the gardens are open at present. But, you see, Ambrose will mostly be working as my Estate Agent, so you'll largely have to look after yourself."

I think he'll manage the job splendidly, thought Lord Dalmane. It was a stroke of inspiration on Sue's part to think of this lad as our Guide.

Not long after that, the Becks, and Jim Sandy with them, left the house having said their Good-byes and Thank-yous to Lady Knebworth. As they came out of the porch to walk back through the garden to the door in the wall, Mr. Beck was carrying his suitcase while Mrs. Beck and Jim carried nothing. The Dalmanes, who had nothing in particular to do just then, said that they would walk with them as far as the door in the wall. Mr. Beck, as he walked, was doing his best to look nostalgically over his former scout-camping site for the last time.

"Right, Mrs. Beck," said Susan, "we'll see you next on this Saturday morning early to pick up Jim on our way home."

"About how early?" asked Mrs. Beck.

"Oh, we'd better say between nine and ten. That should give us plenty of time to get to London, to call at Mrs. Sandy's house for

Jim's belongings, and still be in time for the three o'clock train from Waterloo. We'll give you a ring at Tolmers if there's any change of plan, as you've given us the number." Susan had only known Mr. and Mrs. Beck for about twenty-four hours, but she had a strong sense of saying Good-bye to long-standing friends, rather than to new acquaintances. Certainly a day of travelling with the Becks followed by spending a night with them had left a strong bond of friendship between the two families, a friendship which completely transcended the class barrier between them.

The path to the door in the wall, having lead them through the more open parts of the wood, ended by plunging through a dense, shady screen of closely packed trees, shrubs, and undergrowth, which hid the door from the garden. Leafy branches were all around them, crossing over their heads, and throwing their crossing and re-crossing shadows on the ground. The light in that shrubbery was greenish and one could not see very far.

Susan kissed Mrs. Beck and shook hands with Mr. Beck, and young Sandy felt his heart pounding very fast as he waited for his turn. Would it be a kiss for him, or would it not? Susan turned to him, a radiant smile on her pretty face.

"Good-bye, Jim, but not for long!" she said. "Mrs. Beck will look after you well, I'm sure, so be good, my love, and I'll see you Saturday morning. Good-bye!" She squeezed his right hand between both of hers and planted a kiss on his right cheek. Oh, the bliss of it! Jim felt such a burning infatuation rise up within him that any sadness at the thought of the imminent parting was swallowed up by it.

"Good-bye, Susan," he said, smiling broadly. Then he shook hands with Lord Dalmane, who had slightly raised his eyebrows, as if in mild surprise at the kiss.

"Good-bye, young man, until we meet again," said Lord Dalmane. Jim passed through the door after Mrs. Beck; then, for a moment, he turned round once more to wave a hand to Susan, his face beaming with pleasure. It won't be long until we meet again, he thought. He closed the door behind him, and she was gone from his sight. Then he walked down the lane with Mr. and Mrs. Beck and out onto the road, happy enough on that bright and cheerful morning as they made their way down to the bus stop in the new village (Mr. Beck had said that it would be better to make this journey by bus as it was a more direct route than by railway).

The Dalmanes remained standing where they were for a moment after the door had been closed before they began strolling back to the house.

"Do you know, my dear, that I fancy that that lad has a crush on you?" said Lord Dalmane casually. "I thought I could detect a certain infatuation in his expression when you kissed him."

"Oh rot!" said Susan. "I'm sure he can't be feeling infatuated with me. He just—he's just feeling happy, that's all."

Is it? wondered Lord Dalmane. He knew very well that he <u>had</u> just seen a look of great infatuation in that youth's eyes, but he wisely decided to say no more about it. But Sue <u>is</u> a very lovely lady, he said to himself. I can't really be surprised if he has a crush on her.

CHAPTER EIGHTEEN

About an hour after the Becks and Jim Sandy had left Langley House Lord and Lady Dalmane drove off from Knebworth in a hired car. Still thinking of their recently finished cruise in the <u>Osprey</u> in Northern waters, the idea of going to the Essex coast had greatly pleased both of them, particularly John; and so, having borrowed a road map from Lady Knebworth, they had set off in a car hired from the garage in the village, bound for Soken Hall. They had made one change to their plans before starting: Susan had told her Great Aunt that they were going to stay two nights (Wednesday and Thursday) at Soken Hall with her parents; she had just confirmed the arrangements by talking to her mother on the telephone.

They arrived at Soken Hall, as planned, in time for lunch, having taken turns at driving the car. It was not the first time that John had met his parents-in-law, or seen their home; he had been taken there by Susan shortly before their wedding to stay for a few days with the Marquis and Marchioness of Walton, so now, as Susan drove the car up the main drive to the front of the large house with its conspicuous glass conservatory, he was not feeling shy, nor did the place seem strange to him. On the contrary, John almost preferred Lord Walton's seat to his own Rhodes Castle. Soken Hall had an expansive view to the north, a marvellous prospect of tidal waters and low-lying islands. From the first-floor windows of the front of the house one could look out to the trees and green fields of Horsey Island, some two miles away, separated from the mainland by the winding channel of Kirby Creek, a narrow-looking ribbon of water or mud, depending on the tide. One could also see from those windows Skipper Island, further over to the left, but the wider channel of Hamford Water, which lay behind the islands to the north, was hard to distinguish by eye without the help of binoculars. The house was built on the top of a slight rise and thus commanded this wide panorama to the north, but in the foreground, nestling at the foot of the hill, lay the village of Kirby-le-Soken, stretched out along the road which lead to Walton. As John shook hands with Lady Walton upon their arrival at the house he was already looking forward to being shown to the big spare bedroom he and Susan had occupied on their last visit there— hopefully they would have that same room again—so that he could enjoy again that view of the creek and the islands.

Later that afternoon John and Susan took their hired car into the town. Susan was driving as she said she knew the way, more or less, to the Yacht Club. She turned left off the busy High Street—there were plenty of pedestrians about in Walton on that fine summer afternoon—and drove the car down the narrow cut of Mill Lane (which leads down to the water at the head of Walton Channel), and parked it on some waste ground. The tide was out and close at hand scores of small boats were lying on their sides on the mud.

"Well," said Susan, "we <u>have</u> come the wrong way after all for the Yacht Club—it's a long time since I was last here—but we can easily walk there. It's barely a quarter of a mile further down the Channel."

"Of course," said John. "Anyway, it's delightful just being here. Doesn't it make you feel, my dear, that our sailing holiday is not quite over yet—seeing all these boats, and smelling the bracing tang of salt water in the air?" Susan nodded her head in agreement.

"I'll tell you what, Sue," continued John, "we could do some more sailing ourselves tomorrow morning on the high tide if we could borrow the Soken Hall dinghy."

Susan agreed with this idea, so the next morning, after a reasonably early breakfast, she and John drove with Lord Walton down to his boathouse on Kirby Creek to borrow his sailing dinghy. Lord Walton drove his car through the village and down Quay Lane; his boathouse was at the end of the lane where there was an old barge quay, a house, and a black, thatched cottage. As they went, the Marquis and the Earl were chatting together, not of business in the House of Lords, but of boats. Lord Walton, a small, dark-haired man with a rather sunburnt face, was a retired Admiral in the Royal Navy. He looked much younger than his sixty years and was still a great sailor of small boats, but nowadays he was not much involved in politics, and was seldom seen in the Lords except on ceremonial occasions (unlike Lord Dalmane who spent much of his time there). But Lord Walton did not join Susan and John in the dinghy that morning. There was only just sufficient depth of water at the quayside to float the little boat: the flood tide still had about another hour to make until it would be high water. John and Susan hoped to sail right round Horsey Island and return to the boathouse before the water disappeared from the creek on the ebbing tide. This meant a long, hard pull on the oars at the start, down the winding creek, going between Skipper and Horsey Islands to gain Hamford Water. They took turns at rowing the boat over the incoming tide, but once they had rounded the north-western point of Horsey Island they were able to put up the sail and blow down Hamford Water against the tide on the fresh westerly breeze. They rounded the buoy marking the mouth of Walton Channel off the north-eastern point of the island, and from that point had the tide with them up to the watershed of the road over the Wade from the mainland to the island (this road to the farm on Horsey Island is a causeway at low tide over the mud of the Wade). The westerly wind made it possible to reach up the Walton Channel on the starboard tack without tacking, but when the wind headed them as they rounded the corner at the entrance to the Wade Susan, at a word from John, lowered the sail while John took out the oars and began to row; the Channel was too narrow to tack against the wind. The tide turned against them before they came to the crossing of the Wade Causeway so John, suddenly afraid that the quickly ebbing tide might leave their little boat stuck on the soft mud, began to row as hard as he could. But now all went well, and presently they were rowing up the creek from where they had set off, to return to Lord Walton's boathouse.

Susan was enjoying herself so much as she sat in the stern of the borrowed dinghy with John, handling the sheet and the tiller (the little boat had only a single lugsail), or taking her turn at the oars, that she had never a thought in her head for her new Guide. She had been thinking of Jim Sandy and missing him when they had left Knebworth, but she had soon forgotten about him. When the time came on Friday to return to Knebworth, after lunch at Soken Hall, both Susan and John were very reluctant to depart, so much had they enjoyed their small boating holiday on the Walton Backwaters.

That evening, back once again at Langley House, Susan began planning and writing a letter about Mr. Ruddock to the Committee Chairman whom he had mentioned, remembering that she had given him her promise that she would make efforts by writing letters to have him re-instated as a train driver.

Meanwhile at Tolmers Mrs. Beck had been doing her best to fill Susan's place temporarily as a deputy mother for Jim Sandy. They had reached Mr. Beck's parents' house on Wednesday before lunch time. Jim knew that his mood of happiness was waning all the time now that he was no longer with Susan, but he nevertheless remained cheerful during the bus journey to Tolmers, while he was amusing himself by doing some mental arithmetic. He was calculating the number of hours which would have to pass until ten a.m. came on Saturday morning, by which time, if things went according to plan, he would be back with Susan.

Jim found that most of his stay at Tolmers Hall, the big old house where the elder Mr. and Mrs. Beck lived, was a very boring time; nevertheless he was not unhappy staying there. He thought that the country around Tolmers was at least as attractive as he had found it around Knebworth, but he found it hard to believe that it was significantly nearer to the outer suburbs of London. However, it seemed to be as rural a neighbourhood as anyone could wish for. Certainly what Mr. Beck had said about Tolmers not really being a place at all turned out to be true. The big house, Tolmers Hall, had a drive which opened out onto the small country road from Newgate Street to Northaw, but that was all that Tolmers consisted of, apart from another house on the other side of the road.

On the morning of the next day Nigel and Norma Beck took Jim shopping with them in Hertford, when they also found time to go and look at the house in Bengeo where Mr. Beck had been born and had lived as a child. But Jim was only half-interested in most of the things he was shown, while he was busily counting hours in his head and longing to be with Susan again.

The Dalmanes arrived at Tolmers Hall soon after breakfast on the Saturday morning, having come there by taxi from Knebworth. Jim gathered that it was only about a mile to the nearest railway station at Cuffley, that they were going to walk there, and that the Becks intended to walk with them. They arrived at Cuffley station to find that they had missed a London train by a few minutes, but that the next one went in a quarter of an hour at 11.1 a.m. Here, outside the booking office, before going with John and Susan Dalmane onto the platform, Jim said Good-bye to Mrs. Beck and thanked her for looking after him. He was rather saddened at having to part company with Mr. and Mrs. Beck who had, after all, been near neighbours in Cockermouth for many years; but, of course, the main thing for Jim was that he was with Susan again, and had no more hours to count in his head. Before the Dalmanes and the Becks went their separate ways, Susan invited Mrs. Beck to come with her husband sometime to Rhodes Castle. The Becks were going to walk back to Tolmers Hall without waiting to see Lord and Lady Dalmane and Jim onto the train, when it should arrive; and they were going to stay at Tolmers for an indefinite time while searching for somewhere to live in the South. They were both delighted and very flattered to accept Susan's invitation, although nothing definite was arranged there at the station. Then Mrs. Beck, not to be outdone in hospitality, boldly suggested that she and her husband would be very pleased to receive a visit any time at Tolmers from the Earl and Countess of Saint Helens.

"John and I would love to," said Susan. "Yes, we shall certainly pay you a visit here presently." The nicest thing about it, she thought, is that Mrs. Beck seems to be so much better and more cheerful now. She must have wanted very badly to get away from the North.

The stopping train brought John and Susan Dalmane and Jim Sandy into London before mid-day. Lord Dalmane left his wife and Jim on the platform at King's Cross station; they were going to visit Mrs. Sandy at her home in Ealing, but he was intending to press on and take an earlier train home from Waterloo.

★

"Jim! Well, fancy seeing you! And what brings you here, my love?" said Mrs. Sandy.

"I've come to see about my luggage, mum," said Jim. "You know: what I sent to this address. Has it arrived here?"

"That trunk of yours? It's been here since Monday. You've come to take it away, I suppose?"

"Well, not today, mum, because I'm travelling by train; but I could take it away tomorrow when we come in the car."

"Car? What car?" said Mrs. Sandy. "And who's 'we'?"

"That's me and Lady Dalmane, the Countess of Saint Helens," explained Jim. "She'll bring me here in her car tomorrow, she says. She's the lady I'm going to work for, and she lives at Rhodes Castle with Lord Dalmane. It's somewhere in Dorset. I'm going to live there with them."

"What!" Mrs. Sandy's face looked as startled as her voice sounded.

Jim had been talking to his mother in the hall of her house while Susan remained waiting for him just outside the front door, knowing that he would manage this business best without her being there. When Lord Dalmane had left them at King's Cross, taking a taxi to Waterloo, Susan and Jim had travelled by Underground to Liverpool Street in the City, come up to the surface, and had a quick early lunch snack at a restaurant Susan knew of, a place where she had eaten before on occasions when she had been travelling by train from London down to Essex to her parents' home. The City of London was fairly quiet by that time on a Saturday afternoon (at around a quarter past twelve), but Jim was nevertheless impressed by the busy look of the place, as he looked out through a window at the pavement and a broad main street while he ate. Soon they were travelling again, this time by a Central Line tube train to Ealing Broadway station. As they descended to the Central Line platforms at Liverpool Street station, Susan said that she thought that John would be able to get a train back to Sherborne at one o'clock (which he did), whereas they would aim for the three o'clock departure. Near the station at Ealing they found a bookshop where Susan went in and bought a street map; then, armed with this map, they set off walking to try to find Number Ninety-Six, Lakeland Avenue, W5, Mrs. Sandy's address in Ealing. They found the road—a typically dreary road in that part of suburbia—without much difficulty;

and having struck it at the corner where Number Two was, they had a fairly long walk from there along the even-number side of the street; but when they came to Number Ninety-Six they had been walking for no more than twenty minutes since leaving the Underground station.

It was lucky for Jim that he found his mother in at Number Ninety-Six, Lakeland Avenue; but she had a shopping basket in her hand as Jim came in, and looked as if she were in a hurry to go out. Mrs. Sandy was a large, powerful-looking woman in her mid-fifties, by origin a Cockney. Her black hair, now beginning to fade to a shade of grey, was swept up into a bun, making her appear even taller than she already was. Like Mrs. Beck, she had fled from the northern town of Cockermouth partly out of a desire to return home. Although she was startled when her son broke the news to her of his new job—something about working for some Countess at Rhodes Castle, she gathered—she did not appear to be much interested.

"Well, fancy that!" she said. "I thought you were still in the police at Cockermouth, although I wondered what the devil you were up to when all these things of yours arrived here. But I can't stop now, Jim; I've got to hurry out to the shops, and be back to start cooking the evening meal before my Tom comes home at five o'clock. You said you'd be coming with a car tomorrow to pick up your things, didn't you? Well, we could talk then, as there's no time now, Jim, dearie, believe me. Could you come about two tomorrow afternoon? I'd be in then."

"I think so, mum," said Jim.

"Then you do that, my love," said his mother. She picked up her handbag and shopping basket, which had been put down on a chair in the hall, opened the front door, and saw Susan standing on the garden path outside.

"Hello! 'ho are you, and what d' you want 'ere?" she asked rather sharply. Traces of a Cockney accent had largely disappeared from Mrs. Sandy's speech after many years of living in the North with Mr. Sandy, but every now and then the Londoner's way of speaking would slip out with a few clipped H's.

"I'm Susan Dalmane, the Countess of Saint Helens," said Susan calmly. "I've come here with your son, who has agreed to take a job with me."

"Well!" exclaimed Mrs. Sandy, who did not think of curtseying, of offering a hand to be shaken, or even of being reasonably polite. "Well, fancy; wonders never cease! But you look very young to be a real countess, that you do, young lady. Seems to me you look more like a schoolgirl than a countess—mind now, meanin' no offence, Mrs. Dalmane!—or <u>Lady</u> Dalmane, as I should say, shouldn't I? Sorry, but I'm not used to meetin' people like you, if you really are a countess. But you'll have to 'scuse me, Lady Dalmane, but I'm in a bit of a rush. Shall I see you and Jim tomorrow, if you don't mind?"

Jim was horrified at the casual way his mother was prattling on, but Susan did not seem to be at all put out by Mrs. Sandy's rather insolent manner of speech.

"Very well, Mrs. Sandy, we'll come tomorrow with the car to pick up Jim's things around two o'clock. We're travelling by train today, you understand, so <u>we've</u> got to hurry too; but we called here to find out where your house is, and to make arrangements. Good afternoon, Mrs. Sandy."

"Good-bye, Mrs. Dalmane—Lady Dalmane, I mean. See you tomorrow, Jim."

"All right, mum. Oh, I say, is Ben not here?" Jim suddenly remembered his brother Benjamin, whom he had not seen since he had left Cockermouth with his mother.

"Oh no," said Mrs. Sandy. "Ben's at school. He's a full-time boarder, you know, so he only lives here in the holidays. But I must go, so 'bye for now, Jim!"

"Good-bye, mum."

Mrs. Sandy shut and locked her front door, while Susan and Jim walked away from the house, silently at first, but they began talking again as soon as Number Ninety-Six was well behind them. Jim was feeling ashamed of his mother, and was indeed very shocked at what he thought was the appallingly rude way she had spoken to Susan, but he remembered that she was always inclined to speak with embarrassing tactlenessness to strangers. He glanced behind him, and was glad to see that his mother was not following them, but was standing at a bus stop on the other side of the road, nearly opposite her house.

"I'm sorry mother spoke to you like that—so rudely, I mean," he said, looking rather nervously at Susan.

"Oh, don't worry about that," said Susan. "I don't mind in the least: I'm sure your mother didn't <u>mean</u> to sound rude, so you needn't feel upset about it. But tell me about your brother, Ben, Jim. What school does he attend?"

"Mother wanted to send him to a public school, so he's a boarder at Westminster. Of course, it's not very far from here for Ben to come home in the holidays—I mean, mother's house here in Ealing isn't far from Westminster—but I suppose he thinks of it as home now."

"You don't know how he's getting on as a boarder there?"

"I know absolutely nothing except that he's there," said Jim, "and that he'll have finished his first year at the end of this term, which must be sometime quite soon. But he never writes to me, and I've never seen him since he went off to London with mum, so, you see, I don't know whether he enjoys being at boarding school, or not."

"Yes, I see," said Susan thoughtfully. "You've lost touch with your brother—at the present time."

After that they were silent for a minute or two, as they walked along Lakeland Avenue by the way they had come, each pursuing their own thoughts. Jim was suddenly wishing that he did not have to return to that house the next day to collect his trunk and to see his mother again. Although she had spoken disgustingly rudely to Susan (he still thought), she had otherwise been pleasant enough in her manner, but Jim knew that his mother could be horribly bad-tempered at times, even without apparent reason; and now he knew that he was almost afraid of her, all but dreading the return visit to Lakeland Avenue. As for his brother, Benjamin, whatever he might be doing at his boarding school, it was of no importance to Jim; and Susan, seeming to sense that this was so, asked him no more questions about him.

Very soon, by the time they came to the end of Lakeland Avenue, Jim was once again feeling cheerful; his high spirits had bubbled up again under the effect of his intense crush on Susan, and his other feelings, occasioned by meeting his mother, had receded into the background.

"Now," said Susan, "I should think the best way to return to town would be by the District Line, changing at Charing Cross. But let's have a look at our street map, Jim." After a short consultation of the map, she added: "That's it: look, if we turn right here, instead of going round to the left by the way we came, we could head for Ealing Common station. But it's only a quarter to two now, so we've got masses of time to catch that three o'clock train from Waterloo."

At Sherborne station, where Susan and Jim disembarked from the afternoon express from Waterloo to Exeter, Jim noticed that among the people who were waiting on the platform was one very smartly dressed man who doffed his peaked cap respectfully to Susan as soon as she set foot on the platform. They had travelled down from London alone in a First-Class compartment of that train after Susan had paid both their fares, but it had been a very unremarkable journey, even a rather dull journey, Jim thought, from the scenic point of view; but he had been with Susan all the time, going home now to Rhodes Castle, and his excitement had been rising with every mile the train made as they had approached Sherborne.

"Hello, George," said Susan cheerfully. "It's nice to see you again."

"Thank you, ma'am," said the chauffeur (for he was the Dalmanes' chauffeur). "I have the car in the yard for you. Is it to be straight home, ma'am?"

"Yes, straight home," said Susan.

George, the chauffeur, lead the way out, and Jim was not at all surprised to see a grey Rolls Royce car parked just outside the station. The chauffeur opened and shut the front passenger door for Susan, having first placed her knapsack on the back seat; then he did the same with a rear door for Jim. As the chauffeur drove the car away from the station car park, Jim saw the smoke of the departing train and knew that at last he had come to the last stage of his long progress to Rhodes Castle. The great ancestral home of the Dalmane family was only seven miles from Sherborne, Susan had told him, and already in the train he had been seeing in his mind's eye hundreds of pictures of castles and great houses in spacious grounds. But what would the real Rhodes Castle look like? He could hardly bear any more waiting to see it, and once the car had left the streets of the town, Jim began straining his vision, looking far ahead and trying to catch a distant glimpse of towers on the horizon, which would show where the Castle lay.

They had only driven two and a half miles along the main road when the chauffeur turned the car off onto a small side road; but Jim, looking eagerly around, had still seen no sign of a castle anywhere. The road was a public road, but it ran through Rhodes Park, and before Jim realised it, there was Lord Dalmane's parkland stretching away majestically on both sides of the road, which had no hedges or fences between it and the Park. Huge stately trees spread their leafy branches earthwards, and Jim saw deer, many of them standing in the long shadows for shade, for the evening was still sunny (as the whole day had been) and it was surprisingly warm, considerably that it was getting on for half past six.

"Well, here we are at home, Jim, more or less," said Susan. "At least, we're in the Rhodes Park. That house ahead of us is the South Lodge of the Castle, which is where our private drive begins. It's about a mile from the gates (you'll see them in a moment) up to our front door." The house called the South Lodge was a long way ahead on the right-hand side of the road when Susan had first pointed to it, but it seemed to take only a few seconds for the car to reach it. Then Jim saw that the house stood at a road junction. The chauffeur, having slowed the car down nearly to a stop, was turning right into another road which passed through a gateway between two tall and tremendously ornate stone gate posts, both of which had a coat of arms carved on them. The gates were of massive wrought iron work, painted black, but they stood open; and as the car crossed a cattle grid between them, Jim concluded that they must seldom, if ever, be closed.

And now, at last, he saw it! Far ahead, at the other end of the drive, a distant view of a tower was revealed to Jim's sight. The roadway was lined by a triumphal avenue of trees, and the drive was dead straight all the way to the great Castle, which seemed to stand where the trees of that avenue converged by perspective (the trees did not go the <u>whole</u> way along that drive, but only as far as the next lodge, called Inner Lodge). The chauffeur drove the car fast, smoothly, and silently up that majestic drive. Susan pointed out to Jim the squat, grey tower of a small church which stood a little way off to the left of the drive, and told him that it was Rhodes Church, and that it was not only the special church of the Castle but also an ordinary country parish church, although its churchyard was quite surrounded by Lord Dalmane's Rhodes Park. Then, looking ahead again, Jim saw that a flag was flying from the top of a tall flagstaff above the Castle; the butler had hoisted the Union Flag to signify that the Earl of Saint Helens was in residence at his chief seat (Lord Dalmane had got home some two hours earlier).

"How lovely your park looks!" said Jim involuntarily, unable in his rising excitement and enthusiasm to keep his silence any longer. "And what fine rhododendrons you have here! It's a magnificent place, Lady Dalmane!" She had asked him to remember to address her as "Lady Dalmane", not "Susan", before the other servants.

"I'm glad you think well of your first view of our Park," said Susan. "It *is* a magnificent place and, although I say it myself, remember that I haven't lived here long—only since we were married in April of this year—so I can't claim to know the place well yet. But the rhododendrons are past their best now with only those purple ones left in flower." As well as the trees lining the drive there were many tall, old rhododendron bushes, and it was at these that Jim was looking.

"The purple rhododendrons are the wild ones, aren't they?" asked Jim.

"Yes, that's right," said Susan. "They flower much later than our cultivated varieties—the white, and pink, and red ones, which have been over for some time now. But we have plenty of both sorts."

"So I see," said Jim. Then another thought struck him. "Shall we be driving in this car to London tomorrow, Lady Dalmane?" he asked.

"Oh no," said Susan. "We'll be going in my car, which is a great deal smaller and more manageable than this one, and I'll be driving it myself: I enjoy driving. We've never used this big car much, and in fact we're about to sell it. We don't, either of us, like being ostentatious, so we've decided to part with the Rolls. John says he's going to get himself a much smaller car."

Jim, privately, felt a little disappointed that he was not to travel up to London the next day in the Rolls Royce, but he said nothing more about it.

At about three quarters of a mile from the drive gates, they came to a crossroads: to the left another tree-lined roadway branched off, and to the right a wider road lead into what looked like a large car park with various buildings around it, but they saw only one car parked there.

"That's what we call the Visitor Centre," said Susan, pointing to the right. "You know: car park, tourist's souvenir shop, toilets, cafeteria, and so on: all for the benefit of our many visitors. It's a place you'll have to get to know well. And over there (she pointed to the left) that drive leads to the Stables and to West Lodge. The house you saw by the crossroads is called Inner Lodge, and Major Ambrose, who'll be your immediate boss, lives there."

Jim wondered how many lodges there were altogether in the vast park surrounding Rhodes Castle, but he asked Susan a question on a different point.

"I see. And do you keep any horses in your Stables?"

"We only keep a few horses nowadays for riding, but they're out in the Park all summer. We both ride, John and I, although John very rarely has time for riding."

By this time the car had passed through another gateway, this time a white wooden gate, and was passing up the inner part of the main drive between the Castle Gardens. The chauffeur had slowed the car down nearly to a stop by the crossroads so that Susan could point things out to Jim, and now he was driving slowly along between two great lawns on either side of the drive; one of the lawns was being mowed by a man sitting on a motor mower with a seat. Then, immediately before the drive opened out into a large space in front of the Castle it crossed a sort of causeway between two ponds. A fountain was playing in one of the ponds which had small, Japanese-style ornamental trees overhanging the water; and there were beds of bright flowers round about. Rather further away stood the largest cedar tree Jim had ever seen. It was in the middle of one of the lawns, and like all cedars it appeared to be in a number of layers of heavy-looking branches. The lowest branches would have drooped right down onto the lawn, but they were propped up by stout wooden stakes. And there before them was the Castle itself; however, Jim thought at first that there seemed to be no one about, barring that man mowing the lawn. He asked Susan if the garden was closed to the public that day.

"Yes," said Susan. "We haven't had it open while we've been away. But we're open again tomorrow."

The chauffeur drew the car up to the foot of a wide flight of stone steps leading up to the front door. All that side of Rhodes Castle, Susan explained to Jim (who was looking at it) was a relatively new façade stuck onto a mediaeval castle behind it; however, it had been carefully styled to match the appearance of the older part of the building. The whole place was roughly square, with a rectangle of various buildings surrounding a large central quadrangle or bailey; but the part of the castle in which the Dalmanes lived was shaped like a capital 'L' with its angle at the eastern corner of the buildings. The newer front side of the Castle faced south-east and made up the long axis of the 'L', while the Great Tower dominated the eastern corner; but round this corner, beyond the Tower, the north-eastern walls were ancient and ruinous, as were some other parts of the Castle away from the south-eastern façade.

The chauffeur, who was also one of the gardeners, opened the front passenger door of the car for Susan, and she stepped out onto the gravel. Jim had just noticed two men, who seemed to have been deep in some conversation; they had been standing not far away, but now they were approaching them. They each made a stiff little bow to Susan, moving only their heads, and then shook hands with her. Meanwhile Jim stepped out of the car, and Susan immediately introduced him to these two senior servants (for such they were): the butler, whom she called simply "Jack", and Major Ambrose, a fuzzy, grey haired man, who looked as if he was getting on in years, although Jim at once noted what he thought was a jolly twinkle in his eyes. Just then Jim noticed a face flattened against the window to the left of the front door, a young female face, watching their arrival, but just as he noticed the girl she disappeared from the window.

"Hello, Sue! So you've got home," called a familiar man's voice from somewhere above them. "I was just sitting out here reading while I waited for you to turn up." Lord Dalmane had been sitting unseen in a garden chair on a balcony on the first floor just above and to the left of the front door. Now he had risen from his chair and was looking down over the stone parapet at the group below him at the foot of the stone steps to the front door.

"Oh, there you are, John," said Susan. "I was just wondering where you'd got to. Now then, Jim—oh, hello, Sam!"

The rather plain-looking, fair-haired girl whom Jim had just seen at that window had emerged through the front door and now stood at the top of the steps. It may well have been due to Jim's great infatuation for Susan that his first impression of this girl was of someone who looked positively dull, although she had shoulder-length blonde hair, and was clearly fairly young, probably in her twenties, Jim thought (but he learned later that she was thirty-three years old). She was, in fact, Susan's maid, Samantha Villers; and in one hand she held a duster.

"Hello, Susan," she said, smiling at her mistress. "Have you had a good holiday?"

"We've had a simply lovely time, John and I," said Susan. "This is Jim Sandy, our new Guide. Jim, this is my maid, Samantha."

"Pleased to meet you, Jim," said Samantha, shaking hands with him. She signed to the chauffeur, and he handed to her Susan's knapsack, her only baggage, which the chauffeur had just removed from the back seat of the car. She took it into the house.

"Now, Jim," said Susan, "let's go indoors. I asked them to have some supper ready for us for eight o'clock, so there's time for me to show you to your room, and show you the way around the place a bit before we eat. I expect you're hungry by now?"

"Yes, I am, thank you," said Jim. He certainly was hungry, having eaten since breakfast only a light and early lunch in London and a snack with tea in the buffet car of the train from Waterloo.

He walked with Susan up the steps and through both the doors into the hall; there was an outer door which was a massive wooden affair, quite in keeping with the style of the place as an inhabited castle, while the inner door had a glass window in it. Major Ambrose did not follow them in, but the butler came in behind them and promptly disappeared rapidly down a corridor to the left as if on some urgent business. As Jim passed across the threshold into the hall he reflected that although one adventure was ended, his escapade of running away from the police to look for a new job, he was in a literal sense stepping into another adventure by setting foot for the first time inside the seat of the noble Dalmane family, Earls of Saint Helens for many generations. He told himself that from that moment onwards he was going to be singularly privileged to be a part of that great household, and he guessed that, with such a remarkably friendly relationship with Susan Dalmane already built up, he would quickly be treated as one of the Dalmane family himself. It was too good to be true, and yet he reminded himself, as he looked around the hall, that it would surely work out that way. But the first thing he noticed about the hall was that it was a long, lofty, and rather dark chamber, somewhat depressing; and the second thing he noticed in the penumbral gloom (for little daylight seemed to penetrate into that hall) was a stag's head with huge antlers staring solemnly down on them from an opposite wall, over the entrance to the main staircase. Then he noticed some sombre-looking flags or banners attached high up to the left-hand wall of the place. These first impressions of the interior of the Castle were hardly in tune with his riotously cheerful mood, but although he quickly took in a rather depressing vision of that long, dark hall, it could not affect his feeling of triumphant elation at that moment.

"Well," said Susan, having given Jim a moment to look around in silence, "how lovely it is to come home! But I daresay you're thinking, Jim, what a dark and gloomy place this Great Hall is— and so it certainly is! But we won't linger here. Come on, and I'll show you the way upstairs and to your room—I've chosen a very nice little homely room to be your bedroom, and I think you'll like it. Eh, what's that, Sam?" Her lady's maid, Samantha Villers, had just appeared, coming down the broad staircase at the further end of the hall.

"I've just put your knapsack in your bedroom," said Samantha. "Do you want me to show Jim where his room is?"

"No," said Susan. "I'm just going to do that myself, but do come along too, Sam, if you're not busy now, and we'll all talk together. Only first, just nip down to the kitchen, will you, to tell Cook that we've arrived, and report back to us how the supper's coming on."

"Very good, Sue." Samantha was regarded by Susan as a very special servant, indeed as a close friend and confidante rather than as a servant, and consequently it was accepted that she did not address Susan as "ma'am" or "my Lady" or "your Ladyship", but simply as "Susan". She hurried off towards the kitchen, presently disappearing from Jim's sight down the long corridor which lead to the left out of the hall.

"Samantha is one of only three servants who live-in here, in the Castle," explained Susan as she and Jim advanced towards the wide, grand staircase. "Our butler, Jack, lives-in too, and now there's to be you as well!"

Me! thought Jim. How splendid to be one of the privileged few who live-in here! I'm going to have a great time working and living here: I'm sure of it!

A fortnight later Susan and John Dalmane were having breakfast in the small dining-room which they called the Breakfast Room, with its pleasant east-facing aspect, when Samantha entered, bearing the morning's post. She placed a pile of letters in front of Susan who, looking through them, found one that had a Carlisle postmark and was addressed to her.

"Oh good, it's a letter from Mr. Ruddock, that nice train driver," she said. "Here's your post, John." She passed some envelopes across the table to her husband, and hurriedly opened the one with the Carlisle postmark, ignoring for the moment the rest of her post and the rest of her breakfast (which she had almost finished anyway). She took out of the envelope the following letter.

14th July, 1959   2 Railway Terrace,
                                   London Road,
                                   CARLISLE,
                                   Cumberland.

My Lady,

I am writing to inform you that I have received a letter from the Chairman of the Disciplinary Committee before which I was ordered to appear. The Chairman in his letter to me said that the Committee has decided that I should continue in my job as an engine-driver, and that my suspension from that work was therefore to cease immediately. I am, of course, extremely happy to be back at my work again.

I've no doubt that it was only your intercession, ma'am, on my behalf, which persuaded the Committee to re-instate me. I am deeply grateful to you, ma'am, for taking such an interest in my well-being, and for your effort in writing for me to the Committee Chairman.

I hope very much, ma'am, that if you should come up to the Lakes for another holiday, perhaps next year, or later, you and your husband would take a train trip on the Cockermouth Line. You told me how very much your husband, the Earl, regretted not being able to come with you in the train on June 30th, so may I suggest that you put that matter right with a train trip together sometime. I can't, of course, guarantee to be driving any particular train myself, but I hope very much that I may look forward to meeting your husband and yourself on a train when you're up here next.

With all best wishes,
I am, my Lady,
Yours very sincerely,
Thomas Ruddock.

"How splendid!" said Susan.

"What's it all about, darling?" asked Lord Dalmane, looking at a brown envelope addressed to himself.

"You remember how I told you about Driver Ruddock, and how he had the misfortune to be threatened with the sack because of me?" said Susan.

"Yes."

"Well, he's got his job back! The Committee has re-instated him, he says. Isn't that marvellous news? And he says: why shouldn't we both go up there again, and perhaps ride in his train, next year maybe, or the year after—<u>both</u> of us?"

"Well, why not, Sue? I <u>was</u> dreadfully disappointed at being left behind that time."

"Then let's make it a resolution to do that trip together sometime—it'll be a good holiday to look forward to."

THE END

Lightning Source UK Ltd.
Milton Keynes UK
UKOW03f0123130614

233352UK00002B/6/P